The Unseemly Woman

The Unseemly Woman

A Story of the Plain People

by

Esther Wingert Bennett

DORRANCE PUBLISHING CO., INC.
PITTSBURGH, PENNSYLVANIA 15222

*To my daughter Jean
with all my love.*

Preface

It was not a dream. The red-haired woman struggled up from under layers of sleep just in time to hear the kitchen clock strike three times. The wind in the night moaned. A window blind suddenly moved, startling her as it billowed out from the air whistling in from the cracks around the sash.

It was happening more frequently now, but that did not lessen the feeling of terror it always produced in her. It would start with a sliding sound, soft, like a small body creeping over the rough floor of the garret above. If she were lucky tonight, she might be spared the next horrifying sound. With that hope, she burrowed down into the bed covers and pulled them over her head, but this was not one of the fortunate nights. Although she tried desperately to block out the sound, she heard the thin, burbling cry of an infant. Then came the baby's great heart-wrenching sobs. Her own body shook, and cold sweat gathered on her brow. She would have to get out of bed and go up into the garret to stop it!

It was nearing dawn, but the moon had not yet set, so she had light enough to see. She slid from the bed and crept softly to the door leading to the garret above. Damp, cold air poured down the steep stairs, but she climbed upwards, unconsciously murmuring, "There, now. There, there now."

Seating herself on an old rush-bottomed rocking chair, she took up a bundle of rags lying on the floor. She sobbed convulsively as she rocked, hugging the bundle to her breast. She was conscious of a great emptiness within her. She was adrift in a vast, soundless sea, alone.

Slowly she rocked, and then, as the gentle motion soothed her, she patted the bundle she had clutched so tightly. Crooning a lullaby, she stared unseeing into the shadows of the timbered room. Suddenly a tapping sound came from the direction of the north chimney-end of the garret. She stopped singing and she listened. Peering through the clutter of chests and boxes, she perceived a dark figure sitting with its back against the bricks of the chimney. Goat-like legs were crossed nonchalantly, with one foot tapping the floor in time to her rocking.

She stopped rocking and was halfway out of her chair before she saw the long, greenish-yellow eyes glowing in the gleam of the garret. A reddish snake was coiled around his wrist. She recoiled in horror as she instinctively recognized the figure. An aura of evil hung over him like a stench.

His insolent eyes swept over her, lingering, debasing. "What kept you so long? I've come for you at last."

She felt nausea rising inside of her. "Who are you? What do you want?"

"Oh, come on now. You know who I am and you know what I want. I want you."

"Get away from me. I'll scream!"

"So? What good will that do? Didn't you come up here to rock the baby? No one believes in you anymore." His leer cut through her as he leaned back against the chimney.

"Go away! I've never done anything to you. Stop tormenting me!"

"I've come for your soul. I won't leave you here with that bawling brat that you think lives here in the garret."

"You can't make me go!"

"True, true. I can't force you to do anything. You have free choice. Every mortal does. Even your mother Eve did in the Garden of Eden. But you do have to pay, just as she did."

"And if I come, will I have to hear the baby cry again?"

"I promise that you will never hear it again. There are no babies in my kingdom, aborted ones or any other kind."

"How can I go? I don't know the way."

"Oh, yes, you do. It is easy." His voice purred on. "Stand up on your chair and take that rope hanging from the rafters. Tie it about your neck. It won't take long. Just jump off the chair, now!"

The sobbing creature stood on the shaky rocker, obeying the directions. Just at that moment, a rooster crowed the morning light. Giving a loud scream, she jumped outward into oblivion.

CHAPTER 1

The later afternoon sun tried to force its way through the rain-besmeared panes of the auditorium of Beaver Creek High School. The tightly shut windows could not provide the ventilation so badly needed by the seventy students that made up the student body of this small, rural school. The stale stench was like all schools, where such a mass of humanity had to be forced into close quarters.

Most of the students were the children of local farmers, but a small number came from over the mountain and were boarding with relatives. They were called the Buckwheat Eaters by their snobbish peers and were made the constant butt of jokes and gibes, but none endured the harassment that Rachel Miller, the girl in the blue gingham dress, did. She was the one sitting next to the window where the sun lit up her red hair so that its glory glowed about her like a halo.

No one else in the community had red hair like hers, and because she was not like others, she was ridiculed by her classmates as well as others she met in the course of the day. This particular afternoon, a loutish boy, on his way to the pencil sharpener, reached out to touch her hair. Stopping midway, he quickly withdrew his fingers and yelled, "Ouch!" Waving his hands in the air, he explained, "It burned me!"

His audience tittered, and Rachel's face went scarlet. Her large flecked green eyes glittered. In her shame she hid her face in her arms on the top of her desk.

Just then the door to the hallway opened, and the principal entered escorting a stranger. This man was so different in appearance from the men of that area that everyone dropped their books and stared. The stranger's black hair was worn longer than most, coming down below his ears and curling up at the ends. His narrow, pale face was lighted by large, intense black eyes. He wore a lay-down collar with a flowing scarf tied in a bow in a Byron-like manner. A large, glittering ring adorned his right hand. It was only then that the gawking students noticed he was carrying a violin.

When the principal cleared his throat, the students were quickly drawn out of their reverie, sat up, and gave him attention. "Put away your work, boys and girls. We are being favored this afternoon with a violin concert by Professor Anton Dereck!"

The "professor" made a quick bow, then said, "Before I begin, let us have some fresh air. Will that beautiful young lady next to the window kindly raise it while everyone stands and takes a deep breath?"

The class burst into laughter. Rachel had been called *beautiful young lady*. The professor was surprised at this outburst, but he could not help but take in the girl's slim waist and full bosom with his eyes when she rose to obey him. Her glorious hair so fascinated him that he spent several moments gazing at her. Even the principal seemed to see her in a new perspective. Now all eyes were drawn to her a second time, and once again, she blushed deeply.

The professor mentally shook himself and spoke, "Ah, yes, I will play for you a symphony written by Tchaikovsky, familiarly known as the *Pathetique*."

Rachel had never had the opportunity to hear live classical music before. As the pure golden notes came from this man's violin when he swept his bow across the strings and his flashing ring leaped and glided with his movements, she forgot her embarrassment and leaned forward, her lips parted and her eyes paled to aquamarine. She seemed to have stopped breathing. She was in total rapture.

The professor's attention was once more drawn to her. Aware of her admiration, he was inspired to play as he had not done for many years. He surprised himself as the restless pupils quieted and became enraptured by the magic of this music man. They were even prone to disregard the bell when it rang for dismissal.

A few minutes later as Rachel walked home with her two younger brothers, she hummed some of the airs she had heard that afternoon. The three were taking the shortcut home on the railroad tracks. They were not in danger since the train had already made its daily trip into Peterboro and back. They ran no danger of meeting with it now.

"Beat you walking on the rails!" her younger brother Jacob called out.

"How many ties can you walk over while on the rails, Rachel?" The challenge came from the older of the two brothers, Amos.

Her mind was abruptly drawn to the immediate present. Rachel balanced herself as she walked on the narrow rail. "I just walked seven. Margie White says if you walk over seven ties, the first person you meet will marry you some day," she responded wistfully.

"Ah, Margie White! What does she know? Anyhow, Sis, no one would want to marry a fiery-head like you. Everyone calls you a spitfire," teased Amos. He instantly regretted his words when he saw the pain in her eyes.

"T'ain't so, Amos. You know Sis ain't like that a bit. T'ain't her fault she got red hair!" Jacob defended.

"Thanks, Jacob. I'm glad someone takes up for me." But Rachel still felt that hurtful pang in her heart as she once again was faced with her affliction. In this superstitious rural community, red hair was associated with the DEVIL.

The three continued in a heavy silence. When they reached home, they could smell the fassnaughts that their mother was frying out. The three children realized it was Shrove Tuesday, Fassnaught Day. The boys clamored to sugar the spicy doughnuts and succeeded in cramming fistfuls of the still warm goodies into their hungry mouths.

Rachel retired to her room to put away her books and tied a fresh gingham apron around her waist before helping her mother cut out the circles of dough. Using a thimble, she cut out the centers. The circles were fried in one pot, while the centers of dough were fried in another pot. When they were later salted, they took on the flavor of salted nuts. All were stacked on the long, covered table that was used for the family dining table.

When it seemed that the table could hold no more of the delicacies, large tin cans were brought out from the storeroom in the back hallway, packed with unsugared fassnaughts, and put back into the cold room. Sugar would be sprinkled on them before serving, thus there would be enough fassnaughts to last them the six weeks before Easter.

"That old groundhog sure knew what he was doing when he went back into his hole on Groundhog Day. Six more weeks of winter!" Mother poked the fire in the kitchen range. "Amos, get in a few more sticks of wood. And Jacob, run down to the spring and get some water for the tank on the stove, for it's about dry. Papa needs plenty of warm water to wash in when he comes in from the barn."

In a little while the tank at the end of the cast-iron stove was filled and the table was set for supper with the steel knives and two-tined forks that Rachel had to scour every week. Heavy ironstone plates were placed upside down over the cutlery as was the custom, not to be turned right side up until after Papa asked the blessing.

Pickles, jelly, and the inevitable apple butter were placed on the table along with the fresh butter that Rachel had churned last evening after school. It was the rule to pass the bread first and for everyone to eat a piece of apple butter bread before eating anything else. It was understood. That way, no one got indigestion by putting more heavy foods into his empty stomach.

The two boys sat on a bench against the wall. The quiet Rachel sat opposite, then Mother next to Papa's place at the head of the table. The boys sat patiently while Papa washed up and combed his hair at the small looking glass hung above the bench that held the wash basins. When he sat down, Rachel could smell the redolence from the cow stable on his shoes. She suddenly wondered if all farmers smelled that way and if she were lucky enough to marry, if her husband would. The thought depressed her slightly.

Mother moved from stove to table bearing bowls of food, holding the hot dishes with her apron. She always wore an apron of the same material as her Sunday dress, gathered full like her skirt. It had a v-shaped cape pinned down the center of her front, held back with a black-headed pin. Never seeming to be off her modestly covered hair, she wore a white organdy cap with long, narrow, black ribbons to tie under her full chin. She seldom tied them, but it was not good to be seen wearing a cap without strings.

Papa asked a long blessing, while the boys hungrily eyed the rich fried ham in its own gravy. Next to it was a bowl of fried potatoes and then a bowl of boiled cabbage with a bountiful amount of black pepper sprinkled over it. As usual at family meals, little conversation took place except for requests for food to be passed.

"Rachel, the cream's all," her mother voiced suddenly. "You will have to run down to the springhouse and fetch some more up."

Rachel immediately took the pitcher and ran over a rocky path to the springhouse, slightly relieved to be away from them all with her thoughts. The beautiful music she had heard that afternoon for the first time in her life, that afternoon someone had said she was *beautiful*!

A screened door opened into the old stone building that straddled the free-flowing spring. A shallow, smooth-bottomed basin of water was shored up with cement and it held crocks of milk immersed in the icy water. Every day the crocks and cans of milk were skimmed of their cream, and the cream collected into a separate earthen crock.

While Mother and Rachel were washing dishes after supper, Amos watched his mother out of the corner of his eye, hoping she would not notice while he furtively poured some of the fat from the fassnaughts into a can and then stole out into the gathering darkness. The next morning the family discovered the hex signs, big *X's*, daubed with grease from the fassnaught frying on the exterior corners of the big stone house. Papa went about with a wry smile, but Mother was loud in her lament.

"What will people say? Only the presence of the Devil would be an excuse for marking our house in such a manner!"

"No, Mother, I just wanted to keep evil spirits *away*. Besides a long time ago, people made the panels of their doors to look like crosses. What was that for if it wasn't to keep out the Evil One?"

Papa Miller was eloquent in Amos's defense. "Well, I guess there's something to that. I don't want you to get those ideas the Fletchers have about spells being put on us, Amos."

"Would you believe that Mr. Fletcher has gone down into the lower counties to find a witch doctor?" Amos was as surprised as the rest at this piece of information from his father. "I heard it down at the store the other day. They believe they have been hexed!"

"Why, Papa! I never heard that!" Rachel cried. The Fletcher girls were her best friends in school. "Do they really think they are hexed?"

Mother hushed Rachel and whispered, "I'll tell you all about it when we are alone."

That evening Mother waited until the boys and Papa had gone to bed before confiding in her daughter. "I don't want the boys to hear this. It's this way, Rachel, only a few weeks after the gentleman cow has been with the milch cows, the Fletcher's cows drop their calves. It has always happened so quickly and it's not natural. That's what makes them think they're bewitched." Mother always used the term "gentleman cow" or the "duke." Bull was considered a vulgar, dirty word.

"But Mother, I heard the Fletcher girls say that one of their little brothers also was sick. It is the one next to the baby. Every day he has a high fever, then he cools down. But the next day, he is as bad as he was the day before. He is getting weaker all the time, and no one knows what ails him. They even had Aunt Katie Smith come in and try for him. She said she thought he was bewitched, too."

"I'll go over tomorrow and take some pennyroyal tea," her mother sighed. "We have several bunches left hanging in the store room. I'm glad we gathered and dried a lot last summer."

"But if they're truly bewitched, your pennyroyal tea won't help!" Rachel was concerned and upset.

"Hush! It's a good thing we don't believe in witches. It is the Evil One's doing. That's what it is. If people only behaved themselves and did what was right, there wouldn't be all that trouble."

"But, Mother, the Fletchers are good people. How could they be punished? They go to church all the time. Why, the girls always wear their caps—even to school."

This fact mollified Mother, but she was not quite convinced. "Just the same, Brother Fletcher had to marry Susie Fletcher. Remember their oldest boy was born seven months after they were married. They had to stand up in church and confess to their sin. Believe me, there was never anything like that between your father and me before we were married! We've been married nearly nineteen years now, and you came along two years after we were married. Brother Fletcher and Susie committed an unforgivable sin, and now they are being punished."

As Rachel and her mother climbed the stairs to their bedrooms, Rachel was deep in thought, wondering when she would get married. *I wonder if anyone will ever want to marry a redhead like me?* How could she be a child of the DEVIL? Once more she turned her mind to the violinist, his magical talent, and how he had called her *beautiful*.

CHAPTER 2

The spring rains did their best to wash off the greasy hex signs from the corners of the house, but they were still quite discernible by the time that May came with its locust trees in bloom along the roads. White clumps of flowers hung from the tall, slender trees. These shaggy barked trees were very popular with farmers as a source for fence posts. The honey-seeking bees enjoyed the perfume from their blossoms as much as Rachel did.

Mother had spent many nights with the Fletchers, sitting up with the sick child. In spite of good nursing, it was getting weaker. Then the youngest child came down with the same sickness. Mr. Fletcher took another trip to the Lower Counties and finally he found a hex doctor. Mother reported that there were paper bags with charms inside tied to the garden fence, the barnyard fence, and even to the pigpen. Mrs. Fletcher even called in Dr. Flowers, the local doctor. Nothing seemed to work.

It was nearing the end of the school year and the end of Rachel's school life. She was now over seventeen, older than most of the children from the Plain People. It was the custom for them to leave school at sixteen and help their parents on the farms. Rachel would have liked to have finished high school and prepared herself for teaching, but Mother needed her too much at home.

The first thing she was expected to do was to help with the garden. The lettuce had been planted when the *Hagerstown Almanac* gave the moon sign for it. The quarter horns of the moon had to point upwards in order to plant lettuce, peas, beans, and other vegetables that produced their fruit above the ground. Papa and the boys cleaned out the horse stable and put the good, rich fertilizer into a ridge into which the sprouts from sweet potatoes were put. These had been sprouting in a cold frame for several weeks, waiting for the *down sign* of the moon. Thus the potatoes grew below the soil with great bounty.

Mother often remarked how she would like to have a parsley bed, but was afraid to plant the seed, for everyone knew that death would come to the family that broke this taboo. Finally Mother found out how to thwart this bad luck. Mrs. Fletcher asked the hex doctor, and he said to put the seed onto a paper and let the wind blow the seed about in the place where the herb was wanted. So on a windy day Mother went out with her paper of parsley seeds and the deed was done. Within a few days the tiny parsley plants were starting to grow.

"Now we will have parsley in our pot pie and our rivel soup," observed Mother with great satisfaction.

The first Saturday in May seemed to find everything gone wrong. The hogs had broken out of their pen and had gone into the garden, uprooting the sweet potato ridges and gobbling up the young plants that the family had put in as soon as there was no further danger of frost. The boys had not been around to drive them out, so it was up to Rachel to chase them out by herself. The stubborn animals raced across the spring onion bed, uprooting them and mangling them with their sharp hooves. Rachel raced them and finally got them headed toward the pigpen. She found a hammer and some nails which she used awkwardly to hammer fast the board that they had broken. Her face was scarlet with her exertions and her hair became unbound, forming a witch's mop about her flushed face.

It was a misfortune to Rachel that she had red hair. Her classmates seemed to have had a particular pick on her. Her family often seemed ashamed of her, too, for her two brothers had coal-black hair like their mother. Her father's hair was brown, but she could see red fires in his hair in the sunlight.

"It's a judgment on me!" sighed her mother. "I never liked your father's sister Dolly, and she had red hair. You take after her, but to make up for it you don't have freckles. That's a good thing."

"Yes, and I'll never have to wear any eyebrow pencil, for my eyebrows and lashes are dark, nearly as dark as yours, Mothers."

"Just let me catch you daubing such stuff on your face. That's the worldly influence. You're like the good Lord made you, and we'll make the best of it."

Rachel recalled this conversation when she returned to the kitchen to scrub the floor. She asked herself why God had to punish her by giving her this flaming mop of hair. Then, too, she was quite well-developed for a girl of seventeen, with a full breast but slim waist and curved hips. Many snide remarks and looks came from the high school boys, so she had Mother make her tight waists even tighter. Mother had never bought her any regular bras like the other girls wore. She used the same pattern for Rachel that she used for herself and made these undergarments from feed sacks that had been bleached out in the sun. Even her intimate garments were made from this heavy cloth. Of course her Sunday underclothes were made from muslin and trimmed with homemade crocheted lace that Mother worked on during the long winter evenings.

As these thoughts were going through Rachel's mind, she heard her mother come panting across the porch. "Quick, get that scrub bucket out of here and get cleaned up. Run upstairs and comb your hair and get on your new cap. Here come the visiting brethren!" Mother brushed up her hair as she hurried to open the front room.

Rachel gave a last swipe to the floor, then rushing to the back door, she sent the dirty water in a swirl over the back yard. Hastily she ran to the cistern pump shed, and there in its privacy she opened the front of her blouse and doused the good, cold water over her full bosom and her flushed face. With water-filled eyes she groped for the towel hanging by the pump. She was startled to find she had touched someone instead. Snatching off her apron, she dried her face and saw the surprised person of Deacon Cook standing before her.

"Oh, I didn't see you! Did I get you all wet?"

"No, Sister, I just came to get a drink of water. Will you give me some?"

"This is cistern water and isn't as good as our spring water, but you can have it." As she pumped, she was conscious of her hair streaming over her face and down her back. She nearly forgot her dress being open until she saw the lecherous look the deacon gave her. Hastily thrusting the tin cup of water into his had, she fled up the back stairs to her room in her embarrassment.

The murmur of voices from the front room below rose to her as she dressed and combed her hair. She heard her name being mentioned, so she silently opened the pipe hole that led from the front room through the floor in her room. In winter this pipe from the heater in the front room kept her from getting too chilly in her bedroom. She threw back the rug that covered this aperture and listened.

"But, Sister Miller, it is unseemly for a young woman to look like your daughter." That was Deacon Young's high-pitched voice.

"What's wrong with Rachel? We keep her dressed decent and in the order of the church. What more do you want?"

"It's her hair. It just ain't seemly that a woman would have such fiery red hair."

Mother snorted. "It's what the good Lord gave her. We can't change that. What do you want us to do about it?"

Deacon Cook purred in his silky voice, "We think she should dress plainer, like yourself, with a solid white cap to cover her hair. Also if she wore longer skirts and a cape and an apron, she wouldn't be such a temptation to the brothers of the church."

"A temptation! Why my Rachel never tempted a man in all of her young life. The very idea!"

"Yes, Sister Miller, a temptation. She brings evil thoughts to the minds of the brothers of the church. Rather than being the means of leading a soul to sin, don't you think she'd better cover up all that smacks of the DEVIL and his pernicious ways?"

Rachel jumped to her feet and looked into the small mirror that hung in her room. She could not see her figure. She had never had a full view of herself, but she often wondered. How could she tempt a man? Then the hot blood rushed to her face as she remembered a time when she was thirteen. She had been embarrassed about her budding breasts. Something had happened when she had gone with some other youngsters to their home for Sunday dinner. It shamed her yet to think about it.

A visiting evangelist from a distant congregation had been sitting in the front room waiting for his dinner. Tired of playing with her friends, Rachel had wandered into this room looking for some books to read. She was unaware of the preacher until he came over to the couch where she was reading *Pilgrim's Progress*. Then she was surprised to find the man sitting on the end of the couch and beginning to inch over to her side. He put his arm over the back of the couch, all the while talking in low tones about the pilgrim in the book. Then he accidentally touched her breast, stroking it and running his other hand over her neck and hair. He captured her hand and drew it to his body. A glassy look had come into his eyes. She sensed an aura of animal desire as he rhythmically stroked himself with her limp, reluctant hand. A feeling of nausea had come over her as she pulled frantically and jerked away. The man collapsed onto the sofa while she ran outdoors to seek the other children. She had never dared to tell her mother, and every time she thought about it, she felt like vomiting. So perhaps that was what the deacon meant by her being such a temptation.

When Rachel went down to the front room, her heightened color and fiery hair seemed to be living proof that this colorful gift should be dimmed. She scarcely heard the deacons repeat to her what they had already told her mother. Papa was called in from the fields, and he looked very troubled when these righteous men explained their errand.

A few days later, Mr. Miller hitched up the buggy for his wife and Rachel to drive to town. They drove by the sweeping lawn that extended to the road from a gentle rise of ground where some large ivy covered buildings stood, surrounded by spruce and maple trees. This was Miss Priscilla Pringle's School for Young Ladies. A number of young ladies were strolling on the campus.

Rachel stared in fascination at these exotic creatures that resemble the hollyhocks in the garden at home. They were from a world that Rachel only read about when she was allowed to borrow a book from the school library. Mother did not approve of her reading "ten cent novels," so she could read only books that were recommended by her English teacher.

These town girls had their hair "bobbed," and their beautiful dresses made them appear like royal personages.

"Mother, why don't we dress like those girls? Why do we have to dress with caps and long dresses and capes? Don't those girls want to go to Heaven too?" Rachel had startled her mother with questions similar to these when she first joined the church at the age of twelve.

"Those are proud girls, Rachel. Proud people are not willing to put on the whole armor of God. We are expected to suffer for Christ's sake."

"But why does dressing different make us any better? Does God not want us to be kind and good to others? Doesn't he want us to live a life that is happy?" Rachel trembled in her earnestness. "How do clothes make us any better?"

"Oh, hush, Rachel! You will understand when you are older. In the meantime I am going to see that you are not going to be called *unseemly* again."

There was but one dry goods store in the town, and the black-aproned saleslady pulled down several bolts of dark cloth when she saw who was asking for dress goods. No bright voiles or silks for these sober people. The store kept materials for these Plain People, for there were several sects of them in the community. They all insisted that their womenfolk wear dull and uninteresting colors.

"Here, Rachel, this brown will do for a Sunday dress, and I believe that dark green would make another one. I draw the line at putting black on you."

"Oh, thank you, Mother! I like green, but I wish you would get this light green voile. It's dark enough and it would be so cool for summer."

"All right then, but it will have long sleeves like the other ones. Now we will have to get some cap goods."

"We have some fine bobinet in stock, Mrs. Miller," ventured the clerk.

"No, no bobinet. We want some heavy organdy."

Rebellion rose in Rachel's heart. "Oh, Mother, do I have to wear organdy? That's an old woman's cap! None of the other girls wear organdy!"

"Yes, we have to cover that red hair of yours." Mother's eyes could hardly meet the sorrowful eyes of her daughter.

"Why, Mrs. Miller," the clerk spoke before thinking, "What in the world makes you want to cover that beautiful red hair? Why I have heard that many women in the city are paying out good money to dye their hair that color! It's all the fashion."

Mother sniffed. "All the more reason why it should be covered up. I promised the visiting brethren that we would cover it up, and cover it up we will."

The saleslady retired in confusion. Mrs. Miller paid for her purchases and she hurried Rachel from the store.

"Oh, Rachel, you aren't ugly by any means. You take after your Aunt Bessie, and she had the red hair and dark brows just like you have. She was often accused of painting her eyebrows, but I know she didn't, much as I didn't like her."

"Why didn't you like her, Mother?"

"Because she broke your grandmother's heart. She took off her cap and bonnet and went to the city to live."

"What's she doing now, Mother?"

"She got married to a man outside the church and she never came back home again, not even to your grandmother's funeral. Poor old Grandfather Miller often cries about it."

The dust rose from the road as a Maxwell car passed them. "That was Brother Hadwell in his new car. I guess he bought a Maxwell because the name rhymes with his," snickered Rachel.

"Well all I have to say is that pride can get into the church through the members buying their fancy cars as well as girls wearing bobinet caps without strings instead of organdy caps with black strings."

There were several members of the church that had bought new cars. Even Deacon Cook had bought a Model T. No one seemed to think it was worldly if they bought the smaller cars, but a few were like Mother. Big cars smacked of pride. The more conservative groups of the Plain People had forbidden their members to own cars, but they were the ones who also forbade mirrors, gasoline motors of any kind, and even rocking chairs.

Chapter 3

Rachel was hoping that her mother would take a different road home than the one that led over Black Creek Bridge, for it was a sinister place and had always frightened her ever since she had heard about the couple from town that had perished there. The story went that the two had been so busy making love that they had dropped the reins and let the horse go where it wanted. When a large buzzard had been startled suddenly from the road ahead of them, the horse bolted, throwing the man and woman into a deep pit where the road curved to the right. Their broken bodies were found a few hours later as the horse ate grass peacefully by the roadside.

To heighten the malevolence of the bridge, a dark cavern formed by trees intertwined overhead led to the field where the buzzards fed on the carcasses of dead farm animals that had been hauled there to be skinned by an old man who supported himself by this distasteful job. The skins were sold to a tannery in the next town, but the corpses remained there. These ominous birds, symbols of death, could always be seen circling over the field or feeding on the decomposed flesh.

Rachel always felt relieved when the horse pulled the buggy past this grisly spot, and she looked forward to seeing the little cottage that was a quarter mile beyond the old bridge. Miss Lucy lived there in her little doll-like house. The tiny, quaint place was painted white with pink gingerbread trimmings and had pink shutters. Tall hollyhocks and rambler roses grew inside her whitewashed shed across the road from her cottage. Rachel secretly admired Miss Lucy; she was the only woman in the countryside that drove a car.

As they approached, Miss Lucy could be discerned rocking herself on the porch, dressed in a pink wrapper, her bright yellow hair piled high and fastened with a fancy comb. Rachel thought that the woman looked like a life-size doll in her dollhouse. Before her mother could stop her, Rachel waved and called out, "Hello, Miss Lucy!"

"Hello, yourself, Rachel! I hope you are well, and you, too, Miz Miller!" the friendly woman called back in a cheerful voice.

To Rachel's surprise her mother snubbed Miss Lucy, turning her head away and clucking to the horse. She drove by as fast as she could make old Maude go.

"What's the matter, Mother? Don't you like Miss Lucy? I do. I think she's so pretty!" Rachel turned back to look longingly.

"I love everybody, Rachel. It's my duty to love them, but Miss Lucy is a bad woman, and I don't want to have any truck with her until she turns over a new leaf."

"How can she be so bad, Mother? Every time she sees me, she is so kind to me. She never teases me about my red hair either." Rachel defended the one she considered a true friend.

"You stay away from that painted hussy! Many's the man who's committed adultery with her. And people say there's many a woman from town who have come sneaking around here at night to have her chase away their unborn babies."

"Chase away unborn babies! Oh, Mother, how could anyone possibly do that?"

"It's called abortion. Seems like she was once a nurse in the big city, and that's where she learned to do it. She lost her job on account of it. It is murder and sinful, and I don't want to talk anymore about it or Miss Lucy!"

Ever since Professor Anton Dereck had decided to visit some nearby schools to try to get a few extra dollars by recruiting new pupils, his delicate nervous system seemed especially trained. The studio seemed to close in about him today when his fifth pupil of the day had just left, a giggling teenage girl clutching her mail-order violin.

"My daddy says that I have to learn to play the fiddle real good. Of course I told him it was a *violin*, but Daddy says it's the same thing and he wants me to learn to play square dance music so that he can take me and my mother across the mountain to play in hoedowns."

But Anton had shivered with every painful screech of her bow. How could he *bear* three more pupils this afternoon? More importantly, why should he? Just then the thunder of stampeding feet answered the question as three of his seven children came slamming into the house and dashed up the uncarpeted stairs to the second floor where Mamie, his wife, lay in bed with the youngest, a newborn girl.

In the kitchen, an inexperienced maid could be heard trying to cope with the whining toddlers. Each one seemed to be screaming in a different key. How had he, once a promising, young violinist with the New York Symphony, managed to lower himself into this state of meager existence? He thought back to the time when he had met the spoiled, darling daughter of the first violinist. Mamie had been curvaceous and blonde. Her blue-eyed loveliness blinded him to everything but his passion for her. A few visits later to his apartment and within a few months, she told him the disastrous news that she was pregnant. The only thing that could be done was to slip out of town to Maryland and have a quick marriage ceremony, come back, and face her amazed parents with, "We are married!" The enraged father had thrown out the bridegroom, and his weeping daughter had packed up her things to follow her new husband. The next day Anton appeared at a rehearsal only to learn that he had been fired from the orchestra.

Life seemed to grow increasingly more difficult after that, Mamie proved to be a good breeder, and baby after baby followed in quick succession during the ten years of their marriage. There were seven mouths to feed on the salary that Miss Priscilla Pringle deemed was expedient to pay her resident "music master." After hours, Anton took as many pupils as time permitted in order to support his family, but even his best efforts fell short of meeting its needs. The doctor had cautioned that Mamie could not take anymore pregnancies, for she was exhausted. There was but one solution to that; he had been sleeping on the couch in the studio for three months now.

The small mountain town where they had settled to seek anonymity offered little in the line of culture. Anton never heard any music except his own or that on a friend's victrola. His friend, Mears, had invested in some really good records, including a few of Caruso's.

One Sunday in April, Anton walked over to Mears's house for some intellectual stimulation and to listen to records, but his friend was not in. Since it was unseasonally warm and beautiful, Anton decided he would take his precious violin and find a quiet spot to play, someplace away from the noisy, depressing place he had to call home. So getting into his shabby, little car, he headed out into the countryside in a direction he had never gone before.

Every fence was resplendent with its row of locust trees in blossom. Fruit trees were in bloom, too, giving promise of the autumn's treasure to come. The worries and frustrations of the little, overcrowded house were suddenly behind him as he drove out over the back roads, thrilled at the sight of the green wheat growing and rippling in the breeze-like waves on the ocean. He passed the odorous field of the buzzards near the stone arched bridge, startled at this, the only jarring note in the pleasant countryside. When he spotted a large, shady oak tree near the side of the road, he decided it was the perfect place. Pulling up there, Anton parked his car and taking his violin, he excitedly climbed over a rail fence into a meadow.

The bees seemed to buzz in harmony with a bullfrog that supplied the bass, and he was delighted. A bird whistled from the top of a sycamore tree, while another started up in terror from under his feet. It fluttered so realistically in front of him, crying plaintively, "Kill dee, kill dee," that it nearly fooled him into thinking it really was injured. But then he remembered that this species of bird did this when its nest was near. Sure enough, there was a nest hidden in the grass, but he was careful not to brush the fledglings so that the mother bird would return.

He followed the lazily flowing stream for several miles, going upstream, growing more and more elated at the sharing in the joy and beauty of nature, for long sorely missed until now. Anton ventured on into the deepness of a woods, on and on, until at last he came to a large bed of moss. There he lay down to rest his weary body and soul, and clasping his violin in his arms, he fell asleep with all the beautiful sounds of spring in his ears.

Rachel wore her new green voile dress with apron and cape to church the very next Sunday after the trip to town. She felt self-conscious as she entered the church, her organdy cap tied tightly under her chin. Mother had put in an order for a new black bonnet like her own, a sunbonnet style instead of the wire frame kind that Rachel had always worn since her baptism at the age of twelve. Her new one would be considered more modest. The girls in her Sunday School class stared at her, nudging one another. Rachel was conscious of how her face had turned as crimson as the defiant wisps of hair that showed from under her cap.

By the time the preaching services were over, Rachel was in a state of exhaustion from her physical surroundings as well as her emotional anguish. Her back still felt the cramp of sitting on the hard wooden bench while Elder Hachman had expounded for a full hour and twelve minutes. Then the congregation knelt to pray, facing away from the preacher. Each person seemed to be shut in by the pews around him, kneeling on the splintery floor. The young people had whispered to each other, the boys on the men's side of the church being a little bit louder than the girls from the women's side. But Rachel had had no one to chat with since her Aunt Becky was on one side of her and Cousin Grace was on the other, so she had spent the twenty minutes of prayer watching the clock. Its hands moved so slowly!

At last, with a loud clearing of throats to relieve the tension and a bustle of rising from the kneeling position, the congregation sang the closing hymn led by Deacon Cook. He pranced to the front of the church on his neat little feet as immaculate as his black suit, its collar cut off in the approved way of the church. He wore no beard, but was so clean-shaven his pink cheeks shone. He tapped his pitch pipe, and everyone sang lustily. There was no organ or piano to accompany them, for the use of a musical instrument was considered a way of the "popular churches."

After dismissal, the women lingered near their door to greet one another with a customary kiss. When Deacon Cook's wife swept out of the women's door, she pulled aside her voluminous skirts so that they would not touch the Martin girls. These "rebellious" sisters, Golden and Patience, always wore their caps without strings. They even dared to make little curls of hair around the edge of their caps, and worst of all, they wore gold wristwatches instead of the silver ones, the only kind approved by the church. However Sister Cook looked approvingly at Rachel in her new clothes and kissed her. Her chin felt scratchy to Rachel, and she wondered if the rumor was true that Sister Cook had to shave.

Rachel saw her father being saluted by the deacons as well as the preachers in the greeting of a hearty kiss bestowed fully on the lips. All Plain People kissed, but all kissing was confined to members of the same sex. In fact Rachel had never in her life seen her father and mother kiss each other, and after the last baby left infancy, the children were seldom kissed. She never thought to question this.

When the good Sister Gray appeared at the church door, her gentle glance took in even the disconcerted Martin girls. She quickly moved over to them and lovingly kissed each one, inquiring about their invalid mother with sincere concern. Then she turned to Rachel and said quietly, "You are getting prettier every day, my child. Keep well and the Lord's blessings be on you."

Tears of joyful emotion sprang to Rachel's eyes. Being such an outcast because of the color of her hair, seldom had she experienced such tenderness and concern, even from her own family.

Brother Gray had been a preacher for years, yet had not been asked to preach very often. Rachel could not understand why, for on the few occasions he did, his sermon was made up of what St. John had to say, "Little children, let us love one another," and she for one was always moved. Other people felt good about this, but the Elder seemed to think that there should be more hellfire preached.

Brother and Sister Gray were much poorer than the other members of the church; their farm was small and not very productive. Brother Gray's buggy was almost as old as his weary, gray horse, but whenever inclement weather prevented him from working in the fields, he would hitch up his horse and with Sister Gray, go out to visit the sick and afflicted. The good, generous couple never left a home until he had prayed with its family. Many times Sister Gray would take chicken or beef broth and noodles to Granny Glacker who lived alone without any income except what a selfish son would spare her.

Some of the church members felt Brother Gray's poverty was an indication of a spiritual lacking, quoting, "The Lord helps those who help themselves," when they spoke of him. But Rachel alone noticed the peaceful, joyous look on this saintly couple's faces and saw that many other people did not have such a look of inner contentment and happiness.

When Rachel's brothers had brought around the horse and surrey, Papa let them take turns driving home. The two horses did double duty by being Sunday carriage horses, and farm horses the rest of the week. On the way home, Papa pointed to a faint haze of smoke hanging over the crest of the mountains to the south.

"Arbutus hunters, most likely, and they manage to start a brush fire every year. Somebody drops a cigarette in the leaves, then us fellows soon have a mountain fire to fight! Ought to be a law," he drawled.

Mother spoke up. "It seems to be a little late in the season for arbutus. Those little flowers like the snow. It seems too warm, even if it is April."

"Can us boys go up to the woods and see what is burning?" asked Amos suddenly.

"No, it might be dangerous," Papa muttered.

"Then can we go over to Willie Smith's place this afternoon? Please, Pa?"

"If your mother agrees."

"I guess it will be all right if you don't play ball or go fishing. Such things are not for the Sabbath," Mother admonished.

"Well we can go to the foot of the mountain," Amos persisted hopefully. "That way we would be out of danger and still see if the fire is burning yet."

"All right, but don't get caught in the storm. I'm afraid a thunder gust will come up this afternoon by the looks of the sky. See the clouds there to the left of the Cove. Your Grandfather Folk always said if a storm came up from over the Cove, it would be a bad one," Mother cautioned.

"A gust in April, Wife? It seems a little unseasonable, but those clouds aren't for nothing, I guess."

After the heavy midday dinner, the boys raced off to join their friends while Rachel helped her mother with the dishes. Because she felt she had much on her mind, she told her mother she would take a walk in the woods. "If the storm comes up, I will be close to the house and won't get wet." How Rachel longed to spend time away from her dreary life and go to her secret place.

Reluctantly Mother gave in. "I think I will slip over to the Fletchers to see how the little ones are. I'm going to take them another bunch of pennyroyal tea. It seemed to help them the last time." Her voice trailed off, and Rachel sensed the sorrow there. She wished the babies would get well, but so far her mother's nursing efforts had really not helped them to recover. With a slight pang of sadness tugging at her soul, Rachel sought the escape of the outdoors.

CHAPTER 4

Rachel loved music, yet had seldom experienced the elation of it. Her church congregation sang without any instrumental accompaniment, and at school only occasionally would she hear some student play on the piano. Rarely during assemblies would she hear some student play in an amateurish way on a clarinet or trombone. But since Professor Dereck's surprise visit and awe-inspiring performance on the violin, she often caught herself humming snatches from the *Blue Danube* Waltz, although she couldn't remember the name of that melody.

So humming a little tune, she whistled to Shep, the family collie, as she strolled out the back door. She started off across the fields and down a neighbor's lane to their back pasture. Golden shafts of light touched her head, still covered by the white cap she was expected to wear. Under her cap her bright hair was combed back severely, braided, and pinned in loops about her head. But she was so happy to be alone with her fantasies, even the harsh restrictions of reality she carried with her couldn't daunt her spirit.

As she approached the big pine tree and the stile that marked the edge of Bentley's Woods, the tender green of the willows and elms along the creek seemed to reach out to her, beckoning her to come to something magical. Sitting on the stile, she took off her shoes and stockings, and hiding them under the bottom step, she sprang down onto the lush grass. How sensuous was the feel of the grass on her bare feet! It made her feel free, so far from her drab life.

A brook flowing from a spring had watercress growing along its edge. Gingerly she advanced a slender foot into its icy current hoping to pick some, but gasping with the shock of its coldness, she drew it back. Just then a bird trilled comfortingly to her from the copse of elder bushes. A bee buzzed by. High in the top of a hemlock tree a crow cawed at her, and she smiled. The heady incense of fallen pine needles rose from a stand of white pines. She was at peace.

Secure in the knowledge that she was alone, Rachel took off her apron and the cape to her everyday dress, and finally shook her hair free from its pins and braids. She made a tidy bundle of these symbols of a dogmatic religion before running her side combs through the unbound hair. Giving it a toss, she began humming again the tune that had been haunting her, the one she had heard the violinist play that magical afternoon. Her eyes gleamed with emerald fires as she luxuriated in the freedom of the woods. Her simple green dress, now freed of the restrictive V-shaped cape and full apron, was a sheath to this exotic tiger lily.

Lifting her arms, Rachel laughed loudly and twirled around in her own dance of freedom. She leaped and glided deeper into the woods, overjoyed at her newfound physical freedom. Now there was purpose to her dance; she was going to her secret place. She had long ago discovered this perfect circle of green moss at the foot of a rocky cliff along the creek where it lay behind a low evergreen. All winter she had kept the secret of this delightful spot to herself, promising herself she would visit the place again when the warm spring returned. A break in the trees allowed a shaft of the hot April sunlight to touch her mass of flaming hair. Her green eyes, rimmed in their dark lashes and eyebrows, glowed in her face. Suddenly she stopped at the sound. Her startled gaze did not comprehend what she saw, nor did her ears believe what she heard.

A man was standing in the middle of the fairy ring of moss, with his back turned toward her; she could not see his face, and he did not see her as he tuned a violin. Suddenly Rachel knew who he was; it was the music master from the girls' school in town! But what a strange place to bring a violin! Then he started to play such delicate trills and tender notes that Rachel sank back onto the moss to listen. She was as quiet as a leaf dropping on a still pool as she crept even closer. Unconsciously she knelt directly behind him, a nerve throbbing in her throat, and her body quaking with emotion.

On and on went the trills, then sinking into a lower, more passionate chord, the music climaxed into an exquisite caress. By now Rachel's face was wet with tears. Her hands were clasped. She had momentarily forgotten who she was; she had become one with the music.

Hearing a soft sob, the master stopped playing in surprise and looked around sharply. "Are you a dryad? Am I imagining you or are you a real girl?" He walked over and helped her rise. "What glorious hair! I have never seen anything like it before in my life—no, wait! I *have* seen you before. Where?"

The quaking girl could not speak. The lump in her throat hurt with a physical ache. Unconsciously she pulled shut the open neck of her dress and stared at him with tear-filled eyes.

"Didn't I see you somewhere around here before? I seem to remember a girl with your glorious hair in a school somewhere around here. Was that you?"

Rachel nodded.

"You are crying! Why?" The man smiled and gently touched her wet face, then reaching into his pocket, he brought out a square of linen and carefully wiped her tears. "Now blow!" he commanded as he held the handkerchief to her nose. "That's better. Now tell me, why do you cry? Was it my music?"

Numbly she nodded her head, then finding her voice, she murmured weakly, "Please play some more."

He was moved by the emotion in her words. "I've never had a more appreciative audience. Never before has anyone cried at my concerts."

Again the violin's imprisoned spirit cried out. Again sobs rose from the depths of Rachel's soul. The fragrance of the earth seemed to fill her lungs as the world stood still. Even the birds ceased their songs to listen.

Eventually the man laid down his violin and again gazed with incredulity at this exotic creature in her simple attire. Why, she was even barefoot!

"How did you get here? You look like a wood sprite," he teased softly.

"No, I'm only a girl," she giggled, comforted by his kind face and gentle manner. "Please, play some more music! I've never heard anything so grand."

So on and on he played. They were both so involved in the music that they were unaware of the ominously darkening sky. Suddenly the rumble of thunder sounded from the southwest, and before the startled pair could move, a sharp crack of lightning and thunder preceded the abrupt downpour of rain. The woods instantly became as dark as night.

"The storm is coming from over the Cove. That's where my mother says all of the bad storms come from," Rachel shouted over the sound of the thunder. "Come, we must find a place to get out of this storm! It's too dangerous to stay here."

"Are there any houses nearby where we can seek shelter?" the man inquired.

"Yes, the Bentleys live just a step away. Come on, quick! I'll show you."

Tucking his precious violin under his coat to shield it from the rain, Anton grabbed Rachel's hand and raced through the trees, turning sharply to the left away from the creek. They came to a barbed wire fence. Rolling under its sharp barbs, they picked themselves off the drenched grass and sped across a field in the heavy downpour. They arrived panting at an old, run-down, brick farmhouse.

A chicken had taken shelter on the porch, but otherwise the house appeared to be deserted, for no one answered the man's frantic pounding on the door while trying to shield his violin. Crash after crash of thunder sounded and sharp streaks of lightning played about them as though seeking to destroy them. Still no answer came, and the door remained solidly closed. It seemed the heavens were bent on destruction, and each grew secretly fearful.

Rachel was too frightened to remain there. "Come, we must run for the barn. Let's go up the barn bridge, it's closer."

Suiting words into action, they raced up the bank of earth behind the barn that was known as the "barn bridge." A small door had been cut into the larger barn door that was opened during haying season to accommodate the hay wagons. The two soaking refugees fell through this small door just as hail was heard beginning to fall on the tin roof of the barn. The blackness of the interior seemed as cold as an arctic night.

Sinking into the hay, Rachel began to shake uncontrollably, both from fright and the cold rain that chilled her to the bone. Their dripping clothes soon made the hay become wet.

"Come, we will have to get out of these wet clothes and rub ourselves with this hay to restore circulation," her companion suggested. "Get out of your wet clothes, and I will hang them up on this rope. Wring them out well."

Rachel lost her inhibitions in the emergency of the moment, but still she tried to shield her nakedness with a large handful of hay. But she was too numb to let it worry her that she was undressing in front of a strange man. Even as they huddled in the hay trying to get some warmth, Rachel still shook in her chill. The man drew her to him to warm her quaking body, and then they buried themselves in the hay, up to their necks.

The storm raged on, long into the evening. Lightning flashed through the cabalistic designs left open in the brick work of the gable ends of the barn, which were meant to keep away evil spirits. Although the hail seemed to have abated, the rain persisted, pouring down in torrents.

Rachel began to feel a strange tenderness stirring in her body. She tried to remember what her mother had taught her, but as she drew more and more of the physical warmth from her companion, a feeling of great security rushed over her. How right it seemed that this man, a stranger no longer, lay here beside her, caressing her body with hands and lips.

The lovers were so insistent in their demands that time stood still. The only world that existed for them both was here in the haymow. Then came a burst of ecstatic delight that eclipsed anything Rachel had ever known. She moaned in fruition.

They slept, and when they awoke, they could hear movements below them in the cow barn. Then came the drawling voices of people milking the cows. The rain was slackening.

Anton looked at the girl, his eyes full of tenderness. "What's your name? Do you know I have loved you and do not even know your name?"

"Rachel," she whispered.

"Will your people miss you? Do you live far from here?"

"About three miles if you follow the crick. I don't know what I'll tell my mother. You don't suppose I could get a baby, do you?" For the first time Rachel's conscience started to hurt her. It had been a dream.

"Not likely, at least not for the first time. But I should not have let you do it. I'll take all the blame. But what will you tell your parents about where you were during the storm?"

Rachel thought for a moment. "I'll simply tell them the truth that I spent the afternoon here in the barn to get out of the rain. They don't need to know that you were here, too. But we must not let the Bentleys know we are here. They have a couple of sons who could make trouble for us. We'd better be very quiet until they leave the barn."

Anton crept over to where their clothes still hung and felt them. "Our clothes aren't any drier than they were before. We may as well stay the rest of the night. It is still raining."

As he slid back to her side, she met him with an embrace, once more opening her soul and body to him.

A rooster's crow told them that it was morning. They could no longer hear rain pounding on the roof, so reluctantly they slipped into their still-damp clothes. After a final embrace, Rachel promised to meet Anton again on the following Sunday afternoon in the woods.

The rain-laden branches of the trees still dripped as Anton walked briskly through the woods to his car, while Rachel ran swiftly to the place where she had left her shoes, cap, and cape. She clasped the sodden bundle to her breast and gaining the back door of her home before anyone could see her, she crept up the back stairs to her room. She found dry clothes, and braiding up her hair, she donned a fresh cap in time to dash downstairs when her father called her.

"Is Mother home yet? Wasn't that a terrible storm? I found shelter in the Bentley's barn and I sure was scared," she told him nervously. Would he be able to tell by looking at her what she had experienced?

Papa didn't seem as interested in hearing how she got home in the larger news that the Fletcher's barn had been struck by lightning. "It did some damage. Mother just told me when she got home. She's upstairs now, so you'd better start some breakfast."

Since her father expressed no further curiosity about her whereabouts during the storm, Rachel relaxed a bit as she set about getting breakfast. Soon Mother came downstairs to take up the reins of her household duties. The conversation at breakfast was full of reports of the damage to the Fletcher's barn.

"Do you know," said Mother as she was frying out strips of mush at the stove, "I think there could be something to it that the Fletchers are bewitched! Here they have sick children, sick cows, a sick shoat, and now their barn is struck by lightning. I hardly blame them for going after a witch doctor."

"Don't say such things, Mother. You will bring trouble here!" Papa poured some sorghum syrup over his fried mush. "We must put our trust in the Lord."

"Well anyhow, the snakes certainly got awake from such thunder as we had last night. By the way, boys, where were *you* during the thunder gust?" Mother still had not gotten around to questioning Rachel, and now her fear was renewed that her exploits of the previous night would be discovered.

"Willie Smith's mother made us stay in their house during the night," Amos answered quickly, "We knew that you wouldn't worry because we were at the Smith's place."

Rachel was now sure she would be questioned about her movements of the previous afternoon and night, and she felt a hot wave of shame come over her. But just then a horse and buggy was heard reining to a halt outside the Miller's front gate. As the family turned to see who it was, Grandfather Miller cam limping up the walk.

Rachel silently said a prayer for this respite.

"My, my, you people still at the breakfast table! I've been up a couple of hours and had my breakfast over an hour ago just before I started for your place," the old man chortled.

"Then come in and have some more. There's still some mush left that I can fry up easy. Rachel, set a place for your grandfather." Mother bustled about putting another stick of wood into the kitchen range, as Rachel rose from her place with great relief.

Grateful that Grandfather's arrival stopped any investigations that might come her way, Rachel longed to kiss the old man. But he would have been very surprised if she had. She had not kissed the old man since she was a little girl. As she went about collecting plates and cutlery, Rachel's emotions were mingled as she recalled the night of her transgressions. She had no friend to tell her secret to and felt she could not even if she had such a close friend. Her mother had often warned her about letting a boy "feel her leg," but until last night she had always been unsure of what would happen then. She only knew that she would have to go before the Church if she got into the family way and had to get married, and this thought filled her with dread. Suddenly it came to her again. Was she, in fact, a child of the DEVIL?

CHAPTER 5

During the week following the storm, Mother spent several full days at the Fletcher's house helping with the sickness of the little ones, leaving Rachel with the care of the house and garden as well as helping her father and boys to do the milking. School had ended for the term, and Rachel would never return to school again. Because she was so busy at home this week, she had no time to think of her experiences of the Sunday before until she was alone in her room at night. Then she relived each thrilling moment with relish. Only occasionally did thoughts of guilt come to her, but she was able to force them back into her conscience and she looked forward to the next meeting with Anton with great eagerness.

The following Sunday afternoon, Mother decided to take an afternoon nap while Papa went over to see a neighbor, taking the boys with him. Elated at this stroke of good fortune, once again Rachel stole off for the woods. She was confident that no neighbor could see Anton's car, for he parked it several miles away on the other side of the woods.

Once again Anton entered the woods and walked its lovely length until he came to the mossy ring where he had first seen the girl. Again he had brought his violin. He was surprised to find his heart beating so eagerly in expectation of keeping this tryst with the simple farm girl. He looked around anxiously, but she was not yet there. During the past week he often thought of her while he occupied his lonely couch in the studio. He gave no practical thought to any sentiments he may have kindled in Rachel's life, for becoming involved in a serious relationship with her was out of the question since he was engulfed in debt and weighed down with the responsibilities of seven children and an invalid wife. His realistic future looked dim. In this mood of sorrow and regret, he was playing with so much concentration that he did not notice Rachel's arrival until he played the last notes. Again she had tears in her beautiful eyes, and he greeted her with, "How did you like that?"

"It is so beautiful, yet so *sad*! The composer must have felt very lonely when he wrote it or else you must feel very sad."

Anton sighed as he eased himself wearily onto the mossy ring, drawing a fine linen handkerchief from his pocket to dry her tears. Then he caressed her face and her body. At first Rachel held back, then soon he had wooed her so that again she forgot herself in the passion of the moment. A few hours later the setting of the sun and the twittering of the night birds aroused the pair of lovers to thoughts of duty elsewhere.

"Anton, why don't you come to my house and meet my people?" she suggested hopefully. "Since we are in love, we should meet proper. I won't be ashamed to introduce you to my people, then we can get married."

The man looked at her glowing face in disbelief. He realized he had been wrong to give no thought to anything but his own desires. Marry her! How could he ever tell her the truth?

"What do you want me to do, my love? Do you want me to ask your father for your hand?"

She had seen the look of astonishment in his eyes. "I think you had better before I get into the family way! Then I would really be in trouble!" She laughed.

"What would your father do, take a whip to you?"

"Not exactly that, but it would really hurt my folks, for then you and I would have to go before the church and ask for forgiveness."

"Forgiveness? Forgiveness for what? For loving each other? Surely you do not think it is a sin to simply love one another?"

"But I should never have allowed you to—to—," her voice trailed off in shame and horror. Suddenly she realized he had no intention of marrying her. She struggled from his arms as in a nightmare and ran home as swiftly as a deer. He gazed after her in sorrow.

Days went by, cloudy days, rainy days, days of foreboding as Rachel struggled with her conscience. Her body longed to go back to the woods but her mind said *No*! The next Sunday came and the one after that, but she fought the urge to return to the woods.

One day while mowing the yard near the fence next to the road, a car came by and screeched to a halt a few yards away. It was Anton! He stared in disbelief at the white-capped girl behind the hollyhocks.

"As I live and breathe, Rachel! Is that you?" he called. "What is that thing on your beautiful hair? Why are you wearing it? Where have you been the last few Sundays?"

In her shock, Rachel twisted a corner of her apron and self-consciously pulled her cape into place. She blushed so red that her face was as brilliant as her hair.

"Come on, Rachel! Tell me, why do you wear those strange clothes? Are you one of the Plain People?"

"Yes, Anton," she answered. Then with hope, "Why don't you get out and come inside to meet my people?"

"Meet your family! Well hardly—at least not today," he caught himself. "But you must come to the woods on Sunday, for I have something to tell you." With that he stepped on the gas pedal and drove off in a cloud of dust as she stared after him stupidly.

Mother had come out onto the porch. "Who was that fellow? Did you know him?"

"Just someone asking the way," she lied, not knowing what else to say. She could not tell her mother about Anton when it was painfully plain that he did not wish to meet them.

But the following Sunday afternoon, she sped through the woods. This time she was wearing her cap and the rest of her plain clothes, feeling protected in her religious garb. Today they would have to come to an understanding; she could no longer meet him in the woods. She was determined, either they would marry or she would no longer see him.

When she appeared from behind the bushes, he was playing his violin, for he learned how to woo her. Today his music was so wonderful that her knees turned to water and her face to adoration. How could she live without this glorious music? How had she ever thought she could leave him? She had never lived until this man brought her his music. She suddenly realized that.

He stopped playing when he saw her. Approaching her, he gently removed her cap. Taking out the hair pins, he ran his hands through her glorious hair, exulting in its beauty before he crushed her lips beneath his. Stripped of her armor, she was vulnerable again; she had no power to resist him.

Later on, as the sun began sinking, he told her gently he would not be back for a few Sundays since he would be going to Philadelphia on business.

"I'll get in touch when I get back. I will be thinking about you all the time, so goodbye for now. Go slowly so you can hear this beautiful *Liebestraun*. It was written for you." He began to play as she turned to walk away.

Rachel could hear its haunting strains as far as the bend in the creek. She continued home sadly, feeling mysteriously within her heart that she would never see him again.

During the next few days, Rachel suffered some qualms of conscience for her misdeeds, but she stifled them with the decision to convert Anton to her faith. It followed naturally that then they would be married, the ceremony rectifying the transgressions of the secret meetings in the woods. To her it was quite a simple solution.

At home the family prepared for the annual Spring Love Feast. The village seamstress was called in to make up new dresses for both Rachel and her mother for the occasion, for it was unheard of to go to the Love Feast in anything but a new dress, and that a summer one. The colors were dark or muted as always, but the material was crisp and new.

"Stand still, Rachel, while I try this skirt on you," Miss Susie, the dressmaker, commanded. "I declare, I think you are getting fatter than last time I used this pattern." The blue voile material *did* seem to fit snugly, but Rachel thought nothing of it.

The dresses were finished in time for Saturday, the first day of the Love Feast. Mother had the boys pick as many peonies as they could find around the yard; their showy red and pink and white blossoms nearly filled up the surrey. Old canning jars stuffed under the back seat served as vases. But these flowers were not for the church; no one ever decorated the Plain People's house of worship. No, these blossoms were to festoon the graves in the graveyard that adjoined the old limestone church building.

When the Miller family arrived at the Mills Meeting House, a long line of horses and buggies were already lined up at the hitching rail inside an open-fronted shed. Each driver had brought along a bucket of water for his thirsty beasts, for it was a warm day for the last of May. In addition to the more rustic means of transportation, several automobiles were parked in front of the church.

Inside the church, singing had already started, and Deacon Cook was the chorister. He pranced about on his neat little feet, and his hair was combed down so slick that he fairly shone. When the preaching started, Rachel could smell the coffee boiling in the big tin coffee pots in the basement where the church kitchen was located.

As usual the men sat on one side of the church, little boys sitting with their fathers, while little girls huddled next to their mothers on the women's side. Many women were calmly suckling their babies while others cradled sleeping infants in their arms. The more modest women laid handkerchiefs over their bare breasts, but others used only the edge of their V-shaped capes to cover themselves. Rachel tried to avert her eyes from these nursing mothers; the sight always embarrassed her.

Soon the sweet aroma of cooking meat rose from the kitchen. It was the lamb being cooked for the evening service.

During the noon intermission, all of the young people ate at a single long table in the cool basement that smelled of freshly scrubbed wood. Piles of sliced bread were placed at intervals on the table. Rounds of butter, tasting faintly of the first wild garlic the cows ate while grazing had been set on the table along with dishes of cucumber pickles and dark red beet pickles. Steaming coffee was served in tin cups. Everyone was welcome to seat at the midday meal, even "outsiders" who might happen to come to visit.

Tubs for the coming feet washing ceremony were stacked in several piles, and in her distraction, Rachel came close to kicking them as she had finished eating and was climbing the stairs to the outside lawn to join the others. The young men had already started to eye the girls and to wander out under the huge maple trees to talk with them. Many future marriages began here at this service.

But Rachel chose to wander alone. She noticed David Lowe looking her way, but she turned her back on him. He was a widower with a child, and if rumor had it correctly, the child was mentally retarded. David's old aunt Virgie took care of his house and now the child, if her feeble efforts could be so termed. The crotchety Aunt Virgie was up in years and did what little she could. Anyway Rachel was too full of her secret love to let a widower at least fifteen years her senior make any romantic impressions.

The afternoon service of the Love Feast was the Examination Sermon, and usually a vigorous preacher from the lower valley visited to preach an emotional sermon, chastising the sins of the flesh and the pride of life. This young man also preached about preparing one's self spiritually for the most sacred evening service: the Love Feast and the Holy Communion. As he preached, Rachel felt pangs of guilt for the stolen meetings in the woods and discovered that she had committed the grievous sin of "fornication." What a foreboding word it seemed. The sermon disquieted her.

At sundown Papa and the boys went home to feed the stock and to milk while Mother went to the graveyard to see how the peonies were bearing up as decorations on the graves, visiting each and every grave to be sure that the sexton was taking proper care of them.

Left alone again, Rachel stood about awkwardly, trying to avoid the ever-present David Lowe. Finally she went to the screened-in outhouse with its two compartments. In the next side she could hear some giggling girls discussing the beau they expected to have after the next service.

"Aren't you afraid that Rachel Miller has her cap set for Luther?" asked one in a catty tone. Rachel recognized the voice as that of Deacon Nester's daughter.

"My, my, you must think I am ugly! No one would ever look at that redhead unless he was as desperate as David Lowe, who needs a wife to take care of his house and that crazy child."

"I wonder why her mother makes her wear a cape and an organdy cap?" speculated the Cook girl. "My mother would *never* make me give up bobinet caps and put on those horrible capes!"

"Do you know what *I* heard?" the other whispered disdainfully. "My father and mother were talking one night when they didn't know I was listening. I heard that Rachel was asked to dress that way by the church because they considered her a temptation to some of the men. Did you ever hear tell of such a thing! Just imagine, Rachel Miller being a temptation!" Both girls convulsed in screams of laughter.

Rachel's face burned with humiliation. Sobs rose in Rachel's throat, and with tears streaming from her eyes, she ran blindly to the front of the church building. Regaining control, she peered through her tears into the interior. The deacons were raising the backs of some of the pews and sliding them in place to form a table. The alternate pews were then arranged to accommodate a long row of communicants who would later sit on either side of the table, facing one another. Large bowls of broken bread were placed at intervals down the lengths of the long, white-draped tables along with plates heaped with carved, stewed lamb.

At the Holy Desk in front, large crystal decanters of grape juice stood beside the pewter chalices, one for the women's side and another for the men's side of the church. On trays lay the long, flat strips of unleavened communion bread, each strip pricked in rows of five pricks, each prick to commemorate the five wounds of Christ on the cross. Some of the deacons were pulling down the hanging oil lamps and lighting them in preparation for the evening service in spite of the fact that the sun had not yet set.

As Rachel stood there numbly, the congregation began to return and the tables began to fill. A few lingered outside, for it was thought that long-standing quarrels should be resolved; to eat the Love Feast with unconfessed grudges would bring down on them condemnation from God.

Shaking herself back to reality, Rachel humbly took a place beside a humpbacked girl from across the mountain. No one had paid any attention to the unfortunate girl, so Rachel smiled tentatively at her. The girl's face immediately lit up, and Rachel felt her heart easing a little.

At that moment, Deacon Cook announced a hymn, "At The Cross." Everyone joined in lustily.

"At the cross, At the cross, where I first saw the light and the burden of my heart rolled away."

A number of other songs were sung whose theme was that of holiness. The scripture was read concerning the Last Supper, when another of the visiting ministers read, "He riseth from supper, and laid aside His garments; and took a towel and girdeth Himself. After that He poureth water into a basin and began to wash the disciples' feet, and to wipe them with the towel where with He was girded."

There was a general movement at both sides of the church to begin the feet washing by removing shoes and stockings.

Because she sat at the end of the bench, it was Rachel's duty to begin the ceremony by washing the feet of the humpbacked girl next to her. She rose upon completion of this holy service and kissed the girl as was the custom. Then Rachel murmured, "May God bless you."

The girl looked very surprised, for this greeting was an innovation to her. The greeting smacked too strongly of emotion, and the Church did not support too strong of emotions being expressed. Deacon Cook and Deacon Rice brought the lamb's broth at this time and they carefully poured the steaming liquid into the bowls of broken bread. They carefully covered each bowl with a plate to prevent it from cooling off.

As the steam from the bowl entered her nostrils, suddenly the odor of the cooked meat and the broth was too much for Rachel. Her head started to feel too big for her. She felt nauseous. From the heat of the scores of people sitting in rows, the peevish children crying in the sanctuary as well as in the upstairs nursery, where some ancient wooden cradles held them, to the ache in her heart, were all too much. She slumped forward, then to her horror, she felt she was going to vomit. *"Oh, if I can only make it outside!"* she thought as she pressed her handkerchief to her lips. She made it through the door, but to her humiliation she started to vomit near the door step.

Out of the dusk there came a gentle voice, "Here, sister, lean on me. Here's a clean handkerchief." It was David Lowe, of all people! Why wasn't he inside washing feet? "I saw you leave and I thought I could help you. Are you all right now?"

Rachel could only nod her head. How fortunate that she had not taken off her shoes and stockings yet! Her feet would be washed by the girl at the other end of the bench, and they had not reached the middle of the long row as yet.

"Why don't you wait a while before going inside? It will be several minutes before it is your turn to be washed."

"Won't you miss out in your row?"

"No, Rachel, they haven't come to me yet."

"Thank you very much, Brother Lowe. I think I had better go inside now before I am missed and someone starts to talk."

David's sad eyes followed her inside where she participated in the rest of the solemn service that was practiced but twice a year.

The girl next to her looked at Rachel curiously when she had regained her seat. Later, after the feet washing was finished and everyone had washed his or her hands from a basin being passed around, more songs were sung. Then the soup was eaten, four persons eating from a common bowl, and after the plate of lamb was eaten, the tables were covered.

The visiting preachers as well as the elders carried trays of the communion bread and let each person break the bread for the person at his side. At last the symbol of the Lord's shed blood was drunk in the form of grape juice, the chalice being passed from lip to lip. The Love Feast was now over.

Rachel did not tell her mother about her nausea, but rode home in silence. A gibbous moon was rising and the earth looked full of shadows. Her inner conflict seemed more than she could bear.

CHAPTER 6

Two weeks following the Love Feast went by without any cessation of the horrible nausea Rachel experienced each morning behind the cows she milked. Once little Jacob found her gagging and heaving, and he asked her in his innocence, "Rachel, do you have the bellyache?"

She avoided telling her mother anything about her nausea but brewed up some catnip tea to settle her stomach. Then one day while looking at the calendar, the horrible suspicion came to her—she was in the family way! She was going to have a baby! She would have to get married! To have to stand up before the church members and confess, and Anton not even a member! What in the world would she do?

I'll have to tell him, she told herself. But how would she get in touch with him? She did not even know where he lived.

I will have to go to town to try to find him and tell him about the baby, she decided. She knew that he taught at the girls' school, so that was where she would go. Suddenly a beautiful thought came to her. Her mother's old schoolmate, a descendent of a runaway slave that had taken up residence in this community at the time of the Underground Railroad and had settled near Mrs. Miller's childhood home, was a cook at the girls' school. Rachel would go to see her. She would know where Anton lived.

Since Mother had gone over to Grandpa Miller's home for the day to clean house, Rachel started to walk to town. The butterflies were fluttering about the honeysuckles and the mourning doves kept up their incessant cry in the woods as she passed by. She reached the long hill that led to Peterboro Road when she heard a car approach from the rear. To her surprise and confusion, the driver was Deacon Cook. He stopped and smirked, "Going far, Rachel?"

"Just into town," she shrugged, hoping to sound casual.

"Come on and get in. I'm going there myself and don't mind a little company. Isn't it quite a distance for you to walk, and all by yourself?" he added with that evil smile as she reluctantly climbed in beside him.

"Papa is using the horses, so I have to walk. I have an errand in town," she answered, avoiding his gaze.

"Well, now, my dear child, I won't tell if you don't want your people to know that you ran off for the day," and the oily quality of his voice as well as his familiar hand on her knee made her cringe. After that she stared stonily ahead and drew into her corner of the seat, avoiding conversation. It was the longest drive of her life.

"Here we are. Now that wasn't long, was it? Where do you want out?"

"Just put me out at the girls' school."

"I wasn't aware that you knew anyone there." he looked at her quizzically.

"Well everyone knows Aunt Sally, the cook. My mother went to school with her." Rachel couldn't get out of the automobile fast enough.

Seeking the kitchen at the rear of the dining hall, Rachel found Aunt Sally herself, sitting in a rocking chair in her room off the kitchen. She was fanning herself with a palm fan. It was too early to begin preparations for the evening meal.

After they had exchanged warm greetings, Rachel stammered out her request, Where did the music master live? Aunt Sally eyed her keenly, as Rachel felt the woman could see into the depths of her soul. "Why do you want him, honey? He has his share of trouble. His house is full of trouble, seven young ones and an ailing wife. Surely *you* ain't about to bring him any more trouble!"

The shock that registered on the young girl's face confirmed Aunt ally's suspicions. *What! A wife* and seven children! Merciful Heavens! The heat of the room was too much. The room began to spin, then there was blackness as Rachel fell into the abyss.

When Rachel opened her eyes, she found the old lady waving burnt feathers under her nose as she fanned her. Tears were streaming down over her brown cheeks and she sobbed uncontrollably.

"Rachel, what have you gone and done now? May the good Lord have mercy on you if it's like I think it is. Your dear mother will die of shame, and the people of your church will crucify you."

Rachel's face was as white as a sheet and her green eyes stared blankly at the old woman. Her hair stood away from her face as she started to moan and to weep like one having a nightmare. She, Rachel Miller, was a fallen woman, a girl so shameful that no one would ever want to have anything to do with her again. She *was* the Devil's child! They had been right all along!

"Aunt Sally, Aunt Sally, what will I do? I love him so much, and here he is a married man!" she sobbed. "I just met him three months ago!" The two women mingled their tears.

"How far do you reckon you has gone, honey?" asked Aunt Sally soberly after a moment as she blew her nose.

"For two times now."

"Then you are in your third month." Aunt Sally started to fumble down the neck of her dress, bringing out a handkerchief wrapped around something. She opened it, and Rachel saw her take out a roll of bills. She counted out several and pushed them into Rachel's hand.

"There, honey, run along before it gets too dark. The kitchen girls will be coming in soon to help get ready for supper. You keep your mouth shut and go out to Miss Lucy's place. She will know what to do to help you. If that ain't enough money, tell her I'll see to it. I owe your mama that much for old times' sake. Now run."

Rachel looked about her very carefully before she set out, then decided she would cut across the fields so that she would not meet anyone. It would never do to let Deacon Cook see her again with her face swollen.

Sobbing as she crept along, she managed to get to the woods that ran along the buzzards field. Dear God, she would have to cross that field! Well buzzards never hurt live people, and she would go as fast as she could.

The overwhelming stench struck her at the edge of the field. The huge, black vultures were feeding on the carrion that lay scattered about. There was so little light by now that she could scarcely see the way. Her feet caught on something putrid and squashed it, causing her to slip and fall into the obscene stuff. Again came that dreadful nausea, the bile rising in her throat, causing her to befoul the entire front of her dress. She was now as repulsive as the vultures about her.

Screaming, she raced across the bridge, panting up the road and stopping at intervals to vomit. Finally she reached Miss Lucy's neat pink and white cottage set so sedately behind its picket fence. The red ramblers reached out tendrils to catch at her hair as she went through the gate.

"Miss Lucy! Miss Lucy!" Hysteria gave her strength to cry out.

The curtained glassed door opened and a rose-shaded lamp silhouetted Miss Lucy's dainty figure.

"Who in the world? Why, Rachel Miller, what in the name of Heaven is the matter? You look like God's wrath—and—whew! You smell worse than a privy! What have you been up to?"

But Rachel sank at the foot of the porch in her second faint of the day. When she regained her senses, she was lying on a narrow, white-sheeted bed, without blankets or quilts. She had on a clean, white gown and her stinking clothes were in a heap on the floor.

"Here, Rachel, drink this tea. It's good for you. Now tell me all about it."

It took the shaking girl a long time to get out the whole wonderful, sordid story. While she told it, Miss Lucy shook her head again and again. "Poor babe in the woods! How innocent you are."

Then Rachel produced the money Aunt Sally had given her and asked Miss Lucy to help her. The older woman went into the tiny living room and extinguished the rosy lamp, then drew the shades and said in a very businesslike way, "All right, since that is the only way. At least I will give you the right kind of abortion. I learned this well when I was a young nurse, keeping my eyes open in the hospital where I trained. Cleanliness and a steady hand are the main things. With any luck, you will be as good as new in a few days. But you must keep your mouth shut. I could end up in jail."

Rachel never realized it could be like that. Miss Lucy had nothing to deaden the pain except a little laudanum. This she was very sparing of, but it did not take her very long. Just as she was tearing up old sheets for napkins, there was a heavy knocking at the front door.

"Lucy, come on and let me in! It's me."

Miss Lucy muttered, "Oh, bother! I can't leave you now. But lie still for a little while, and I will send him away."

"Lucy, come on, let me in!" The voice seemed very familiar to Rachel as she lay half conscious on the narrow, white bed. Who could it be?

"Come on! Let me in, I say! It's Claude!"

Claude! What that was Deacon Cook! What in the world was he doing here? Was he after her?

"All right, coming." Miss Lucy shut the door to the tiny room with her patient on the narrow bed. A murmur of voices came from the frilly pink and white bedroom next to the one Rachel was in. She heard Miss Lucy say, "Hold on a bit, Claude. I have something on hand that just can't wait."

Returning to Rachel, she finished the work at hand, then gathering up the girl's filthy clothing, set them to soak in a sudsy tub in a washroom off the kitchen. Rinsing them, she hung them to dry on a line strung up behind her kitchen range. Bidding Rachel to sleep, she spread a blanket over her and entered the room where the impatient deacon lay waiting.

Dawn was just streaking across the east as a rooster crowed, waking up Rachel. Miss Lucy came into the room, then cried in dismay, "You are bleeding too much to walk home, and I can't keep you here. Good gracious, what must I do?"

A grunt from the bedroom seemed to answer her question. That was it, the perfect solution. "I'll send you home in his car. Neither one of you dares to tell on the other!"

In a few minutes, Rachel was now in her dry but clean clothes. Miss Lucy had fixed her so that no more hemorrhaging was likely to take place, and Deacon

Cook was roused from his peaceful sleep. His expression when he saw Rachel could only be matched by her shame when she saw him.

Backing the Model T out from behind the hedge, he helped Rachel in and set out as fast as the little car would go for her home. There was no conversation, only heavy thoughts. When they arrived at the Miller house, no one was up as yet.

"Remember, if you tell on me, I'll tell on you!" was the farewell from the disgruntled deacon.

Rachel managed to get up the back steps to her room and fall into bed where she experienced a violent chill. Crawling under her blankets and log cabin quilt, she shook the bed in her paroxysms.

Little Jacob came up the stairs to call her, but when he saw her face so flushed, he was frightened. "Rachel, what's the matter? You sick? Can't you get us some breakfast?"

"Where's Mother? Jakey, I don't feel so good."

"Mother went to the Fletcher's place last night. Didn't you hear her? Their baby died."

"Oh, my! Please get me a glass of water. I'm burning up. I think I have a bad cold."

Swimming off into a vortex of shadows, she surfaced now and then to drink greedily of the water her adored younger brother brought fresh from the spring.

"Sis, you look sick enough to die. I'm going over to Fletchers and get Mother."

When Mother came home she decided that Rachel must have the grippe.

"Wading in that cold spring water after watercress the other day brought this on along with your monthly sickness. I'll send Papa to town to get a bottle of Lydia Pinkhams. That will straighten you out. That and some mother's worth salve poultices."

Mother went out to the backyard and found several plants of mother's worth. Taking the leaves she fried them out in lard. She put this hot mixture in a poultice and placed it on Rachel's chest.

The rest of the month and well into the next, Rachel was too weak to do more than stay in her room. She helped her mother string beans or seed cherries by crawling down to the kitchen on occasion, but she soon sought the sanctuary of her room. She cried for hours each day. Horrible dreams came to her, and she felt a great emptiness inside. So devoid of meaning was life that she felt there could never be anything but sorrow in existence. She avoided saying her nightly prayers and never wore her cap. She had not been to church for a month.

Mother and Papa were as puzzled as everyone else, and a horrible suspicion came to them. What if the witches had put a spell on her as they had on the Fletchers?

Finally Papa said, "We are going to take her to the doctor. Old Doc Schluder came from Germany and he knows a lot more than any of these here young doctors. So we'll drive across the mountains and see him."

The old doctor examined her very carefully, then sent his nurse to another room while he talked to her privately.

"Have you just lost a child?" he queried bluntly.

"I am not married," Rachel answered unsteadily.

"Yes, I know that, but the facts I have discovered tell me that you are suffering from an abortion. If I am right, and feel certain that I am, you must never take such matters into your hands again. That is very dangerous. I will give you some medicine that should help you."

To the anxious parents he said, "I have examined her and found her to be a little anemic. I want her to take this medicine, and when it is gone, come back for more. She is to be out in the sun as much as possible and is to drink plenty of milk. She should eat plenty of red meats and get some exercise. She can help with household chores, but no heavy lifting. She could go for walks or drives frequently. She seems to be suffering from melancholia."

As for taking any more walks in the woods as she was once so eager to do, the very thought of going there turned her bowels to water. She would never meet Anton there again, and the wonderful music that Anton played for her was something she would never hear again. Her Paradise was lost.

CHAPTER 7

Mother dosed Rachel with the doctor's medicine as well as the herbs she went into the fields and woods to find. She brewed catnip tea for her stomach, boneset tea for her liver, ginger tea for chills, and pennyroyal for the vapors. These vapors or crying spells were beginning to lessen, but a numbness took over Rachel's body. She could see nothing ahead of her in life.

One evening at the supper table, Papa asked the family, "How would you like to go to the Steven's barn raisin'? Tomorrow is a slack day since the wheat is all harvested, and it is too early to cut the late hay again."

So the next morning, Mother had a big basket of homemade bread, some red beet pickled eggs, a big jar of fresh apple sauce, and she even included a dried apple snits pie. Its dark goodness oozed out from its lattice-work crust.

Mother and Rachel wore clean everyday dresses, and the men wore their blue overalls. Rachel's dress, however, was not one of her new ones with the cape and apron. She came out to the gate where the family had been waiting, with her hair in braids and hanging down her back. She looked like an innocent school girl instead of an "unseemly woman." She had no cap on her head. No one said anything to her, but she noticed her mother's stricken face, so calling, "Wait a minute," Rachel rushed back to her room and hastily pinned up her braids. But she did not put on her cap.

A bobwhite started to call out to the world as they passed slowly in the family carriage. The boys took turns trying to imitate its whistle. A rain dove was calling its mournful song that rain was coming, but there were no rain clouds in the sky. Yellow butterflies flitted about the blue thistles, the day lilies, and the daisies that grew by the dusty road. Scarcely a word was spoken as the horse plodded on, mile after mile.

At the Steven's farmhouse, long tables were set under the trees on the side lawn. Rachel found herself the self-appointed guard at the spring that bubbled up near the sycamore tree at the edge of the lawn. Little toddlers seemed drawn to the place. The regular spring house was a little farther away since the water in the yard spring was thought to be contaminated by the barnyard nearby. Rachel drew the children away from the dangerous spot. Then seeing the flies gathering over the food, she went inside and found a fly bush made of newspapers sewn to a stick and then cut into strips. She busied herself wielding it over the table, chasing away the flies while the other women scurried about setting such delicacies on the table that only this group could produce.

In the kitchen big skillets of chicken were frying, while pickles of all kinds, shoofly pies, montgomery pies, cherry, apple, and custard pies were set out. When the dinner bell rang, Rachel became conscious of the stares of the men at her uncovered red hair. She hid herself in the house until after the first few tables of men had eaten. She wished now that she had worn her plainer clothes and her cap.

David Lowe was with the other men on ladders, putting timbers in place for the frame. After the noon meal they would be ready for the roof and weather boarding. Since there were a good two dozen men working together, they had hopes that the barn would be finished by the next day except for the paint. The barn bridge had been put in several days before the raising took place. This inclined bank of earth led up to the big doors on the back of the barn and would lead through onto the barn floor. On either side there were huge mows, waiting for the winter supply of hay. Next to the mows were mouse-proof granaries for the corn, wheat, rye, and oats.

On the ground floor below would be the stock and horse barn. Next week some of these men, all brothers in the church, would return and give the barn two coats of paint, all free work. Then the barn would be complete, all for only the cost of the materials used.

As David nailed the window frames together, he could see a flash of red out of the corners of his eyes. No wonder he hit his thumb with the hammer! He had thought so much about this girl who looked like a brilliant bird but wore such a tragic face. Why had the joy of life gone out of it? Were her parents forcing her into a senseless existence with her mode of dressing?

Deacon Cook came through the yard after the men were all resting on the front porch and caught Rachel as she was bringing more food for the women and children to eat.

"How are you, Rachel? You haven't let out anything, have you, my dear?" he purred in his silky voice, grasping her by the upper arms. He reached up and smoothed her hair.

Rachel shook herself free from his odious touch, spilling some hot coffee onto his arm as she did so. He looked balefully at her.

"I told nothing. Now please go away from me." And with quivering lips she hurried by him. The very idea! Her family must be very ashamed of her!

David noticed the interchange and his heart gave a lurch. What was that sanctimonious old hypocrite pawing Rachel for? Rachel's father noticed it too and ugly thoughts arose in his mind. Why was Rachel not dressed the way the visiting brethren had asked her mother to dress her? He would have to see, for no one was going to talk about his daughter.

On the way home Papa suggested that she ride in the front seat with him. While Mother and the boys dozed in the back, he questioned her.

"Rachel, what did Deacon Cook say to you today when he put his hands on you?"

Rachel's face grew white with fear, then she turned away from her father and answered in a muffled voice, "It was nothing much, Papa."

"Can't you tell me, daughter"

"He—he asked me if I was well again."

"But why did he put his hands on you?"

"I don't know, Papa, but he's done that before."

"Before—before when?"

"Before I was sick. He makes me feel so ashamed."

"Uh, huh! Well don't worry about it. I'll talk to him about that."

"No, no, Papa. I'll just try to stay away from him. Please don't say anything to him."

"All right, Rachel, but no one is going to hurt you."

No more was said. Mother's gentle snores mingled with the boys' breathing, so Rachel was sure this was something only between her and her father. A warm feeling stole through her heart, the first such feeling to touch her in all these weeks.

All the following week Rachel and her mother were busy gathering in sweet corn, cooking it in the big iron pots that were ordinarily used for heating wash water, then cutting off the corn and spreading it onto big, wire-screen-bottomed trays. These trays were placed inside the outdoor drying house. Papa had made the small building and had put a small chunk stove inside to provide heat for the drying. The narrow building resembled the outdoor privy in size, but in use it had a very different utility. Many hours were spent stirring the drying corn, firing the tiny stove, and finally, gathering the finished product, the dried corn into cheese-cloth bags. These were hung from the rafters of the store room, waiting to be used during the fall and winter. Such savory dishes were made from dried corn!

Next were the early apples to gather, peel, and dry in the drying house. These sweet apples were used for that great delicacy, *schnitz and knepp.* Many of the apples were made into apple sauce and canned. The later apples were to be gathered late in September and stored outside under layers of leaves. Of course most of the late apples would be made into apple cider and apple butter. Then the neighbors would gather for an evening of apple peeling and visiting. The next day the big copper kettle would be set to boiling with the fragrant apple cider. Spices were tied into little cheesecloth bags and boiled along with the quartered apple schnitz while the whole wonderful mess was slowly stirring, the apple butter was poured into stoneware crocks, tied with paper, and set in the storeroom. How good Mother's homemade bread tasted with fresh butter and apple butter on it! No properly brought-up child ever started to eat until he had his apple butter piece first.

By the end of the summer, rows of fruits were stored on shelves down in the earthen-floored cellar. It looked like Aladin's cave with golden peaches, purple plums, green beans, red and green stuffed peppers, all shining in the glass jars like huge jewels!

CHAPTER 8

It was near sauerkraut-making time when the "Protracted Meetings" started at the church. Mother and Rachel discussed it as they knelt on the earthen cellar floor, busy stomping down shredded cabbage in large, stoneware crocks. Mrs. Miller put a layer of cabbage into the crock, then scattered large handfuls of coarse salt on it. Rachel took a carved wooden stomper and applied it vigorously. When the crock was full, an old plate or piece of broken slate roofing was placed on top and weighted down with a stone. There it was left to ferment before being taken out and canned.

"The visiting evangelist will give chalk talks before the meetings begin each evening," observed Mother as she tied a piece of cheesecloth over the sauerkraut jar to keep it clean.

"Will we be going tonight?"

"Of course we will. We seldom miss any if we can help it."

The family rode through the gathering dusk to the meeting house. The yellow light from the hanging lamps welcomed them as they drove up. Already Deacon Cook was up front leading the congregation in songs. He enjoyed every one of the fifteen minutes of song service. Many people came from adjoining congregations, and the singing became more melodious each evening as the meetings progressed.

The drive home each evening under the deep blue sky with its twinkling stars and harvest moon floating overhead caused Rachel's spirits to rise. She resolutely put aside thoughts of the secret place and of Anton. In fact she knew she would never see him again, for she had read a short article in the weekly county paper that said that Professor Anton Dereck had recently accepted a place in the

Philadelphia Philharmonic Orchestra and would be moving to the city with his family. *So much for that,* thought Rachel. *Now I will do what Mother and Papa want me to do and put on my plain clothes willingly. I will settle down to being a good girl so that they will never need to be ashamed of me again.*

The visiting evangelist wore a dark beard in the same fashion as most of the older men of the church did. Even David Lowe wore a beard, having done so ever since his marriage and now after his wife's death. But the evangelist's hair was worn longer than most, and it gave him the appearance of a Holy Man.

One night as Rachel listened rather listlessly to the sermon, the light shining down from the overhead oil hanging lamp seemed to form a halo about the man's head. An electric shock went through her body as she seemingly recognized the Man from Galilee!

"Harken ye! Harken ye, ye sinners! Repent today, for the Son of God cometh as a thief in the night. No one knows the day nor the hour thereof. Get your souls right and confess your sins before God!"

The man seemed to be pointing straight at Rachel, and her very soul seemed to shrivel into dust. In one terrible flash she saw herself as a terrible sinner, guilty not only of fornication, but also of murder—the murder of an unborn child. She gave a gasp and sprang to her feet. Her mother pulled her back by her dress.

"Are you have a fit?" she whispered.

"No, no, I've got to tell!" Her voice rose hysterically. The preacher stopped and looked at her in astonishment.

"Sh—h—h, Rachel. Sit down! What's come over you?"

"No, no, I've got to tell!"

Deacon Cook's face turned white, then blood red. He had been sitting with his arm propped up on a hymn book, but in his agitation, he dropped it. The noise was like thunder in the silent church. Everyone turned from watching Rachel to see what had happened to the deacon, who was shaking his head and moaning, "Oh, no! Oh, no!"

"Surely the Holy Ghost is working here tonight!" observed the evangelist.

The leader rose and walked over to the women's side to where Rachel still stood, trembling and weeping.

"Come, Sister, what is it that you must tell?"

"I must tell that I have sinned—sinned so grievously that I am no longer fit to be called a member of the church!"

"Surely, Rachel, a young girl like you has not sinned that much. You must be mistaken!"

"Yes, I have sinned, and then." Her voice trailed out. Gathering strength, she turned to Deacon Cook and said, "You know about me, you tell them!"

The deacon's stricken face looked ravaged as he whispered hoarsely, "No, no, I know nothing. The girl is mistaken! I don't know what she is talking about!"

"But, Sister," the elder persisted, "How have you sinned?"

"I have committed—fornication! Oh, please forgive . . . ."

"But who is your partner in sin?"

"I can't tell you that," she whispered.

"He should come forward and acknowledge his sin with you."

"He can't do that!"

"Why not?"

"Because he has a wife and family!"

"So you have tempted a man to commit adultery with you?"

"I must have. I didn't mean to."

Rachel stood a self-accused sinner in front of the congregation. Many were in tears or in a state of shock.

Rachel's mother gave a shriek, then fainted into the arms of the nearby sisters. Her father looked dazed, burying his face in his hands. Then he looked up at the quivering Deacon Cook and slowly said, "Brother, can you give me an account of this?"

Deacon Cook turned to the people and cried, "I didn't do it—not to her anyhow!" Then recognizing his self-accusation, he turned and ran from the church. His wife raised herself from her seat and started to follow him, screaming. She fell heavily as she neared the door, and by the time the people had reached her, she was unconscious.

The shocked people heard Deacon Cook's car start up outside in the parking lot. The silence inside the church was so great that they could hear the sound of his car fading far into the distance.

A comforting hand touched Rachel's as she stood before the congregation. "Come, Rachel, let me take you outside to get some fresh air." It was David Lowe who had come from the men's side to offer her condolences.

"But I want forgiveness."

"God has forgiven you. Now forgive yourself!" and David led her gently from the church and to his car outside. Placing her carefully inside, he hurried back to tell little Jacob that he was taking Rachel home.

Rachel felt that she was in a winter's blizzard, so cold was she, and her teeth were chattering with a chill. She could hear the cries from the inside and the sounds of general disorder as they pulled away from the church.

When they reached the Miller homestead, David led her upstairs to her room, loosened her clothing, and laid her on the bed. He spread her log cabin quilt over her shaking shoulders. Gently he stroked her hair until he had soothed her to sleep. Then he went down to the front porch to wait for her family.

Papa came up to him, his shoulders bent like an old man. "Brother Lowe, what do you make of this?"

David slowly sat down on the edge of the porch. "I know nothing except a great sorrow has come to your daughter. She has confessed the bare facts before God and the Church, henceforth she has been absolved from her sin. It isn't up to us to probe into her heart as to what happened."

"But what must I and Mother do? She has just gotten over a grave sickness. Could that be part of the burden she has obviously been carrying?"

"Possibly! but I would like to help her. I've loved her for some time; in fact I have loved her ever since my dear wife died." He paused for a moment. "Give me your blessing to marry her."

"David, you are making a great sacrifice. You have enough burdens to bear. You must realize that because of what happened tonight, Rachel will be looked down on for the rest of her life. God forgives, but we mortals never do; at least we never forget. However if you really do want my daughter for your wife, we will talk it over with her and let you know within a few days."

"Brother Miller, you know that I have an afflicted child. I will keep on my aunt who will help with his care, for I know that Rachel will have her hands full keeping the house," he promised hopefully.

"Yes, and she is still very young, not quite eighteen. But my wife has taught her how to keep house. We will see what can be done to convince her the best solution will be to accept your hand in marriage."

CHAPTER 9

When Rachel awoke the next morning, she wondered how she had gotten home and into her bed. When she got up and started to get dressed, she felt dizzy. Then Mother came upstairs with a tray of food and put it on the dresser. Her face was red and swollen.

"Mother, you have been crying!"

"My poor child, don't you realize what you did last night? You had the church in an uproar. Now I want you to tell me just what happened and how it happened. Who is the man?"

Rachel staggered back onto her bed, then picking up the hem of her sheet, she wiped her eyes and tried to talk over the dreadful lump in her throat.

"It happened while you were going over to the Fletchers so much. I met the man in the woods. He is a married man."

"The very idea, Rachel Miller! How could you do such a thing? Your Papa and I have always tried to raise you right. Who was it? Was it Deacon Cook?"

"Oh, no, Mother! Whatever gave you such an idea?"

"Well you said. . . ."

"But I didn't say that he was the one!"

"Who was it then?"

"Nobody connected with the church. I didn't know until it was too late that he had a wife and a big family."

"In other words, Rachel, you threw yourself away on an old man, a married man who stole away your virginity!"

"Yes, Mother."

"Are you going to have a baby? What does Deacon Cook have to do with it anyway?"

"I can't tell you, Mother. I promised Deacon—I mean I promised I wouldn't tell."

Just then her father's voice was heard calling up the stairs. "Ruth, come down here, right away!"

His voice was so urgent that Mrs. Miller hurried downstairs. Rachel heard their voices strained with doom and ejaculations of horror.

Mother came back upstairs, walking in a daze, her face stiff with terror. "Deacon Cook was found in his barn this morning, hanging in his haymow!"

"You mean he killed himself?"

"Yes, now will you tell what you know?"

"Oh, please don't ask me to tell you. He was guilty of his own sins which I found out. We made a pact. I wouldn't tell about his sins if he wouldn't tell about mine."

"But what did he do?"

"Please don't ask me, Mother. He didn't tell about me, so I must keep my promise, especially now that he is dead."

There was little work done that day. Mother and Papa stayed closed in their bedroom in prayer. The boys hung about the front yard, ducking out of sight whenever a car happened to pass. Rachel was upstairs, lying on her bed, too dazed to cry anymore.

Finally, little Jacob came upstairs, calling, "Sis, David Lowe is here and would like to talk to you."

So Rachel bathed her face and put on her cap before going downstairs. There was David, looking so longingly at her that she dropped her eyes. He came over to her and taking her hands, led her to the old couch in the sitting room.

"Rachel, I've come to see you because I can't stay away any longer. I wanted to have you talk it over with your parents, but now that this new trouble has come, I want to help you. I have already asked your father if I could marry you. What do you say? I love you very much. I will care for you, and if you are going to have a baby, I will claim it for my own."

Suddenly Rachel remembered she had not told about her unborn child and how she had Miss Lucy kill it. How could she tell people that monstrous fact now with all this about Deacon Cook? She would have to keep it quiet, and with the deacon dead, her secret was safe. Miss Lucy would never dare to tell it, and Aunt Sally would remain loyal. She mused how safe she would be now as David's wife. He was so kind, yet uncouth in comparison to Anton. She shook her head angrily—get Anton out of her head.

David saw her angry shake of the head, yet he persisted. "I know you don't love me as I love you, but I promise that will come. I will make you love me someday!"

An aura of goodness seemed to emanate from him as he slid a little nearer. She noticed his fresh-smelling, blue chambray shirt and wondered how many men courted their wives in their everyday clothes. His tender brown eyes searched her face for a reply.

"All right, Brother Lowe, if you want to take the chance on marrying an unseemly woman like me, I will marry you, and I thank you very much. But there is not going to be a baby."

He grasped her hands, then placed a gentle kiss on her forehead.

"Can you be ready by Saturday? I will come and take you across the state line to Elder Winer's place. I have known him a long time. I'll get word to him to marry us on Saturday evening, and we will stay with him and his wife over Sunday. We won't be back for a few days. That will allow time for the talk to die down."

Mother and Papa drew long breaths of relief when Rachel told them about David's plans.

"Thank the dear Lord! Now you will be safe from sinful ways. David is a good man. Of course there is his afflicted son, but you will have to learn patience."

It took Mother the better part of the week to get Rachel ready for her forthcoming wedding. It was decided that Papa and the boys would take the spring wagon of Rachel's possessions over to the Lowe farm during the early evening to avoid much gossip. The church people would all be at the Protracted Meetings, so they could not see the Miller-Lowe activities.

Rachel's dowry was a modest one. She had spent many hours since her childhood piecing quilts, having completed her first one by the time she was ten. The nine-diamond quilt was then set together and knotted with a wool filling to make it into a comfort. She had six more quilts and comforts as well as a dozen embroidered pillow cases and the same number of dresser scarves, all made by her during the long winter evenings. She had no tablecloths so would have to rely on David having some left from his first wife.

Mama gave her a goodly assortment of the fruits and vegetables and jelly they had worked on so industriously the past weeks. So she was not going empty-handed to her husband, even though she was going away empty-hearted.

At last on Saturday morning she dressed in her green voile and got her small wardrobe together. When David came for her in his car she was ready. Kissing her mother goodbye, she thought with a shock of how few times she had kissed her parents since she had grown up. Theirs was not a demonstrative family.

As they rode through the scrub-pine-covered hills between ancient stone fences which protected the soldiers in battle during Civil War days, Rachel thought of the old saying, "Married in green ashamed to be seen." It was closer to the truth than she cared to admit.

They crossed the state line and going to the county seat which was nearest to Elder Winer's place, they purchased the marriage license. Then finding a small restaurant, they went inside to have a small meal. By nightfall they were at the Elder's big stone house set off back from the road at the end of a short lane.

As they approached the house, Rachel noticed a lovely fan light over the front door, a door of such generous proportions that there would be little trouble getting a dead man's casket through it. The heavy brass knocker sounded like the knell of doom. She wondered if David's feet were as cold as hers.

A tiny wrinkled woman in the traditional cape, cap, and apron opened the door. "Here you are, David. And what have we here? A young girl! Don't tell me, David, that you want Ezra to marry you to this pretty little thing! Ezra, they're here!"

Elder Winer was a great, red-faced man towering over his wife. He came to the door, struggling into his plain coat.

"Come in, folks! I got your message, David and I must say that we're very glad that you came to me to be married. You have always seemed to me to be the son we never had. Come in! Come in! Business first, then we'll eat supper."

So David and Rachel were married, with the hired girl coming in from the kitchen to sign the marriage certificate along with Mrs. Winer as witnesses. No music was played, for that was not the custom of the church. Nor did Rachel carry any flowers or receive a wedding ring. Jewelry was forbidden by the church.

After a bountiful supper, Mrs. Winer picked up a lamp and guided Rachel to the nuptial bedroom, leaving David to bring up the suitcases later. Rachel was silent as she helped the old woman remove the starched pillow shams from the bed. They were embroidered in red with a sleeping person on one and "good night" on it. The other one had a wide awake person with the words "good morning" on it. Over one wall were hung several peacock feathers, and a white counterpane covered the double bed. A wash stand with wash bowl and pitcher stood between the windows. Rachel spied a tall, china slop jar with a crocheted lid cover to avoid any noise. Bathrooms were unknown in the country places.

"This is the bed where I gave birth to my two babies." The old woman's voice broke. "But we lost them both. I was too tiny to have Ezra's big boys, and the doctor had to remove them in pieces. Both times. We never had any more. I'll never forget it."

"I'm so sorry!"

"I shouldn't burden you with such sadness on your wedding night. Well good night. I'll have David bring your suitcase, then I'll hold him downstairs until you are undressed and into your nightgown. I can feel how nervous you are. But then, David is a good man. Good night!"

Mrs. Winer left a lamp burning when she left the room, a lamp with pink roses on a globe-shaped shade as well as on its base. The soft rosy light made her think of Miss Lucy's lamp. Should she tell David about what had happened in that small pink and white cottage that night so many months ago? No, she could not do that. It might implicate Deacon Cook, and a promise made to one who was now dead is a sacred promise. Besides, David had asked for no explanation, and she had given none.

Rachel looked all about the bed chamber, thinking of the tragedy of birth and death that had happened here. Could ghosts of unborn babies come back to haunt? If so, then hers could come back, haunting and torturing her for the rest of her days. The very thought made her shiver.

Quickly she undressed and slipped into her best nightgown with its Hamburg lace embroidery trimming it. She was under the covers when David came back from waiting for her to undress. The door had opened quietly and there stood David! Ah, David! How could she endure a wedding night with him when she had so recently received the caresses of Anton?

David's heart gave a lurch when he saw his bride in bed, her hair unbound and spread over the pillow in its unearthly beauty. Her green eyes were blazing with fear. He cleared his throat, removed his coat and vest, and hung them up tidily on the coat rack behind the door. Then sitting on the edge of the bed, he removed his shoes and stockings. Slipping softly to her side of the bed, he knelt, putting his arm protectively over her shoulders. He prayed aloud, "Dear Lord, thank you for giving me this precious one for my wife. Cast all shadows from our lives, and may we walk in the paths of righteousness all the days of our lives. Amen!"

Then blowing out the light, he finished undressing in the dark and carefully got into bed. He whispered to her, "Rachel, my dearest one, I'll not frighten you tonight. I will give you time to get used to me." And after a tender kiss, she felt his breath coming in that of innocent sleep. So breathing a sigh of relief, she, too, went to sleep.

CHAPTER 10

On Monday morning the newlyweds took their departure and jogged along in their car, discovering dewy back country roads. They passed neat farmhouses set by the wayside with purple and pink and white asters growing along orderly vegetable garden borders. Heavenly blue morning glories hung from wire fences, and goldenrod grew in random profusion. Hedge apples lay by fence rows, and locusts were clattering their metallic calls in all the trees. The sycamores were shedding their dry leaves, which lay in drifts, reminding them that fall was close by.

"Look at that corn! I'll bet it is nearly ten foot tall! What a lot of fodder that man will have!" David was more interested in crops at that moment. He talked about the good yield his wheat had given at threshing time.

"Wheat grows better in limestone soil, and I have a hundred acres of it. Some of my farm is too rocky to grow anything on but grass for my cattle. But the Lord has prospered me, and I have some money put away to buy land of my own some day, or rather, I should say, our own land." His eyes shone as he looked at her. "Yes, one of these days I hope we will not be farming for the halves as I do now. But wheat is not the whole thing—no, fattening steers for market is a good money proposition."

"Don't you milk any cows, then?"

"Oh, sure, I have about ten head. I send the cream to the creamery in town after I separate it. I have a good many shoats I fatten on the skim milk. I also use the corn I raise on the bottom land next to the creek. I have a flock of chickens, although I didn't get many pullets raised this year. That will be your job to do next spring. How do you think you are going to like being a farmer's wife?"

"I've never known anything except farm life, so it would be out of my way of life to be anything else."

They rode on in silence for several miles, then Rachel broke the silence by asking, "Do you mind telling me how your wife came to die? I don't think I ever heard."

A spasm of pain crossed David's face as he slowly replied, "It was the second year after our little boy was born, nearly six years ago now, and she was expecting our second child. Ella had been terribly disappointed that the boy seemed to be so slow at doing things. He didn't learn to walk until he was past two. In fact he had just learned to walk a few steps when she was taken. To this day yet he has never learned to say but a few words. At that time he could say 'Dada,' and once in a great while, he would say 'Ma-Ma.' Well one day I had to go into town on business. I fault myself for that still. Well anyhow, the cows broke out of the pasture at a weak place in the fence. Old man Smith, the landlord, was never one to fix up the fences, saying it was up to me. Well Ella went running outside with only a sweater on, and it was January. She ran and she ran, trying to herd the cattle back inside the barnyard. Finally she got them in, but she took a chill, and by the time I got home, she was running a fever. It was pneumonia. The doctor came, but he couldn't save her or the baby. So she died, leaving me with a two-year-old afflicted child."

David's voice broke and tears rolled down his face. He pulled the car to the side of the road until the shaking subsided in his hands. Rachel reached over timidly and stroked his work-worn hands. He looked at her then and reaching his arms about her shoulders, he kissed her lips. Rachel found herself returning the kisses, and a glow of happiness went through her. Maybe she was going to be happy after all.

Starting up the car, David drove through an evergreen lane to the old brick house he called home. It was so aged that the brick had faded to a rose color.

From the time Rachel crossed the threshold into the neat kitchen, she felt the animosity of David's Aunt Virgie. She was a spare, narrow woman of some age. Wrinkles lay deep in her cheeks, and her thin lips were so compressed that the wrinkles gave her a puckered look. She belonged to a still stricter sect of Plain People than Rachel and David. This group was referred to as the Old Order, or sometimes known as the Barn Brethren. They were widespread in the valley, and their dress was not unlike the more conservative members of Rachel's denomination. In fact Rachel's dress was made over the same pattern as the Barn Brethren women. All women, married or single, wore the cape, the cap, and the apron as had been prescribed for Rachel. However, few single people belonged to the church group, their parents preferring that they get a taste of "worldly life" so that they would be willing to settle down by the time they were married. It was unusual that any of the young people would go "plain" by the time the first child was expected. The men started growing a beard, and the women put on the dull colors and organdy caps that were considered necessary to their salvation.

One sharp difference between the two sects of Plain People in this neighborhood was the fact the Barn Brethren had no established church building for worship. Services were held biweekly in the members' houses. Their farmhouses had a style of architecture peculiar to these people alone. Each of the first floor rooms, with the exception of the kitchen, was connected by means of a folding door. On the Sunday it was the family's turn to hold meeting, the doors were open. Backless wooden benches were brought in from the porch or kitchen, and thus a small auditorium was formed. When the noon hour came, everybody was expected to stay for dinner, and they took turns eating at the big extension table set up in the kitchen.

In the spring, the highlight of the year occurred when the haymow was at its lowest and the granary was empty. Then the barn floor was swept and scrubbed. The wooden benches would be set up both in the haymow as well as the granary and barn floor. Many outsiders attended, and everyone was welcome to eat at the long tables set up in the wagon sheds. Their men as well as women worked hard at showing their hospitality.

The meeting went on all day, and when evening came, long boards on trestles were covered with strips of white linen and set up for the Love Feast. There the communicants sat, women on one side of the barn floor and men on the other. There they washed feet and partook of the Holy Meal and communion. Barn lanterns hung from the rafters. The long meter tunes, to which they sang each hymn, rose to the roof, drowning out the uneasy lowing of the cattle in the barn below. Hence the vulgar term of *Barn Brethren* was attached to these people.

Members were prohibited the use of automobiles, gasoline engines, and tractors. Many homes had no carpets, using only the rag rugs that were plaited and sewn together during the long winter evenings. It was considered sinful to have idle hands, "for the DEVIL finds mischief for idle hands." In some homes even mirrors were avoided since the men wore whiskers and had no need to see to shave, and the women wore the standard mode of hairstyle. The hair was left to grow as long as it would, parted in the middle, combed back tightly on both sides of the head, then gathered into a tight knot on the back of the head. Very little hair escaped from the white organdy cap such as Rachel wore.

Aunt Virgie wore her sparse hair like this. She wore black and white calico, starched stiffly, and no less than three petticoats were worn under her dress. Her "good dress" was solid black, so that Rachel thought she resembled one of the black crows that flew about the fields. Her narrow body surely was adequate for her narrow little soul, so thought Rachel after she had attempted to shake hands, only to see the old woman wipe off her hands on her apron after she had been touched by Rachel. She made no effort to kiss the bride, so Rachel realized that her reputation had reached this house before she did.

The child was rocking himself in his little rocking chair, humming a tuneless song. He had fair hair, but no spark of intelligence seemed to shine out of his wide blue eyes.

"Jonathon, come here, my son." David put down the suitcases as he entered the kitchen and saw his son. "This is your new mama. Say the word. Say 'mama.'"

The child paid no attention, still rocking and singing his little song. Finally the old woman said, "Supper's ready," and left the room to go into a small room next to the kitchen, evidently her bedroom.

"Aren't you eating with us, Aunt Virgie?" David's color was high as he got no reply. He picked up the child and set him in a high chair. Food was put on his plate which he grabbed with both hands when David attempted to ask a blessing. The meal proceeded silently.

After they had eaten and washed up the dishes, David asked Rachel to come on a tour of the house. A wide hall led from the front door to the back door, allowing a sweep of air to cool off the rooms in summer. The front parlor door was shut, and when they entered it, Rachel was thinking it was like opening up a tomb. Big wax flowers were on a marble-topped table in the middle of the room. The furniture was upholstered in a cotton brocade, each piece a different pastel color. A gold-framed picture hung on the wall showing a much younger David without a beard, and a fair-haired girl, evidently his wife. *But then,* she mused, *he is gallant or else he would never have married me.* In one corner sat a gramophone with a stack of records on the table. She wondered if any music that Anton played would be among them. It seemed to her that this would be the epitome of luxury.

Seeing her eyes light up when she saw the gramophone, David stepped over and selected a record at random. A tinny rendition of "Tell Mother I'll Be There" caused Rachel to flinch. David saw her disappointment, so suggested that she find something she might like.

"Another time I'll look for something. Come on and show me the rest of the house."

A balustrated staircase led to the second floor. In spite of many spokes missing, there still remained some beauty of an earlier day. Three bedrooms were on the second floor besides the one that was David's. A hall led back to the garret door that led to the third floor.

"One bedroom faces the east so if we oversleep the sun will wake us up."

Rachel blushed at the reference to "our bedroom," yet she was not prudish enough to think she would have a separate bedroom. The child's room was next to that of his father. Everything was extremely clean and neat. The windows were hung with stiffly starched curtains, and a white counterpane was on each bed. It all seemed very nice to Rachel, and she felt that her life would be a happy one here if Aunt Virgie would accept her.

CHAPTER 11

During the days that followed, Aunt Virgie went about her work in a businesslike precision that belied her age. Rachel found herself acting like a green-haired girl who was all thumbs. Whatever Rachel volunteered to do in the kitchen, the old woman did it over again or else snapped a quick, "No!"

Aunt Virgie would venture no conversation. David was quick to see the state of affairs but felt helpless to do anything. The child was used to the old lady and refused to allow any ministrations from Rachel.

One evening she caught up little Jonathon in her arms and started to cuddle him. She had not seen her family for several weeks and was suffering from a fine case of homesickness. She thought to gain comfort from the little child's presence in her arms. But he remained stiff and unbending, then flailed his arms about screaming, "No, no, no!"

Rachel recoiled in shock, then jumped when Aunt Virgie spoke sharply, "Now see what you've done! You'll never take the place of his mother, not someone the likes of you! Never, never, never!"

The howls of the child rose at her sharp tone. Rachel's tears brimmed over, and in spite of her best efforts, she started to sob. All of the unhappiness of the past few months rose in her consciousness, and her sobs became hysterical. The child stopped crying in amazement at seeing her so upset. David, coming in at this time from the barn, was greeted by a hysterical wife and tear-stained child. Aunt Virgie looked frightened.

Without a word, David picked up his wife and led her upstairs to their bedroom. Sitting on the edge of the bed, he gathered her into his arms.

"There, there, my dear one. Cry it out on my shoulder and tell me all about it."

But Rachel found she could not put into words the homesickness or the hurt the old woman was inflicting with her silent treatment or the guilt she was hiding. Finally she stirred in his arms and murmuring in his ear, said, "David, you are so good to me. Let me make it up to you now." And there David and Rachel first consummated their marriage.

They talked long into the night and decided that the best thing to do was to leave the housekeeping to Aunt Virgie for the time being and Rachel would go out to the fields and help David with the corn husking.

The days that followed were golden autumn ones. Every morning David and Rachel went to the fields as soon as they had finished the milking and other chores. In order to spend as much time as possible in the field, they carried a basket of lunch for the noon meal and a wooden keg of water. The odor of the ripe corn rose to mingle with the sweet air and the tar of the twine they tied on the shocks of corn fodder. Great piles of golden corn lay in their wake as they proceeded across the sloping fields.

These were the happiest days that Rachel had known before in her life. She was delighted to be outdoors and doing something useful. David's delight in her was apparent, for he would sing to her as they worked side by side. His rich baritone voice pleased her as he sang Stephen Foster's songs, ballads, and even some of the sentimental songs of the day. "Juanita" was one of her favorites, and when he sang, "Lean thou on my breast!" thrills ran through her. His tenderness with her and his fervent lovemaking were a delightful paradox.

One evening in mid October David said, "It's getting late. See the moon is already up. It is a gibbous moon. We have husked enough corn for one day. Let's quit now and go into the house."

As they gathered up their lunch kit and water keg, the mists started to roll from the creek up over the corn fields with their row after row of corn shocks, not unlike Indian tepees set among the campfires of the tribe. An eerie feeling came to them as they walked along, holding hands. Then they heard it! At first it came from far in the distance, the baying of hounds. Then nearer, nearer, until it seemed to be nearly over them.

"The Everlasting Hunter!" murmured Rachel in awe. "Have you ever heard it before?"

"Yes, I have. I was a small boy when I first heard it. I think this is the third time I have heard it. My father told me that an old man went out over a hundred years ago to hunt with his hounds. He swore he would never return until he had found a stag. He never did. Now folks think he roams the valley every fall hunting, hunting!"

Rachel shivered in the cool autumn air. "My grandfather says he has heard him during the winter months, too. There must be something to it, for very few people around here keep any hounds, so what else could be making the sound?"

David walked along thoughtfully. "Have you ever heard of death tokens? My grandfather had a token before Grandma died." David continued. "A sharp click was heard in the walls just a few hours before she breathed her last."

"My mother received a token before her mother died," said Rachel as they climbed the last hill before reaching the house. "A bird flew up against the window. She said anytime a bird flies against the window or else gets inside the house, it is a sure sign of death."

"What are we talking about death for, Rachel? We are alive and just starting out in life. So think about something pleasant."

"There's something I would like to ask you to do. Would you take me over home next Sunday? I haven't seen my people now for about six weeks." Rachel looked longingly at her new husband.

"Of course, Rachel, we can go, except it's Aunt Virgie's Meeting Sunday. I always take her over to the Martin's, and they take her to the meeting. I have never taken the boy off of the farm, unless he has to be taken to the doctor. Can you wait another week?"

"Yes, it's all right."

But the week turned into a month, and still it was not convenient for Rachel to see her parents. Aunt Virgie had come down with a bad cold so it would be impossible to ask her to look after the boy in her condition. But to Rachel it seemed like the silver lining to a dark cloud, for she got to do as she chose in her own kitchen. She rearranged things to suit herself. She had learned to cook as a child, so the meals she turned out were good ones even though Aunt Virgie declared they weren't fit to eat.

One day after she had been unusually peevish and irritable, she flung out at Rachel, "Well when are you going to have that baby?"

The question alarmed Rachel, and she came near to spilling some broth she had prepared for the hateful old woman. "What are you talking about?"

"Well you are trying to put another man's child onto David, ain't you? Why else did you get up in the church and make such a show of yourself?"

David caught the last of the ugly statement as he entered the kitchen. He came to the door of the bedroom where the old woman was lying on her narrow, white bed. He addressed himself to Rachel, "Will you please go out in the kitchen and shut the door? I want to talk to Aunt Virgie."

With trepidation, Rachel withdrew, but she could hear loud words at first, then a murmur of voices. When he came out, he said to her, "I think things will be going much better now."

As soon as Aunt Virgie was able to be up and around, David took Rachel to visit her family. They arrived at noon just as the family had returned from church services. It had been over two months since Rachel and David had gone to church, since David thought it best they remain away from the church for a time. They had seen no one from the church, so Rachel was interested in hearing the news.

Mother eyed her quite sharply, and while washing up the dinner dishes asked her, "Rachel, you don't seem to be showing up at all. How soon are you expecting your little one?"

Rachel was so surprised that she dropped her dishcloth. "Why, Mother! I told you I wasn't expecting a baby. Don't you remember?"

"You might have thought you did so at the time, but I had the distinct impression that you were in the family way. Why then did you fool David into thinking you were?"

"He knew that I wasn't. He told me he would claim the baby if I was, but I told him different."

"I'm so glad, Rachel! Now you don't have to bear the disgrace of bearing another man's child. Praise the Lord!"

"What are the people in the church saying, Mother? Does anyone forgive me?"

"I don't know, child. I believe many of them will speak to you when you go back. Sister Cook won't, I feel sure, because she thinks Deacon Cook was the guilty one. She has suffered a great deal, so if you can find forgiveness in your heart for her, do so. I do wish you would tell me who the man was that robbed you of your purity. It would help so much."

"I don't see how. The man has left the community with his wife and family. Please, Mother, don't bring it up again."

So the rest of the day was spent in pleasant conversation.

At bedtime while David was brushing her long red hair, he said, "Do you know, sweetheart, you have streaks of hair that are pure orange and some as red as fire. In fact your hair looks like fire. I have never seen anything like it. I hope our little ones will have hair like this when the come."

"Oh, please don't wish such a thing onto our little ones. If you could only realize the pain I've endured because of my hair. I've been called all kinds of names, including the *unseemly woman*, and I've been treated like I was a harlot. According to the Visiting Brethren, I am a temptation and lead men astray."

"That's not your fault. You tempt me plenty, but that's a wife's privilege. I guess you raise the carnal in me, but I love you for more than that. You seem to be my second self. I really do love you, Rachel, more than I can ever tell you."

"I love you, too, David. I have never met anyone as good and kind to me as your are. What I felt for the other one was not love." Blushing, she kissed his hands as he continued to brush and stroke her hair.

"I want you to get rid of those organdy caps that hide your hair. Didn't St. Paul say that a woman's glory was her hair? I want to see yours all the time, not just at bedtime."

"Oh, David, you wouldn't want me to run about the house with my hair hanging down around my face like this all the time."

"I guess that wouldn't be very practical, but let it hang sometimes, just to please me."

"What would Aunt Virgie say? But I will promise that you can always brush my hair at night whenever you want to."

"So be it! Anyway I want you to buy some bobinet and make caps from it so that I can see my girl's hair through the net. And another thing, take off that cape and apron and get some dresses like other young women. You are my wife now and you only listen to me."

CHAPTER 12

It was with delight that Rachel followed her husband's wishes concerning her clothes. Now she would be dressed according to other young women's fashions, not the advanced ways of the world, but the way the girls of her church did. David took her to town, and she selected some brighter colors for dresses. A natural pongee silk was purchased as well as a green silk crepe and a printed challis. She did not fail to get bobinet for her caps, and a few days later David hitched up a horse to the buggy for her. She drove to the nearby village to the dressmakers. She was on the road every day that week, much to the disgust of Aunt Virgie.

One day she stopped at the girls' school, and going inside the kitchen entrance, she found Aunt Sally.

"Child, why for are you back here again? Not more trouble?"

"No, I'm not in trouble again and I'm not likely to be. I'm married and to the best man in the valley. I came by because I think I owe you some money. I've come to pay you back."

"You know, honey, that man has done gone away—all the way to Phillydelfy. You know he done gone owing everybody in town. Did he ever know about you, Rachel?"

"No, I never saw him again. I've never told anyone, not even my husband about Miss Lucy, and I want you to promise you won't ever let it out."

"You don't have to ask me that. I'll never tell anybody. Just you go ahead and enjoy your new life."

Finally came the day when the tan pongee dress was finished. Rachel had her bobinet cap made in the new round style and without ribbon ties on it. Her beautiful hair shone from under it. She wore her hair in a new style, thinking the severe style she had worn before was not becoming.

It was a warm November Sunday that David and Rachel decided to go back to church. Rachel wore a light wrap over her new pongee dress, and David looked handsome with his beard trimmed close. He was spotless in his new dark suit he had bought in honor of the wedding. They slipped into the back seat, sitting together, and not on opposite sides of the church as was the custom.

A whisper went around the young ladies' class as they ended their Sunday School lesson. They sat on a raised tier of seats near where the young couple sat. Rachel could see the shock on the face of the late Deacon Cook's daughter.

After the service, she and David slipped out of the door, but not fast enough before Clara Cook came up to her. "So—o—o, you Jezebel, you have the gall to come and flaunt yourself with a good man like David Lowe who's too pious to see how really dirty you are!"

Rachel could only stare at the agitated girl. David made a movement to steer her around the screaming girl. A crowd gathered.

"You know you made that whole thing up. You're not in the family way and you never were. You sure tried to fool a lot of people, including my poor father. Whatever my weak father ever saw in you, I'll never know."

"I never blamed your father!"

"You liar! Take that, you deceitful wench!" And to everyone's horror, she spat on Rachel's pretty new dress. Again she spat, this time right into Rachel's white face. "There, I hope you never have any children to carry on your sinful ways!"

The Elder came out just in time to see this incident. He looked at Clara in horror. "Sister, is this the Christian way? You must forgive! Now I want to see you make it right with her. After all, your father denied she was the one."

"Never! My father killed himself over somebody, and I just know she is the guilty one. After all, everyone saw her drawing him on at the barn raisin'."

"If you keep on with such hatred, you will have to be taken to Council. What you are doing is hating, and you know that Christ said that he who hates is the same as a murderer."

The rebellious girl burst into tears and was led away by her angry mother. "Why can't you let us alone? We have enough to bear!"

Rachel stood alone among the people who stared at her without kindness. Only Sister Gray and her Godly husband thought to speak to her. The good sister kissed her saying, "Rachel, we are so glad to see you again."

David took her to the car and tucked her in. "We'll not be coming here again soon. We will go to church someplace else next Sunday. There are other churches of our faith."

The tears ebbed from her eyes as they drove home. Aunt Virgie noticed them as well as her swollen face. *Ah, hah! Quarreling already!*

That night Rachel felt frozen in spite of David's caresses and could not respond. She fell into an uneasy sleep. While she slept she dreamed of Anton. Once more he was playing the *Pathetique*. She sobbed as she listened. Her sobbing awoke David, and when he reached over to comfort her, he heard her murmur, "Anton!"

So that's who he was, he thought. *Poor child! No wonder she couldn't tell. He was a prominent man of the town, if he guessed the name right. At least he was the only one around by that foreign name.* He awoke her and kissed away the memory of the dream.

This seemed to herald a series of bad dreams, for a few nights later she dreamed she was in an open room and heard an infant crying. It awoke her and the memory was so real that she sat up in bed to listen, thinking it was Jonathon. David woke, too, and she told him about the sobbing baby. He went to the child's room, but found his child sleeping peacefully.

However the dream was recurring so often and was so shattering to her nerves that she dreaded going to bed. David interpreted this as being a sign that she was pregnant, but wishful as he was, he was doomed to disappointment at the end of the month.

They now started to attend church services in a congregation farther down the valley. Few people there had heard of her story, and these did not act like they had heard anything.

One Sunday they were invited to go along home with the Wamplers to dinner. They were a young couple with a curly-haired, little, year-old daughter.

"How cute she is! How I wish we could have such a darling daughter!"

"How long have you been married, Rachel?" inquired the child's mother.

"Ever since the end of August. You see I am David's second wife."

"Oh, I see. You seem to be younger than he is. You have plenty of time. You will get started on your family before you know it. Does he have children by his first wife?"

Rachel spoke sadly. "A little boy. He's—well, he's not very well, so David's aunt lives with us and takes care of the child."

On the way home, Rachel spoke of it to David. "Would you like a little girl first or a little boy?"

"Whatever the Lord sends us, only I hope He sends us a goodly child this time."

"Poor little Jonathon! I believe he is happy in his little world, David. When he sings and rocks himself in his little chair, the song has no tune but it sounds like a happy song."

So Rachel started to pray for a child, a normal, happy child. For many weeks she did not hear the baby cry in her sleep. Perhaps this was a good sign.

CHAPTER 13

Winter began to set in. Frost had come, and the leaves were almost all gone from the trees. Butchering day had arrived during the week following Thanksgiving Day. The whole household was put into a fever of preparation.

The butcher and his wife arrived in time for breakfast. After a hasty bite, David and Mr. Keets went to the barn. Rachel could hear the squeal of the pigs destined to be their winter's supply of meat. Three times she heard the report of a gun. Then each animal's throat was cut, and after bleeding, the carcass was lowered into a barrel of scalding water. Then it was hoisted up and scraped to remove the bristles.

Meanwhile Mrs. Keets, the butcher's wife, with Aunt Virgie and Rachel, got out the butchering spices, the knives, and the butchering utensils. A fire had been built in the wash house under the huge, black, cast iron kettles which were filled with more water to scald each carcass. Mr. Keets brought the odorous mass of emptied intestines to the women folks to be scraped and cleaned for the sausage casings. This was a meticulous job.

Lean slabs of "sausage meat" were brought inside and ground into a pale pink mass. This was mixed with spices and seasonings and put into the sausage press. Then the casing was fixed onto a spout running from the side of the press. Soon long links of sausage were curling inside a wicker basket as one of them turned the handle. These sausages were put aside in a cool place for the next day when they would be cooked and coiled inside earthenware crocks and sealed with lard before being set in the storeroom.

Lard was rendered from the cooked slabs of fat, then pressed out in a special press. The cracklings were kept for special dishes.

The heart, liver, and head meats were cooked and ground up into "puddin'," a thick meat sauce. This, too, was stored in crocks and sealed with melted fat. This served as a basis of the farmer's breakfasts. "Puddin' and corncakes" was oftentimes the whole breakfast of the farmer.

After a hearty noonday meal, David and Mr. Keets rubbed the bacon slabs, the shoulders, and the hams with salt, pepper, and salt peter. Then they were hung in the smokehouse to be cured before being smoked with hickory chips.

Once during the day, Rachel felt something on the back of her dress. Reaching back, she was chagrined to find out she had been pinned by the pig's tail. Everyone had a hearty laugh, and she was pleased to see Aunt Virgie had joined in.

It took Rachel and Aunt Virgie several days to finish up the butchering cooking. They worked silently for the most part, but after Rachel said, "Aunt Virgie, will you show me how to make souse and pawn haus? Mother never did get around to showing me how to do it." The old lady seemed to thaw a little.

"I never called it pawn haus. It was called scrapple as I was growing up, but it's the same thing. You have to stir corn meal into boiling broth that comes from cooking the head meats. Don't strain out the little bits of meat. Some people put in a little garden sage. To make souse or head cheese, you must cook the pigs feet and ears after they have been cleaned real good. Cook it until the meat falls off the bones. Then take out the bones, add a little sage and vinegar to taste, and set it in a cool place. Then it will jell, and you can slice it down."

So with such simple household tasks, the ice gradually thawed between the two women.

During the early winter days, David hauled in his corn crop. Rachel again helped in the fields, but the weather was colder, and her hands became rough and red. She selected the best ears of corn and set them aside in baskets. Some of this was reserved for seed corn for the next year's crop, but the most was destined for cornmeal. Every day a basket of corn was taken into the house and the ears were put into the oven of the kitchen stove. The oven door was left open while the corn slowly dried all day long. During the evenings, David and Rachel would sit in the kitchen by the light of the kerosene lamp and shell corn. Now and then they would find an ear that had gotten parched, and Rachel found pleasure in nibbling at the brown kernels. They had such a satisfying taste so basic to life. David would sing to her after Aunt Virgie went to bed.

After an evening of such music, Rachel would crawl into David's arms and return his fervent lovemaking. It occurred to her that music seemed to bring out the passion in her body just as the sight and feel of her hair brought a similar reaction to David.

Finally all of the corn was shelled, and she went with David to the nearby gristmill. Tucked away on the edge of the millrace edged with huge willows, now bare, the waterwheel turned merrily, grinding out their winter's supply of corn-meal. They brought home several dozen sacks of the golden flour.

Aunt Virgie showed Rachel how to stir the mush made from this meal. A round iron pot was filled with water, and when it came to a boil, the golden meal was stirred into the boiling water. A wooden paddle called a *mush paddle* was used for this. Rachel remembered how her mother used to threaten her as a child with the mush paddle. It was a handy tool for spanking small children.

By the time David came in from the barn with fresh frothy milk, the mush was cooled in bowls by each one's place on the table. With a few vegetables and some fresh pork, the heavy meal was ready. The leftover mush would be molded and sliced down for breakfast, the slices being fried a golden brown and eaten with puddin' or sorghum.

Aunt Virgie often stirred up pancakes from the cornmeal using buttermilk from the weekly churning. She also taught Rachel how to make corn pone. The activity of hard farm work kept these people from putting on weight from this heavy diet.

CHAPTER 14

The first snowfall came near Christmas. Rachel coaxed her husband to let little Jonathon go along to the county seat "to see Santa Claus" in the stores, although the Plain People do not teach their children this rendition of Christmas. She thought the boy should have a change of scenery, and she was right. He learned to say a new word, *Santa Claus*.

They bought him a red ball, a teddy bear, and some clear candy made in the shape of zoo animals, called toy candy. For Aunt Virgie they bought a new winter shawl, for her old one had faded from black to brown, and half of the fringes were gone.

Rachel bought David a squeeze box accordion, and he bought her a new record for the gramaphone. He realized what music meant to her. He also got her a bottle of toilet water.

So with these purchases they were content and they returned to the farm to do the evening chores.

On Christmas Day the toys were given to the excited little boy, who shouted, "Santa Claus! Santa Claus!" as he bounced his ball.

Rachel played the Strauss waltzes and *Santa Lucia* until Aunt Virgie grumbled about this worldly music filling the parlor. They had built a fire in the isinglass-sided heater. The red glow from the fire reflected on the pastel upholstering of the "good" furniture and on the tinfoil ornaments they had strung on the cedar tree they had cut on their own farm.

By the process of trial and error, David was able to pick out several tunes on his accordion. He even gained confidence enough to sing to his own accompaniment.

A few nights after Christmas, after Aunt Virgie and the boy were both in bed, David suggested that Rachel let her hair down. They were planning to spend an evening singing by the kitchen stove, for they had let the fire go out in the parlor. Before David could go to get his accordion, a loud knock came at the back door. David went reluctantly to see who was there. A group of weirdly dressed people stood on the back porch.

"It's Bel Snicklers, Rachel. It's getting kind of late, but do you want me to allow them to come in?"

Rachel hurriedly pinned up her hair, then said, "Oh, let's have them in. I haven't seen any Bel Snicklers since I was a child. What fun! Do you know any of them, David?"

"I'm not sure. That fat boy looks like one of the Henderson boys. But no matter. They aren't any of the church people, that's for certain. Come on in, folks!"

About a dozen people entered, all in homemade disguises and some in masks. The week between Christmas and New Year was the time Bel Snicklers, a German name for Santa Claus, visited the farming communities. However these gay characters expected a treat instead of giving a treat or gift. People of all ages participated in this charming practice. Often times they went to a different farmhouse every night of the Christmas week.

As Rachel rushed about getting out popcorn they had raised on their own farm and replenishing the kitchen fire, she was unaware of the stares of the tallest member of the troupe. He wore a homemade black domino, and through the slits could be seen long yellowish-brown eyes.

While bustling about, Rachel's hair became loose and fell about her face. She tried to knot it back up again, but she had lost her hairpins. The tall stranger's yellowish eyes lighted up when he saw the blazing hair. Rachel's eyes turned green in excitement, for this was an unusual experience to be entertaining Bel Snicklers. Plain People frowned on it. It was too worldly.

She got out the old iron skillet and filled it partway with the shelled popcorn.

"Here, let me pop it," the tall man requested. He soon had a bowl of the white, fluffy flakes ready for eating. Rachel set out cake and pie on the kitchen table, and David got a pot of coffee ready.

One of the boys had brought his banjo, so answering the pleas of his companions, he started a lively hoedown. Everyone clapped their hands and started to dance. Rachel was very disturbed when the tall man grabbed her around the waist and started to dance her around the kitchen. She had never danced with anyone, let alone a man who held her so tightly she could scarcely breathe. She could see David's face looking its disapproval. She managed to pull away and went over to stand by the hall door. The man followed her, his eyes never leaving her bright hair. She became very worried for she was afraid that the noise would awaken Aunt Virgie. How could she tame this worldly bunch? Then she had a good idea. David's accordion! He could play some of his tunes and perhaps they could turn this into a song fest!

Leaving the hall door partly ajar, she ran down the hall to the parlor, now dark and cold, and got the instrument. There was but a dim light coming from the noisy kitchen so she didn't see the tall stranger until she was grabbed by the waist and drawn to his chest. There he fondled her hair and then kissed her firmly on the mouth.

Rachel gasped in surprise. "Stop that! What do you think you are doing?"

"Golly, but you're pretty! Where have you been all of my life? How about letting me come again to see you? Reckon your pa would let you see me?"

Rachel gasped in surprise and mortification. Sticking his head around the open door just in time to hear the fellow's words, David spoke sternly, "Stranger, that is my wife you are manhandling. Get your hands off her!"

The man made a start for David before he realized where he was, then muttered, "You'd better keep this sweet morsel under lock and key then, for I'm going to make it my business to come back again and see her!"

As he put down his hands, Rachel was startled to see a coiled snake tattooed on his left wrist. It was dark red, and to her excited senses, it seemed to glow in the dim light.

Calling his friends to come on, the garish group silently departed. They were traveling in sleighs, and David could count four sleighs with two horses apiece already champing at the bits to get along over the frozen countryside. As they pulled out of the farmyard, the tall man called out, "So long, Cutie. See you again soon!"

Rachel was near tears of vexation and she felt deeply humiliated. She was unprepared for David's reaction.

"Why did you lead the fellow on, Rachel? Did you enjoy his kisses?"

She stared in disbelief at her husband, he who never had a fault! Never a harsh word had ever crossed his lips before. Surely David Lowe was not jealous! This then was the first weakness she had ever seen in him! She must be very careful and never allow strangers to see her with her head uncovered or her hair down.

There was no ceremony of hair brushing that night, and for the first time they went to bed without saying their prayers or saying good night to each other. The evil snake had entered their Eden!

Rachel could not sleep. Too many thoughts were going through her mind thoughts she had pushed back into her subconscious for too long. Once again she was stumbling through the buzzards field, through its filth, and across the bridge, and then down the dusty road to the little pink and white cottage, under the rose arch, and to the door, and to the narrow, white bed, and—and—oh! How could she face it again? She shook uncontrollably. Her eyes burned, but there were no tears. Was this what Hell was like—no tears? Were tears only to moisten with tender solicitude the burning to be endured in life? She groaned aloud.

David, roused from a fretful sleep, heard the moans and felt her shaking. How cruel he was! She really had not meant to hide in the hall and lead the fellow on, for too late he had seen her clasping the accordion in her arms and understood the significance of it. Only his pride would not let him tell her how sorry he was at the time. Now just see what he had done! Reaching over to her, he gathered her to his heart, soothing her like he often did little Jonathon.

"Rachel, don't take on so hard. Of course I don't think you led on that tall DEVIL. I am so sorry. Hm—m—m! Come to think of it, he was something like a DEVIL, wasn't he? Did you notice his eyes? They were brownish-yellow, much like a cat's. I have never seen anyone like him around here. I wonder where he came from!" So kissing her trembling lips, he soothed her into an uneasy sleep.

That night the baby cried again, the first time in over two months. She awoke and crept from her bed and into little Jonathon's room where a rocking chair was kept. There she rocked and rocked and rocked herself until she fell asleep. David found her there the next morning, and cold fear touched him for the first time.

CHAPTER 15

M ore snow fell after New Year's Day, and it kept falling for two days. Every fence post wore a joker's cap, and the trees were bent over with the dry, feathery flakes that turned into a hard crust by the second day.

David had gotten all of the corn hauled in from the fields and the corn cribs were filled. A huge stack of fodder stood in the barnyard which the steers enjoyed while they grew heavier and heavier. David visited the barn twice a day to feed and to milk. He even gathered the eggs from the chicken house to spare Rachel the extra steps through the heavy snow.

On the third day a pale, wintry sun came out, so the storm was over. David spent several hours digging paths to the barn, the henhouse, to the privy, and to the well.

After two more days, David decided to go to a stock sale at a farm several miles away to see if he could get a draft horse to help with the spring plowing.

"While you are gone, David, can I take Jonathon for a sled ride? He hasn't had a chance to get out since we took him to see Santa Claus."

"All right, but stay close to the house. Try the barn bridge. It's frozen hard enough to slide down. Be sure to bundle up good. You know how easily he takes cold."

After David left, she got out the old sled from the woodshed. The steel runners were rusty so she got a little grease from the lard can and coated the steel runners with the grease. Little Jonathon was very excited at the unexpected pleasure.

"Santa Claus! Santa Claus!" he cried, for now he used that term for everything that seemed good to him.

Aunt Virgie had not gotten up that morning as she had one of her colds. She had her old shawl wrapped about her for added warmth, and in spite of the good fire burning in the kitchen stove and a fire in her little wood burner stove in her bedroom, she was still chilly. Rachel had put a hot brick wrapped in a towel to the old woman's feet. She could not stay outdoors very long, for she would have to come in soon to keep up the fires.

After bundling the boy and herself in heavy wraps and boots, she seated Jonathon on the little sled and away they went! The runners screeched on the hard-packed snow paths. The barn bridge was covered with a heavy snow crust, so thick it did not break through. She pulled the little boy to the top of the slope then cried, "Whee!" Down he slid with cries of delight.

"Santa Claus! Santa Claus! Ma-ma!"

"Oh, Jonathon, you darling! You finally said it! You called me Mama!"

"You're too pretty for a mama!" A voice came from back of her.

Rachel whirled about in an instant. There standing in the doorway that led into the haymow was a tall stranger.

"What are you doing here? Who are you?" Rachel was very frightened.

"Oh, come on now, Cutie. You know who I am. After all you sure can kiss in the dark!"

So that's who it was, the Bel Snickler with the yellow eyes—the one David said was a DEVIL! "I never kissed you in the dark. It was the other way around. You had better get off this farm before I call my husband!"

"If you mean that old bearded fellow that looks old enough to be your daddy, you will have to have a good set of lungs to reach him. I saw him drive out of here a half hour ago. Unless I miss my guess, he won't be home until evening. So you and I will be all alone here except for the brat there. I know he can't help you."

"So you've been hanging around our barn, huh? You had better go or I'll scream. Aunt Virgie will hear me. We have a telephone, you know!"

"What good will an old woman do you? No, my cute little redhead, you and me are going to spend a real nice time right here in the haymow where it is nice and cozy. I'll bet it's not been the first time you've been in a haymow."

Rachel was terrified. What could he know about any haymow as far as she was concerned? He really must be a DEVIL. She opened her mouth and screamed as loud as she could. He pushed open the little door to the barn floor, dragging her with him. She screamed again and again, biting and scratching, kicking and beating him with her fists. In her struggle she remembered the little boy.

"Have pity on the child if you don't have on me. Please let me send him to the house. He's a delicate child and he will get sick."

"Get sick, get sick! Do tell. Let the kid take care of himself. Come on now, you may as well give in and enjoy it. That way I won't hurt you."

"Never! I'll kill myself first!"

"Now how are you going to do that?"

The beast pulled off her wraps and grabbed her hair as she struggled. All of her hairpins fell out and her hair cascaded down over her body. She bit his arm while she continued to struggle and kick. The man swore savagely at her.

Then an idea came to her. She seemingly relaxed her struggles and staggered back against the wall of the granary. A three-pronged pitch fork was propped against the wall. The man relaxed his grip on her for a moment in order to fumble with her dress fasteners. Taking advantage of that moment, she whirled, and grabbing the fork, plunged it into his torso. Some blood gushed out. She had not been strong enough to kill or even maim him!

"You witch! Can't trust you for a second! Well now you are really going to get it!" He slapped her face, then aimed a heavy blow at her head. Fiercely he tore off her clothing so that she had only her hair to cover her. Blow after blow he rained down upon her.

Her screams came in faint gasps now, weaker and weaker. By the time he had dragged her over to a pile of hay, she had fainted. She was mercifully spared the knowledge of the further indignities he inflicted upon her defenseless body.

Little Jonathon sat patiently on the sled at first, but hearing the screams, he started to walk up the slope. Not understanding how to open the door, he could not realize where his mama had gone. He turned, then slipped on the ice, and fell.

"Ma-ma! Jonny's cold! Wanta go home." But poor Jonny was alone with his problem. He picked himself up and trudged down the barn slope. However in his confusion, he turned towards the woods instead of the house. Valiantly he trudged along through the snow, falling, picking himself up, until at last, too exhausted to go on, he lay still.

"Jonny's sleepy. Want Ma-ma!" and humming his tuneless little song, he fell asleep on the snow.

CHAPTER 16

When David returned home in the late afternoon, he was surprised to find Jonathon's sled at the foot of the barn bridge. Puzzled, he gathered it up and carefully put it away in the woodshed. Then through force of habit, he picked up an armful of wood and started for the house.

The kitchen fire was out and a strange chill was in the house. He went into the sitting room where a small round "chunk stove" usually held a half day's supply of firewood at a time. That, too, was cold. He called out, "Rachel, where are you?" No answer.

Opening the door to Aunt Virgie's room, he saw the old lady on her bed breathing fast. Her face was deeply flushed. It looked like she was very sick indeed. Her room was like ice, for her little wood-burning stove too was cold. Where was Rachel? Where was the boy?

Frantically he searched the house. No one! Then he searched the barn, starting with the cow stables, then the horse stable. No one! He hastily mounted the rough stairs to the barn floor, and there he found her! There was his wife—his beloved!

There she lay, her hair matted with blood, her face so beaten it was hard to recognize her by her features, and she was completely naked. *Oh, God, no! Is she alive?* He touched her. She felt cold, but she was not stiff as in death. He hastily wrapped his coat around her and raced to the house with his burden. He put her on the lounge used in the kitchen.

Thank the Lord he had put in a telephone last fall. Cranking the handle, he yelled into the mouthpiece, "Help! Help! Operator, send a doctor! I have two dying women and a lost child here on my farm. Send a doctor as soon as you can!"

He had presence of mind to tell the operator his name and how to reach his farm before he hung up.

He dragged the lounge in front of the kitchen stove and opened the oven door. After building a roaring fire, he warmed a blanket and wrapped it about Rachel's lifeless form, then tried to massage her cold hands.

Her eyelids fluttered a little, so he knew she was still alive. He found himself sobbing, "Oh, God! Save her, save her!"

But where was his son? He dared not leave Rachel to find him. He knew he would have to call for help, but who? Rachel's parents had no telephone. Ah, yes, he remembered the Fletchers. They had one. He was sure Rachel said that. He would get them to take word to the Millers. He would have to be very discreet, for he was sure about what had happened to Rachel, and he wanted no more gossip about Rachel than necessary.

Suiting his thoughts to action, he got through to the Fletchers. "Please go over to the Millers and tell them to come over to David Lowe's place as soon as possible. Rachel is very sick."

He did not count on the party line, for it was but a short time before he heard a call from the driveway. He went to the door and found a neighbor riding horseback.

"Hi, neighbor! We heard you were in some kind of trouble over here. The missus heard it on the telephone."

"Yes, my wife's had some kind of accident and my little boy is missing. Can you go look for him? I can't leave my wife long enough to look for him, for I think she is dying. Start looking by the barn bridge, for I found his little sled there when I got home a few minutes ago."

The neighbor, Mr. Overman, got off his horse and started for the barn. There were no tracks until he got off the barn bridge, then he saw a trail left by little feet in the softer snow drifts. They were headed for the woods. In several places he found the snow crust had been broken, and it looked like the child and fallen but had eventually picked himself up.

In a little copse of elderberry bushes there was a bundle of clothes. One glance told the man that this was a child, all curled up as though he was asleep. But the boy was in his eternal sleep and was already frozen stiff.

Hurrying back to the house, he broke the news to the distracted father. "We'll have to call the sheriff. We shouldn't move the body until he gets here."

Long afterward David wondered just how he got through that awful day—a dead child, a dying wife, and an extremely sick aunt. *Trouble certainly comes in threes,* he thought, *for it has certainly come to me that way.*

The doctor arrived first. He examined Rachel long and carefully. Then he turned to David. "This woman has been badly beaten and raped. I've never seen anyone as badly abused as she is. Where did you find her?"

"The barn—on the barn floor. She had all her clothes torn off her. Do you think she will live, Doctor?"

"I hope so. But that blow on the head—um—um! I don't like that a bit. She should be taken to the hospital, but right now she can't be moved. Now if we had ambulance service here in the country like they do in the cities, that's where she would go right away. Can you find a room here on the first floor where we could put her so it would be easier to care for her?"

David thought, then he hurried to the parlor and started a fire in the isinglass-sided heater. He would have to have help to move a bed from the second floor, but it could wait until the Millers came.

"Doctor, my boy is lying out there in the fields dead. The same fiend that attacked my wife is responsible for his death. But we will have to wait for the sheriff. Can you find time to look in on my old aunt. She looks like she is in a coma."

So the doctor left Rachel for a time and went to see Aunt Virgie. She was indeed in a coma. Poor old woman! Pneumonia had caught up with her. So they had two critical patients, and it was a gamble which one would be the first to join Jonathon in death.

CHAPTER 17

The sheriff arrived in his official car about the time the Millers got there in their buggy. Since the two Miller boys had not yet arrived home from school, their parents left a note for them to take care of the feeding and the milking, and as soon as Mrs. Miller could gather her first-aid bag, they hurried as fast as the horse could take them over the wintry roads to their son-in-law's farm. How surprised they were to see the sheriff and an assistant heading out across the fields in the direction of the woods. Mr. Miller started to follow, but David spied them and called, "In here! Quick!"

There they saw the doctor working over their daughter's seemingly lifeless body. A few words from David struck terror into the mother's heart. "Oh, who would do such a thing? It must be a DEVIL!"

It was too important to waste any more time in talk with all the many things needing doing. It was hard to decide what to do first, what with Aunt Virgie so sick. Mr. Miller and David went to the second floor and found a single bedstead. They carried it, with its accoutrements down the staircase and set it up in the now cozily warm parlor.

Mother was overcome when she saw the bruises on her poor daughter's body. The doctor had cut out a portion of her hair and had dressed the ugly wounds on the top of her head. Mother found a clean nightgown and after bathing Rachel's once beautiful face and body, attired her in it. Then using the ironing board for a stretcher, she had Papa and David carried Rachel into the parlor to her freshly made bed. Ice was applied to the bruises.

While Rachel slept on in her deep coma, Mother turned her attention to Aunt Virgie. The doctor had left several bottles of medicine for her, saying, "Give her this every hour, day and night, but unless we can break up the congestion, she won't live but a day at the most."

Mother got out her mother's worth, an herb she used in the pneumonia and chest cold season. She fried out some of it in lard and cutting up an old sheet she had found, she spread a portion of this concoction and applied it, still very warm, to Aunt Virgie's shrunken chest for a hot poultice. Every hour she changed the poultice as well as gave the old lady her medicine. The doctor looked very serious after taking her temperature for the second time. He found her pulse very erratic.

"I think, Mrs. Miller, you will have to have another nurse in here with you. Both these women will have to have constant attention. I want ice on the young woman's head, and her medicine will have to be given to her every half hour. This will have to continue all night long. I will be here as early as I can in the morning. Careful nursing will be the only thing that can save these two women now."

Mrs. Miller's mind went to Sister Gray, the sweet-faced woman in the church. She got Papa started in his buggy to go to the Gray's place and see if she would come to help.

David now felt free to go out to see about Jonathon. He found the sheriff making out a report. He said, "We will have to call the coroner. In the meantime you can notify the undertaker to come as soon as the coroner is finished. You can move the body to the house now."

So the little boy who wanted to go home was moved to his little bed on the second floor. The coroner confirmed Mr. Overman's first impressions that the child had died from exhaustion and exposure. But why was the child running for the woods? Was there no one to watch him?

So David told the sheriff about Rachel's tragedy. Once again the sheriff went to the barn bridge. He noticed a few drops of blood on the icy slope, but they were few. Opening the small door to the barn floor, he found more blood on the floor. Then he discovered the blood on the pitchfork.

After the doctor and the sheriff had a consultation in the house, the sheriff said to David, "There were no stab wounds on your wife, so she must have found an opportunity to use the pitchfork on the fellow. But a stab wound like that could seal itself off so that he would still be in condition to do his dirty work and get out without leaving any bloody trail behind."

Several other neighbors came to offer help, and then the Grays came. Brother Gray went with the neighbors to do the evening milking and feeding while the two women took turns watching over the sick. Mr. Miller and Brother Gray sat with the dead, now laid out in the sitting room in a little, white casket.

Mrs. Overman came across the field and set to work to put out a meal on the kitchen table for those who could eat.

It was decided not to hold a funeral in the church but to hold a brief service in the home on the following afternoon, then carry the casket to the cemetery for burial. David announced that the services would be private because of the tragedy in his home. Since Plain People do not have flowers at funerals, he requested that flowers be omitted. Brother Gray had charge of the simple service.

During the following week the snow was worn thin in the lane leading from the highway to the Lowe farm. The Barn Brethren came as soon as the news was noised concerning Aunt Virgie's illness. These fine people brought soup, custard, and delicacies of all kinds to tempt the sick woman's appetite.

As soon as the mother's worth poultices broke up the worst of the congestion and Aunt Virgie could say a few words, she immediately called for her elder to come and anoint her. The deacons and their wives also came in their straight-sided buggies pulled by bay horses. Elder Trumpacker came by himself. He was assisted by his deacons to perform this ancient service, as old as Christianity itself. The anointee was given a chance to reaffirm her faith, then asked if she had any hidden sins to confess.

Aunt Virgie said weakly, "Yes, I have had hatred for Rachel. I did not show her Christian love. I want her to come to my bedroom so that I can ask her for forgiveness."

Elder Trumpacker gently told the sick woman that Rachel had met with an accident and could not leave her bed. At this the old woman began to cry.

"I can't meet my Maker with hatred in my heart that has not been made right. I will not die until I can tell Rachel!"

As the Elder poured the drops of oil on her still-fevered brow, he prayed for the sick woman and asked that she be given an opportunity to carry out her desires for repentance. And from that hour on Aunt Virgie started to recover. The doctor was amazed at her daily progress.

"By all the laws of averages, that old lady should be dead by now. Her faith has brought her through, plus assistance from me and that good woman who has poulticed and nursed her. What is the name of that herb again?"

"Mother's worth. It grows wild in the fields and back yards. I have helped many a person with this plant. It looks very much like catnip, the tea that relieves colic in small babies."

"I have seen many cures that cannot be explained in medical terms," the doctor said. "For example a niece of mine had a rash that bothered her for years. I had treated her with all the known remedies, but to no avail. She heard of a 'pow-wow doctor' of your faith living in a village near here. She went to him, and after he said some words over her, she went away. Within a day or so, the rash disappeared and has not come back. My niece made a point of telling me that the old gentleman was blind and would take no money for it. He said his gift was from God."

"Oh, yes, we knew him," replied Mama. "He has passed away now, but he did a lot of good with his healing powers. He used to clear up thrush in small babies' mouths."

David added, "I often saw him *try* for bleeding. In fact I had cut myself bad when he happened to be around. That was when he had his eyesight. He had been helping my father in the fields. I was a small boy and I got too close to the mowers as they were coming down one swath of hay. Suddenly I felt warm blood going down my leg. It was gushing, but old Brother Dillman said, 'Lie down,' and of course I did. He bent over me and said some words, holding the wound together. I don't know what the words were, but they were holy words like a prayer. The blood stopped right away. He always claimed he could never give away the words except to a good woman, and she in turn could give the words to me."

"There are many mysteries. I must go now, but I will be back as soon as I can," said the doctor as he started his car and headed for the town.

CHAPTER 18

O n the sixth day following the funeral, an out-of-state car drove onto David's
farm. To his surprise and joy he saw Elder Winer and his tiny wife get out
of the car. This was the first time he had seen them since the wedding so many
months ago.

"We have heard of your troubles here, David, my son, my spiritual son, I
should say, so Martha and I felt it to be our pleasure to come for a few days to help
out. I'm a pretty good nurse, at least Martha thinks so when she gets sick. I know
that she is good at nursing. So here we are."

Mrs. Winer's face shone with sympathy and love. They carried their suitcases
to the bedroom that was across the hall from David's and that was heated from a
register carrying heat from the parlor. After consulting with the two tired nurses,
they decided to take over for the rest of the week. So Mother went home to look
after her neglected family and household. Sister Gray went home, promising to
return the following week.

The sheriff came the same day and questioned David concerning any
strangers that may have been on the farm prior to the attack on Rachel.

"The only people to set foot on the property for weeks was a bunch of Bel
Snicklers. They were here the third night following Christmas. Oh, yes, I do
remember . . ." and he stopped, feeling embarrassed.

"Remember what?"

"I'd rather not say now."

"Come, man, a crime has been committed. If you suspect anyone, now's
the time to tell what you know."

"Sheriff, it is a part of what I believe, 'Do not bear false witness against thy neighbor.'"

"Let me be the judge of that, so let's have it."

So David drew a long breath and told how the tall man with the yellowish-brown eyes was with the group of Bel Snicklers that night. He very reluctantly told how the man had watched Rachel and had followed her into the dark hall.

"Yes, yes, man, go on. What happened then?"

"Well I hate to tell you this part. I thought at the time that my wife had drawn him on to follow her. I know now that she only went to the hall to fetch my accordion. I caught him trying to manhandle my wife. How ashamed I am of my vile suspicions of her!" For the first time in all of that tragedy, David broke down and cried great, racking sobs.

The sheriff turned away and let him cry a while, then asked, "Did the man say anything?"

"Yes, he said I'd better keep her under lock and key, for he was coming back."

"What did you do about that? Didn't you knock him down?"

"The people of our belief do not sanction violence. We believe in turning the other cheek. But I did scold my wife, much to my sorrow. When I found out why she went into the dark hall, I found she was perfectly innocent."

"Did you recognize any of the Bel Snicklers?"

"I thought one of them was a Henderson boy, the chunky one. Of course they were all masked. Do you think he would know who the tall fellow was?"

"Leave that to me. Now tell me where the Hendersons live. You will be advised as to whatever we find out." The sheriff went off to make his investigation.

Several days had gone by. The sheriff questioned each of the party that had gone Bel Snickling together. Each one said he did not know who the stranger was.

"He seemed to come out of the dark when we left the Overman farm. There were four sleigh-loads of us, so no one really gave it a thought who he was or who was responsible for him. I knew he acted a little fresh with the girls, but then I don't think he was with us very long. Come to think of it, I don't believe he was with us when we went in to the next place after the Lowes. We talked about it afterwards and wondered where he had gone."

The sheriff put out a description of the tall man with the yellowish-brown eyes. No one knew the color of his hair since it was covered with a stocking cap. No one had even seen his face, but one girl said she had spied a tattoo of a snake on his wrist. It was a coiled snake!

CHAPTER 19

One afternoon Rachel opened her eyes and looked around. She discovered a patch of deep rose and vaguely wondered what it was. Finally after concentration she decided it was the rose brocade chair in the parlor. But what was she doing here in the parlor? She gave a gasp and then saw David sitting nearby, holding her hand.

"David! You're here?"

"Yes, Sweetheart, have you decided to wake up?"

Just then Mrs. Winer brought in some chicken broth and lifting her from the pillow, David encouraged Rachel to drink it.

"That was good," and closing her eyes, she slept—not an uneasy sleep as she had before. This time no baby's crying came to keep her awake.

When the doctor came, he was relieved to see her progress. "Soon we will have to take her to the hospital for some repair surgery. I know a good gynecologist who will fix her up like new. But we will have to wait until she has more strength."

For several days Rachel was not able to do more than say David's name. She did not want him to leave the room. The patient fellow sat there holding her hands by the hour. Mr. Overman, the neighbor, came over to help Elder Winer with the farm chores.

By the time Aunt Virgie was able to sit up, Rachel was beginning to eat solid food. One evening she opened her green eyes and saw David looking at her with such love and devotion in his eyes. She asked him, "Where's Jonathon?"

David stroked her hair and looked out of the window. "Look, Rachel, the sunset's color matches the isinglass stove's glow. The whole room is a lovely rose color, but your hair is the most beautiful."

"David, why are you trying to put me off? Where is Jonathon?"

"I can't tell you, Beloved."

"No, no! Tell me it isn't true!"

"Yes, Rachel. He has gone to be with God. Don't cry, it's bad for you."

"He called me 'Mama.' We were sledding. Then something happened—I can't seem to remember anymore. I think, yes, I really did see a snake!"

"Don't try to remember anymore. Now go to sleep."

Rachel slept an uneasy, restless sleep. The Evil One had her and there was a snake. She then heard sobbing. It must be the baby crying again. But this time the sobs were so close. She must stop that terrible sobbing.

But David once again recovered from the terrible anguish that tore through him. He knelt by her bed for a long time, begging for God's help. How he needed it!

Another snowstorm swept through the valley so that the doctor was unable to get through to see his patients at the Lowe farm for several days. By the time David and Elder Winer had dug themselves out, the road crew came by with a snow shovel hitched to several horses. A large gang of men helped by digging by hand.

On the fourth day the doctor came and found Aunt Virgie up and dressed and sitting in her rocking chair. She was stubborn in her efforts to see Rachel, but the doctor told her to stay in her room for several more days. No one had told her the true story of Rachel's attack, so she had the impression that the girl had fallen on the ice while sledding with Jonathon, thereby getting the concussion. It was explained in easy stages that Jonathon had wandered away from Rachel while she was unconscious, hence he had lost his way and had died of exposure.

"Poor little fellow! He's better off with the Lord. Let us not mourn, for our loss is Heaven's gain!" So with this cliche her faith was her comfort.

It was decided that Rachel would be taken to the county hospital within the week. There she would have the necessary surgery.

Mother came over to help again, but one of Aunt Virgie's church friends came to help nurse her, so Mother helped David to get Rachel ready for the trip to the hospital.

As she was carried through the kitchen in David's strong arms, Aunt Virgie was sitting by the stove. She held out her trembling arms and cried, "Rachel, my child, I want you to forgive me for being so hateful to you. I promised God if I was spared I would try to make it up to you."

"Of course, Aunt Virgie, as soon as I get well, we will have plenty of time to get to know and love each other."

The gynecologist did not tell David all that he had found. He had found evidence of an infection that could have only come from an abortion. Treatment cleared it up during the following days at the hospital. One day he came to her bedside. Drawing her curtains shut, he spoke softly to her.

"Mrs. Lowe, we have repaired all of the damage done, so you should go on now and live a normal, married life. I have cleared up the infection found that could have caused sterility. It could have come from an abortion. Can you tell me about that?"

Rachel stared at the doctor with horror in her eyes. "I don't understand. How could you tell a thing like that?"

"My dear young woman, somebody has really bungled. It could only have been an abortionist. Now will you come straight with me and give me the name of the person who did this to you? I can guarantee that your secret will be safe with me, but we will put an end to this dirty business before she or he kills somebody. Certainly you won't protect that person who might cause someone to lose her life!"

Through tears Rachel said, "But she said all it took was time and cleanliness. She said she learned her business in a hospital in the city. She was a nurse there."

"She could not have been a trained nurse, for nurses are like doctors. They try to preserve life, not destroy it. Of course there are times when we have to abort a fetus in the interest of the patient's life or sanity. Now tell me who it was."

A fit of weeping ended the conversation, and the doctor left in frustration. That night Rachel once again fled through the buzzards field, across the bridge, and down the dusty road to Miss Lucy's pink and white gingerbread house. Once more she endured the pain and shame on the narrow, white bed. She screamed and screamed.

The night nurse came and found her trying to tear out her hair. The other patients in the ward looked on in horror.

"It's this hair! Cut it off! Tear it out! It's been my ruination!"

The frightened nurse got the doctor, and only after tying her hands and giving her a sedative could peace be restored to the ward.

The next morning when the doctor came in to see her, he found a subdued woman. Her green eyes were slate-colored and dead. Her hair was disheveled. She did not respond to his greeting, so he called in a psychiatrist, Dr. Lewitt.

Dr. Lewitt's bedside manner was so reassuring that he struck a note of response. He reported to David on his next visit, "I cannot betray the confidence of my patient, but I can say that she is suffering from something that happened to her in her past, something that has frightened her very much, something that preys on her mind. Has she been open to you concerning this thing?"

David was thoughtful. Here was a man he felt was trustworthy. "My wife had a secret when we were married. I never tried to find out what it was. I took her for better or worse, and that's that way it is."

On one of the psychiatrist's visits, he asked Rachel about her dreams. Little by little he got her to tell about the buzzards field and crossing the bridge. "And where do you go after you cross the bridge?"

"Up a long, dusty road."

"Yes, and then?"

"There's a pretty, little, pink and white house. A rose bush is over the gate. It always catches in my hair."

"And then what do you see?"

But when she had gotten this far she would not say anymore. The fact of her abortion would not come out in words. She tried, but she could not say it. Again she sought refuge in tears. She refused any further communications, so the doctor advised that she be sent home. Her body was healed.

The fact that she had been raped had never come out in any discussion. She had no remembrance of it, only of the snake that the evil man had tattooed on his arm. She was not even sure of that but put it down to a bad dream. She had blotted out the entire tragedy from her consciousness.

CHAPTER 20

Rachel returned home from the hospital by Groundhog Day. It was a raw dreary day, but at noon the famous animal was expected to make his sortie from his winter's sleep. But he was not able to see his shadow and so was not frightened by it into going back for another six weeks' sleep. To his devoted believers, spring would soon be there.

David took an inventory of his grain and hay, and finding that half of it was left, felt that it would see him through to harvest time.

Although very weak, Aunt Virgie was able to be about and could see after her own personal needs. With two semi-invalids in the house, David decided he would have to get a hired girl. Overriding Rachel's objections, he hired a middle-aged garrulous woman named Hilda. David warned her never to speak of the attack and rape to Rachel, explaining to the good woman that Rachel had no remembrance of this cruel event. All newspapers having any references to it had been kept from her.

It was hard to keep Hilda back from housecleaning during the cold early spring. David had to keep the two stoves going, not counting the kitchen range. It took a large amount of wood, and he was glad he had sawed up an extra amount of it last fall.

When Shrove Tuesday came, Hilda baked a large number of fassnaughts like Rachel's mother had done the year before. But no greasy hex marks were drawn on the corners of the house like Rachel's brothers had done. David believed that man made his own mistakes, not witches.

It was soon time to plant tomato, pepper, and cabbage seeds in flats to be later transferred to the vegetable garden. The *Hagerstown Almanac* was consulted, and when the moon's horns turned upwards, the seed was sown. All vegetables producing fruits above the ground were planted when the moon was in its *up sign*, and when later the potatoes and other root vegetables were planted, the moon's horns were in the *down sign*. The little seedlings were placed in a south window to flourish.

At last March "came in like a lamb," and before long the lamb-like weather was being enjoyed. Hilda started to clean house, starting with David and Rachel's bedroom. She carried down the chaff tick which was used in the country instead of mattresses and took them outside to the barnyard and emptied them. Then the ticks were laundered. The rag carpet was taken up from the floor, carried to the clothesline where it was beaten and aired.

Hilda allowed a day or two to air each room, causing Rachel and David to take a new bedroom for the duration. The bare floor was washed with lye soap and warm water, fresh newspapers were spread over it for padding, and then the clean carpet was stretched and tacked back into place. Rachel helped by waxing the furniture with a mixture of turpentine and beeswax. The windows were washed inside, and Hilda hung precariously out of the windows to wash the outside. Curtains were washed, starched, and stretched.

Finally Hilda asked Rachel to help her fill the chaff tick, and taking the freshly laundered bag to the straw stack, they dug underneath the outer layer of straw to where the clean straw was still to be found, and proceeded to fill the tick until it was bulging. The open end was sewn shut. Hilda made an amusing figure with straw sticking out from her sunbonnet and standing near the amazed steers while she sewed the bag shut.

The two women carried the enormous bag to the second floor and made up the bed with fresh-smelling sheets and a clean counterpane. The room smelled so clean it was a delight to go to bed in it.

"I feel like I am on top of the world," David laughed as he tried to find a spot in the bed to hold onto. Finally by clasping Rachel tightly in his arms, he found a place in the middle of the bed. By morning they had worn a valley in their mountain of straw.

Housecleaning went on for two weeks before it was time to start the garden, so one day Hilda asked permission to have her little grandson come to spend a few days with her. The little fellow was five, but as his grandmother explained, he was not "broken yet."

"His mother doesn't know what to do about him when he goes to school next year. I've told her several times what to do, but she won't heed."

"What can you do when a child keeps on wetting himself?" asked Aunt Virgie.

"This one wets the bed at night, too. I've been told a sure cure. At butchering time, take the two lumps from a male hog that are near its hind part, clean them off real good, and then cook them and have the child eat them. You'll have no more trouble with him wetting after that. My daughter-in-law says it's nasty, but when it works, what's the difference? It ain't no worse than having to put warm pee in the ear for earache. Everybody knows how good that is to do. But these old tried and true remedies are no good for the younger generation."

Rachel walked across the kitchen to put a stick of wood in the kitchen range and in doing so had to step across the little fellow who was stretched out on the floor partly asleep.

"Oh, please, missus, now you've done it. That stops the growth!"

"What does?"

"Stepping over a child on the floor. My cousin Minnie had a child that would never grow after it was four years old. It was a dwarf all of its days. It was claimed that it happened because the family kept stepping over the child when it was on the floor."

Now that the house was cleaned, Hilda decided it was time to make soap. She had David get a can of lye when he went into town and she gathered all of the "fryings" collected from the roasts, sausage, and puddin'. This she put into the cast-iron wash kettle, dumping in the lye and a measured amount of cold water. A chemical reaction took place and the mass became hot and bubbly. When it stopped and settled in the pot, there was a mass of white soap. It was then allowed to stand until it was nearly hardened, then Hilda took a knife and marked it off into squares. The next day she lifted out these cubes of soap and set them aside to cure for use in laundering and dishwashing.

"This soap is a lot whiter than what I used to make when I was a girl," Aunt Virgie remarked. "In those days we had to make our own lye, too. We had a box called an ash hopper. All of our wood ashes were thrown into this hopper and a bucket of water thrown over it once a week. This would ooze through the ashes into a pan under the hopper. This was a dark brown liquid or lye. It was just as good as the lye we buy now, but the soap was always brown. Of course that was long ago. But I mind that we often used that lye soap to shave up and make a poultice for boils. There was nothing better than brown lye soap."

The energetic Hilda decided that the next thing to do was to whitewash the picket fence around the yard as soon as she could get the onions and radishes planted. It was the *down sign* of the moon. "It looks to me that the fences haven't been whitewashed for quite a spell. Also the cellar walls need it. Does the Mister have any lime burned out yet?"

"I think he opened one of his kilns yesterday," Rachel replied.

David had been burning out lime, digging the limestone rocks from the abandoned quarry at the edge of the woods. The kiln would burn for days until all of the huge logs were consumed and the intense heat melted the rocks, releasing the lime which was formed into a white powder. This lime was put into a lime spreader and sifted over the fields as soon as they were plowed and harrowed. For a day or two, the fields looked like they had an unseasonable snowfall. His eyes and face would be irritated by the chemical.

So Hilda was given an allotment of the fresh lime. She put this into a tight wooden barrel and mixed it with water. Swathing themselves in their oldest clothes, their hair bound up in big bandanas and wearing gloves, Hilda and Rachel sallied forth to apply whitewash to the fences, the woodshed, the privy, and even to the trunks of the trees in the front yard. Everything looked as pristine as a snowfall. However David questioned their taste in decorating the tree trunks.

"It isn't natural to whitewash a tree."

One day David came in from hauling rocks from the quarry, looking pale and wan. Rachel noticed it right away. "What's wrong, David? You don't look so good."

"I'm fine, but I want you and Hilda to go into the back lot and mark off where you want the sweet potato ridges thrown up. I'm about to clean the horse stable and I don't want to handle the manure twice. I can put it on top of the ground today and then plow it up in a day or two."

"Right now?"

"Yes, right away. I want to get it done as soon as I can."

So the two women went out to the back lot and drove in stakes where the sweet potato ridges were to be placed. Sprouts from the hot bed would be put into the ridges so that their long winding stalks would be kept out of the mud when it rained.

As soon as they were out of the house, David went to the telephone and called the sheriff.

"Hello, Sheriff, I was down at the quarry hole here on my place—what's that? Oh, yes, this is David Lowe. You know the place where the attack took place on my wife back in January? Well I found a body down in the quarry hole here on my place. Can you come out and take care of the details? Please leave your car out on the road. I don't want my wife to know about this. I have had quite a time with her, and now that she is getting better I don't want things all stirred up again. Will you see to it that no newspaperman comes to the house? I'll talk to them at the barn where she is not likely to be."

By the time Hilda and Rachel had gotten in from the back lot, David had cleaned his horse stable and had started to scatter the horse manure on the ground destined to be the sweet potato patch. Then he called to Rachel.

"Sweetheart, I see some dandelions by the fence. How about you and Hilda bringing out a bucket and pick enough for a mess of dandelion greens for supper?"

So the two women did not see the arrival of the sheriff and his men. Once again they came and walked over the fields, but this time David led them along a grassy track back through some scrub cedars and down over a steep bank to an abandoned quarry hole. At the foot of the cliff was a badly decomposed body of what had once been a man. It was partly eaten by buzzards and varmits. The man's chest and left arm were still intact since they had been submerged in water that had just melted from the winter's ice.

After the coroner and his assistants arrived, they discovered three stab wounds on the chest. It was assumed that they had been made by a pitchfork.

"This undoubtedly is the attacker who violated your wife. It is without a doubt that she tried to fight him off with the pitchfork. See, here on the left wrist is the tattoo of a snake that the girl saw when they were Bel Snickling."

"What do you think caused his death, Coroner?"

"From what I can find, he has a broken neck. He fell over the cliff, that's certain. I think we have enough evidence right here to close the case on your wife's attacker, Mr. Lowe."

It was decided to hold the formal inquest the next day at the county courthouse, and David was asked to be there.

CHAPTER 21

The next day David announced that he would have to go to the county seat on business.

"Can't I go along, David? I would like to get away for a change."

"I'm sorry, but I can't take you this time. Tell you what I'll do though. How about my taking you over to visit with your mother for the afternoon? It's on my way to the courthouse?"

"Why are you going to the courthouse?"

"Well it's like this," David groped for an answer. Above all he must shield her from finding out about the discovery of the tall stranger's body. She had blotted the memory of the attack from her mind. With things so well now, he could not take a chance in recalling disturbing things to her memory.

"Well it's like this," he began again. "Dear, you know I want to buy my own land some day and not be a tenant farmer all of my life. Well I am trying to find a place that is delinquent in the taxes so I can bid it in at a tax sale."

What a lie that was! Since Jonathon's funeral and Rachel's sickness and hospitalization, David had no extra money at all. He was feeling the drain very forcefully. But as usual he would not worry his beloved Rachel with his problems.

The day following the hearing, the mailman brought the county weekly paper. There the whole story was spread over the front page. It even went back and recounted the story of the attack and rape upon Rachel. There was no picture of Rachel, but to David's disgust, a photographer had taken a picture of him looking at the remains in the quarry. He hid the paper in the woodshed.

"Missus," said Hilda the following day, "Will you please read to me the receet about how to make Montgomery pies? I never got much book learnin' so I can't read."

"Why, Hilda, you have made Montgomery pies before, haven't you?"

"Oh, yes, but I always get mixed up about how much brown sugar and how much molasses to use. I have already lined my pie pans with the crust, and I always stir up a two-egg cake receet for the top, but it's the middle that I forget."

"All right, Hilda, here it is. 'Grate the lemon rind, beat in one egg, a cup of brown sugar, two tablespoons of flour, beat this, and then add a pint of water.' It doesn't say anything about molasses. This is the part you put on top of the crust before you put in the cake mixture. But this makes six pies. How are we going to eat so many?"

"We'll find a way. The Mister is right fond of pie, and so am I."

"Well don't make your oven too hot. Remember this is partly a cake."

"Sure thing, Missus! Excuse me, I have to get in some more wood."

The good woman went to the woodshed muttering, "Now I've got to find some good pie-baking wood. Well, well, here's the county paper. I bet the Mister forgot and left it here. I'll take it into the house."

So the paper reached Rachel after all. She was sitting listlessly paring potatoes for dinner when she happened to glance at the front page of the newspaper and see a picture. When she read the caption and recognized the picture to be that of David, she read the whole terrible story spread out there on the front page of the newspaper. She gave a choked cry.

"What's the trouble, Missus? You sound like you are choking."

But Rachel was too busy reading about the discovery of the body of the man who had manhandled her on the night the Bel Snicklers came. Then part of the truth flashed through her mind of how the DEVIL trapped and attacked her in the haymow. So that was how she was so badly hurt! That was how little Jonathon met his death!

While she was reading, the telephone rang. She went to answer it, moving as in a dream.

"Hello! Yes, this is Mrs. Lowe."

"So, you old Jezebel, you are up to your old tricks, driving men to their deaths! You are lower than dirt! The DEVIL will surely get you! Murderer! Murderer!"

Rachel started to scream, leaving the telephone receiver dangle as she ran out the door with but one thought—she must find David! Who hated her that much as to call her such names? What did the paper mean—rape? Then the truth flashed across her mind. She had seen the Evil One in her dreams and she had always dreamed of a coiled snake! So her dreams were true after all! Just as true as her running through the buzzards field, across the bridge, up the dusty road, under the grasping rose arbor, and into the cottage with its narrow, white bed! Oh, David!

Her screams reached David as he was working in the field. He jumped off his cultivator and ran across the field to see her coming, her flaming hair and her green eyes fixed in terror. Hilda came panting on behind.

"David! David! Am I really a murderer? A hateful voice on the telephone said I killed a man—a man who had raped me! Oh, David, what have you been keeping from me? A Jezebel, she called me!"

"A Jezebel! You know who that was. It's that hateful Cook girl, the one who spit on you at church that time. But who told you about the dead man? Did she tell you about that, too?"

"I read it in the paper."

"But where did you get hold of a paper?"

Hilda was weeping with all the excitement. "Oh, Mister, I found it in the woodshed! I didn't know, for I can't read. I gave it to the Missus, not meaning any harm!"

"Don't you cry, too, Hilda, for you didn't know. Help me to get my wife into the house."

So the two supported the hysterical woman into the house and got her into bed. Hilda held her down until the doctor came and administered a sedative.

The doctor told David he should explain to her how the attack came about and how the man met his death. He spent several hours with her, but her mental state was not at all good. That night the baby cried and cried. Rachel tried her best to awaken and go to the sobbing infant, but she could not escape the sedative. When morning came, she greeted David with dead-looking eyes. David warned Hilda not to allow her out of bed.

When Hilda went upstairs to take lunch to Rachel, she found her looking out of the window in a dull, listless fashion.

"Hilda, will you do something for me? I have been having very bad dreams, but I'm not asleep now. I hear a baby crawling across the garret floor overhead. I can hear it cry, too. Don't you hear it? Please go upstairs and see if there isn't a baby there."

"All right, Missus," and the faithful woman toiled up the steep steps to the third floor. When she came back there were smudges of dirt on her face and cobwebs adorned her dress. "My land's sake, we have really forgotten the garret when we cleaned house. Next week you and I will have to go up there and really clean out that place. No, Ma'am, there ain't no baby up there. Now you rest yourself, and I'll get you a fresh drink of water."

Several more days went by with Rachel leaving her bed and going to the attic to quiet the phantom baby. David became more and more alarmed. Her whole personality seemed to be under a blight.

Even the weather seemed to be in sympathy with the mood of the stricken family. A cold rain came, and the weather was bad for several days. David was almost frantic with worry.

It was on a Friday night that David was awakened by a scream overhead in the garret. Jumping up, he raced to the end of the hall where the garret door stood open to its dark and mysterious third floor. There was light enough from the moon and the beginning of daylight to show the horrible sight of his beloved hanging by a rope from the rafters. The knot around her neck was tied too loosely so that her neck was not broken, but her breath was cut off so that she was unconscious.

He called loudly for help and after cutting the poor thing down, Hilda helped get her to bed. Her pulse was very weak, scarcely perceptible.

The doctor came once again and shook his head. "I was afraid of this. You will have to have her committed to the state hospital. Unless you do this, you will be responsible when she again tries to take her life, for she will try it again."

David bowed his head in anguish. "Why can't we watch her here at home? I can't think of my dear wife having to be shut up in an asylum with all those crazy people. Oh, what can I do?"

The doctor looked at him in compassion. "The doctors in the state hospital will be able to help her. They can try to get to the bottom of her trouble."

"What do you mean, Doctor?"

"It is plain that there is something your wife has on her mind other than the attack and rape she suffered. She has a secret she is afraid to tell you. When she gets that off her mind, it is my opinion that she will be a normal, happy woman again."

"God grant it!"

Chapter 22

After several weeks had gone by there came another spell of depressing weather. The mountains to the west were blotted out by clouds. Every leaf on the trees dripped dismally. David saw that the bricks of the old house seemed bleached by its tears.

Aunt Virgie had already eaten her noon meal and had retired to her room for an afternoon nap. When David entered the kitchen for the noon meal, he found Hilda sitting listlessly on the lounge idly examining her hands. It was strange to see her idle, for this bundle of energy usually found things to do that were often manufactured.

David merely touched the fried ham, sweet potatoes, and wilted lettuce that she had prepared. His appetite was nil.

When Hilda cleared the table, David decided to spend the rainy afternoon with his accounts rather than clean out cow stables, although anyone could see that it was needed.

He found a letter from the bank. He was overdrawn. The note he had made to buy a new wheat binder was due. How could he pay it? How could he hold on until the wheat was harvested and threshed? How could he pay Hilda her wages? Would he have to sell off some of his livestock? This was hard to do, for they represented his investment, and when a farmer has no stock to make money, he may as well shut down.

Clearing his throat, he said, "Hilda, I hate to do this, but I'm afraid I am going to have to hold back your wages for a month at least, or until I can get the wheat harvested and sold. As you know, I have been under a great deal of expense, what with a funeral, doctor bills, and my wife's expenses. If you can't wait that long, then I'll have to let you go, much as I hate to. I will try to manage with whatever help Aunt Virgie can give me."

"Don't you worry, Mister. I know you're good for it and I ain't under no expense here, so I can wait for it."

Hilda went upstairs to her room for a rare afternoon's nap. David sat by the table and read from the Bible, seeking comfort from its passages.

How long wilt thou forget me, O Lord? Forever? How long wilt thou hide thy face from me? he read. Forever? The word stuck in his mind. Oh Lord not forever! Heal my beloved!

The meaningless days and nights followed one another through the summer and into early fall. Then another blow fell, another sorrow, and with double force. Elder Winer and this tiny wife were on their way home from their county seat when their car was struck by a gasoline truck. These two sweethearts of fifty years were both taken at once, perishing along with the truck driver in a blazing fire. David's sorrow made him numb. How much more could a human stand?

That month he did not go to see Rachel, for he thought he could not afford the long drive to the state capital. The last time he had seen her she looked at him with vacant eyes. Her only comment was, "Shave off that ugly beard. I don't like it."

He had been so depressed he could hardly get home in his car. He was tempted to go off in another direction and never go back to the old farm in the cedar hills where he had found so much misery. Only the thoughts of Aunt Virgie waiting for him kept him on the road back to the farm.

One day, on impulse, he decided to do as Rachel said. He shaved off his beard. When he came to the table that Sunday morning, Aunt Virgie looked him over critically.

"Well you certainly do look different, but come to think of it, you look younger—almost like you did when you were first married. Do you recken that Rachel will know you?"

"It's hard to say. She didn't seem to when I saw her the last time."

One day the telephone rang and a voice requested Mr. David Lowe to come to the county seat near where Elder Winer lived. An appointment was set up for the following week, so David set out in his car to the south and across the state line. He stopped at the cemetery in back of the church where Elder Winer had once attended, and there he found the two mounds where the two lay. Carefully David pulled out a few weeds from the fresh soil and looked at the gravestones. It gave their birth dates and the date of their death. He pondered. Is this all that a man is—a date to be born and a date to die? Certainly man has a better record elsewhere, but how is it recorded? Is it recorded in the wind? No, absolutely not, reason replied. The deeds of man are reflected in the lives of others, in his children, in the kindness he shows to others, or in the record he makes for his country. A record is primarily with God.

But where are my children? mused David. Could he hope for the future?

When he arrived at the lawyer's office, he was beginning to feel curious. He was no relative of the Winers, so he would never inherit their estate. It was possible that they left him a small bequest.

"Mr. Lowe, my clients who are now deceased as you well know, made a will about five years ago. Since the Reverend Mr. Winer and his wife had no living children, they made a will naming several bequests and an heir to their estate. They lived very simple like people of their church often do, so their estate is quite considerable. After taxes, bequests to various distant relatives, and a gift to the church's home for the aged, the bulk of the estate including the farm goes to you. The household furniture has already been sold and the residue has been added to the bulk of the estate."

"The farm! How remarkable! I never expected to own a farm of my own!"

"Not only a farm, Mr. Lowe, but stocks, bonds, and a savings fund in the neighborhood of at least ninety-five thousand dollars."

David was speechless! He closed his eyes to keep back tears that began to flow at the generosity of his friends. How often he had heard them call him their spiritual son! How they had come to his farm to help at the time Rachel was attacked! His head was in a whirl as he drove home. When he entered the kitchen door, his step was lighter and his voice seemed a little more hopeful.

"You sound like you have some good news, David," observed Aunt Virgie.

"I do have some good news. What do you think Elder Winer and his wife did? They left me their fine farm! And that's not all. They left me a great deal of money besides. How do you like that? Now I can get Rachel into a hospital where she can get better care. Then maybe she will soon be well and can come home to us again!"

"Do you mean we will move to the Winer farm?"

"Not until spring. I will have to arrange for someone to put out my winter wheat there. The house is empty, so before we move in we can have the house fixed up to suit ourselves. If I remember correctly, it was in good shape. You know, that's where Rachel and I were married and spent two days of our honeymoon. The house has only happy memories for us, and that is what Rachel needs, happy memories."

"I am not sure I can go with you, Nephew. It is harder for old people to make a change than it is for you younger ones. But I have time to make up my mind."

CHAPTER 23

Rachel never had any recollection of how she got to the state hospital or who went with her. She remained in a state of horrified shock for days, screaming until sedatives were administered. It was a good thing that David was spared the sight of her then.

She was securely locked inside a cell. The sides and floor were padded, and there she was left to wallow in her own misery and filth. She sobbed, even in the induced sleep of the sedatives. No one could go near her except a very strong and no-nonsense female guard. She would cram food into Rachel's protesting mouth until nausea and subsequent vomiting forced her to stop.

After several days of this, Rachel ceased her screaming, and then she was moved into a room with a bed. She was locked in. When David arrived for his first visit at the end of the month, he was so horrified at her appearance that he could only weep. She had lost so much weight and was so wild in her appearance that she was unrecognizable except for her hair. That was dull and sadly matted. He was not even allowed to enter her room, so she was unaware of his visit.

One morning when the matron came, Rachel looked at her and said, "Are you one of the devils?"

The matron turned her back on this inappropriate remark. This woman had many females to deal with, and up until this time the doctor did not have a chance to see Rachel. After all, there were eighteen hundred patients in the hospital. Public funds did not run into hiring more than three psychiatrists for the entire hospital. When the doctors got around to seeing each patient, it took over three months. Not much help could be given them, and each man felt keenly the fact that few people were being dismissed to rejoin society, while each week more people were being admitted. Where would it end?

The hospital also seemed to be the dumping ground for the aged with their little personality quirks. One man claimed to have been there eight years, his only problem being that he talked to himself. He told the doctors that he had a son who craved his farm. The easiest way to get it was to have him committed for insanity.

An old woman had a well-to-do daughter but had no income except through the daughter. When she suffered a broken hip, the daughter wanted no part of caring for her, so she had the mother committed to the state hospital.

Many patients were there because they were in the last stages of venereal disease. The mental patients, however, were in the majority.

When David returned the next time, he found Rachel reduced to utter apathy. She had to be force-fed. She gave no indication that she was aware of anyone else in the world. Her appearance became even worse. They had to clean her up before she was led out to the visitors room. She spied David and pointing a finger at him, said, "Shave off that ugly beard. I don't like it."

A sense of power seemed to possess Rachel when she noticed the hurt that was in David's eyes. She started to make the most of it, taking great delight in humiliating those around her. She became quarrelsome and one day slapped a fellow patient.

She had been allowed to have a partner in the room with her but since she became quarrelsome, the roommate was removed. It was not until she had slapped her second person that she noticed the frightened patient began to cry, great tears running down her face. Rachel walked over to the crying woman, lifted up her wrapper, and dried the woman's tears.

The matron was delighted at hearing of this episode. "She is starting to think of others now. Before this she was only concerned about herself. We should see some progress now."

When David missed the next month's visiting day, she realized something was missing. She turned her thoughts inward onto herself. *Who am I?*

The episode of the buzzards field, the stone bridge, the long, dusty road, the pink and white cottage—all whirled in her mind so that it was like a phonograph record with the needle stuck.

Finally at the end of the second month, a doctor sent for her. He asked her what she thought about. She told him about the dream, but stopped short when she reached the door of the cottage.

"What is inside this beautiful cottage that frightens you so much?"

"I can't tell you."

"Why not?"

"I promised not to tell, and the man there promised not to tell."

"So it's a secret?"

"Yes."

"Does your husband know?"

"My husband is not here in Hell."

"Why do you think this is Hell?"

"Can't you hear the lost souls screaming? I hear it all the time!"

"That is no reason to think this is Hell. It is a hospital."

"No, the DEVIL, the one in my garret, told me I could go with him to his kingdom. He even told me how to get here."

"What did he tell you?"

"He told me to wrap a rope around my neck and step off the chair. I did it, and here I am—in Hell!"

"Why did you think the DEVIL told you to do that? Could you see him?"

"Oh, yes! He had a snake coiled around his wrist. He had first come to our place at Bel Snickling time. He tried to kiss me, but David chased him off that time."

"What was his name?"

"His name is Satan."

"Did your husband see him, too?"

"The first time he saw him. Then he came back and beat me and hurt me. Somebody told me he raped me. What does that mean?"

"It means you should not listen to what people tell you."

"While I was unconscious, little Jonathon ran away and died."

"That is something else you want to forget, because none of it was your fault."

"But what happened in the little cottage," she stopped herself in consternation.

So the doctor began to get the idea that there was something else beside the attack and rape that was causing the mental condition of this frail, unhappy girl. He decided that on his next visit he would try to find out what was behind the door of that pink and white cottage.

But Rachel's mind went round and round like water in a whirlpool and then escaping from the vortex. She then began to regress when she recalled the garret with its old rocking chair and its bundle of rags she had rocked and sang to while the DEVIL with the yellow eyes and the snake coiled on his wrist made fun of her. Again her horrible screams rang through the wards and again she was put into the padded cell. She had a tiny handkerchief that she rolled into a miniature baby. She sat on the floor rocking herself back and forth, crooning a lullaby to her "baby." Then she started to massage the place on her neck where the rope burns were.

This stage went by and she began to cry more quietly, tears spilling over her face. Then one day the "baby" stopped crying. Looking up she saw David outside her door looking in.

"Are you an angel from Heaven down here in Hell?"

"Why do you say that?"

"You seem to bring love with you, and there is no love in Hell."

"I will tell you who I am if you promise to stop crying."

"All right, who are you?"

Calling the matron, David asked permission to go inside the cell door. The matron was very reluctant to do this, but grudgingly she unlocked the door and David entered. The door was quickly locked after this, and he was alone with the wasted person of his wife. He had brought a comb and brush with him, so he spent the next twenty minutes brushing out her dull and matted hair. He then combed and braided it rather clumsily into long braids. He had brought some food that Hilda had put up, and coaxing her, he got Rachel to eat some of it.

"Can you tell me now who I am?"

"You feel like David, but he wouldn't be here in Hell."

"My darling, I would go through Hell if I could get you out of here."

"Is there a way to get out?"

"I think I know of a way. Just be patient, and the next time I come, I will take you away."

Rachel thought about that for several days. Having passed into a stage of being quiet, she had her last privileges restored. She was allowed to return to her small room, and now that she was cooperative, was allowed to have a roommate.

Minnie was a small girl who had been beaten most of her life. She was frightened of her own shadow, and when the two girls were allowed to go to the huge dining room, Minnie ran, cowering by Rachel's side. They ran down the dark hallway as fast as they could, for Rachel could not rid herself of the fancy that she might meet the DEVIL with the yellow eyes and the coiled snake on his wrist. She spared Minnie this fear for she reasoned within herself that Minnie had enough to worry her.

The two girls were as happy as they ever had been in this place, and the doctors and attendants began to have hope for the two.

One day Matron took them to the therapy room, and there they found women patients busy working on some project or other. Matron suggested that the two find a project that they might like to do. It took them several hours to decide, and then they had to return to their rooms for a rest period.

The next day they decided to try basket weaving. The patient volunteer did her best to teach Rachel the intricacies of basketry, but Rachel simply could not do it. Minnie took to it at once, and before the week was over, had finished a basket, crude as it was. She immediately gave it to Rachel.

"Thank you, Minnie. No one here has been so good to me. I shall keep it forever."

Rachel then turned to watercolor painting, and to her pleasure, could really turn out quaint little pictures of houses, barns, and trees. One day she decided to paint the mountains at home as she remembered them. She thought of the sweet redbud trees in the spring time. She put so many redbud trees on the mountain that it was all nearly pink. This picture she decided to save for David, for she was now giving him some thought from time to time. Then she decided to make something for Minnie, for didn't David promise to take her away from here soon? She must leave something for Minnie to remember her by.

She drew a baby chick breaking open his egg as he hatched. "See, Minnie, I have made a picture of a peepie. It has just broken out of its shell. This is to remind you that we are something like a peepie. We can break out of this place when it is time."

"What is a peepie? I never heard of such a thing."

"People around where I lived call a little chicken a peepie. I guess they do that because of the noise they make."

"Poor little peepie! I shall always love it because you made it for me. I'll bet it isn't afraid of anything, but why not?"

"Maybe it hasn't met up with bad things. Chicken hawks and rats are enemies that it should fear."

"What are we afraid of, Rachel? We are always afraid that something will get us."

"People and the DEVIL. The DEVIL is the one who sent me here to Hell."

"Not me. It was my stepfather and my drunken, old mother. They beat me so much that it hurt my head. Now I am always afraid. I have never had anyone to love me."

"They must have been devils, too, because he has many devils helping him."

"Come on, Minnie. Matron said I must stop talking about the DEVIL. That makes me feel worse, and if I want to get out of here, I will have to think of something else."

So life went on. Some days Rachel spent hours contentedly painting scenes she remembered. Those were the days she thought of David. But there were other days when she remembered the long, dusty road and the little, pink cottage. Then she would again cry and refuse to eat. Minnie did her best to bring her out of these horrors. She would sob in her sleep and remain for days in her bed. At last she even forgot David.

CHAPTER 24

The windy and rainy month of March had passed. Hilda had been packing for days, She had barrels of dishes wrapped in newspapers and labeled. They sat in the front hall. Aunt Virgie had to write the labels in her cramped handwriting. All of the cans of fruit and vegetables were also wrapped in newspapers and also put into barrels. Mrs. Miller came over to help a day. She cleaned out all dressers, closets, and last of all, the dusty garret. It was hard for her to go up alone, so Hilda went along. No comments were made, but each woman was conscious of the tragedy that nearly took place there. Nothing was judged to be of any value, so the sticks of furniture that were stored there were carried down and burned outside in a big bonfire.

Mrs. Miller and her husband came a second day to help again. Papa helped David to load up his harness and as much grain as they could take in one load. They hauled it down to the next state to the new farm. The Millers were sorry to see David go, but rejoiced in his good fortune. They agreed with him that Rachel should be removed from the state hospital into a smaller one where she could get better care.

While the men were gone, the womenfolk began to get food ready for the Flitting Day, which took place as a tradition, on April first. Mr. and Mrs. Overman offered to help, as well as the Grays. These good friends had helped so much when Rachel suffered the tragic attack and Aunt Virgie was so sick, so it was no more than right that they should be invited to help on Flitting Day.

April first dawned bright and clear. Breakfast was a fast one, and before daylight was underway, Papa and the two boys had arrived with the "stick wagon" and started to take the fresh cows and other livestock to the new place. They had many weary miles to go, but hoped to be there by nightfall. They took a route over back country roads that would eliminate some of the dangers from traffic. Hilda had provided a huge basket of fried chicken, pie, homemade bread and butter, and some crisp apples still left over from the winter hoard.

The hay and grain had already been moved several days ago and was already in the barn on Elder Winer's homeplace. The chickens were also there in the trim red and white chicken house. All was now in readiness for the household furniture.

It took three wagons to carry all of the furniture, dishes, bedding, canned gods, and food for the Flitting Dinner. That left the three women, Mother, Aunt Virgie, and Hilda after Mrs. Gray and Mrs. Overman had gone ahead to get the fires started in the new house. David had his car good and warm with hot bricks and fur robes. He carried out Aunt Virgie, saying, "I am so glad you are going along with me. What would I do without you, Auntie?"

"David, I am going to try to stay alive until Rachel gets home again. I have asked the dear Lord to let this happen. I want to be by the front gate the day when she comes home."

David's voice was so choked that he could hardly tell Hilda to lock the door behind her. He also failed to notice she was carrying a small bag in her hands. Hilda had already looked into every room to see that no speck of dust would be left behind. It simply would not do to leave a dirty house.

David did not look back, for that house held little but unhappy memories. There he had seen the death of his first wife, his son, and the near destruction of his beloved Rachel.

The kitchen stove was already in place and a fire was burning when the three women got to the new house. Mrs. Gray and her husband had the table set up for dinner, and the other men started to set up beds in the upstairs rooms.

David missed Hilda and started looking for her. He was amazed to see her walking around the yard fence bending over in a strange way.

"What in the world are you doing, Hilda?"

"Salting the house, Mister."

"What do you mean, salting the house?"

"Well, Mister, it's like this. I was brought up among the old-time Germans. They believed that the DEVIL wouldn't pass over salt, so to keep him out, they poured a stream of salt all around the property. I do want good fortune to come to you here. You've had your share of misery." The honest woman's blue eyes clouded over and she hastily wiped them with her gingham apron.

Hilda then went into the house and was soon busy supervising the placing of each article of furniture. Finally she left Mother in charge on the first floor until the beds were fixed up with the new mattresses that David had insisted on buying for the new home. There were no rag carpets for this house either. Instead he bought rugs and had a painter stain the floors around the edges. He made plans for more interior painting, but wisely decided to wait until after they had settled in.

After a bountiful dinner and an afternoon spent in unpacking, it came time to say good bye to these faithful friends. They now represented the past, and although the ties would not be broken, they represented an era that was now history.

Mother, Papa, and the two boys drove back through the night with but few words spoken. Finally little Jacob said, "Do you think Rachel will ever get to live in that fine house?"

Papa flicked the whip briefly over the horses and said, "I hope so, Jacob. I truly hope so. We will pray that a new day dawns for her."

Mother was thinking of practical things. "Isn't it nice that they have running water in the kitchen? I wonder why Elder Winer never put in one of those new bathrooms."

"Well, Mother, he was a close man. That's how he accumulated his wealth."

"I don't think that was saving money. He and his wife both could have enjoyed the comfort of a bathroom. He did get a furnace under the house."

"Yes, and that should be a great comfort to Aunt Virgie. Maybe she won't take cold so much."

"Well whatever David has, he is deserving of it. My only hope is that Rachel will get well and come home a happy woman."

CHAPTER 25

It was a small, well-staffed hospital and clinic that David found after a conference with his doctor. It was close enough so that he could go every week to see Rachel. How grateful he was to have the money now to care for her! He would never cease being thankful that the Winers thought of him when making their will.

After Flitting Day, David went to get Rachel. She did not remember him but huddled miserably in the corner of the car. Minnie had clung tearfully to her when it came time to leave the state hospital.

"Goodbye, Minnie. I hope you will get out of Hell here, too, some day. Don't be afraid."

As they drove the long miles across the state line to the new hospital, Rachel looked fearfully at David at first. Then she said, "Who are you? Are you an angel come to take me from Hell?"

"No, Rachel. Don't you remember me? I am David, your husband. Do you remember how we husked corn a year ago last fall? I sang to you then."

"Yes, now I remember that. You have David's kind eyes and you talk like him, but you don't have a beard like he wore."

"Beards can be shaved off, you know."

"Is that what you did? Why?"

"Because you told me some time ago that you didn't like me with it."

But Rachel was still not convinced. Soon she turned her face the other way and went to sleep.

The mountains were a tender green interspread with shadowy evergreens. Rounding a corner, David heard a gasp. Rachel was awake and sitting up.

"Oh, it is my painting! See the beautiful pink mountain!"

Indeed the mountain did seem pink. The whole side of the slope was covered with redbud trees. How profuse were the trees, like little girls in pink party dresses!

From his first glimpse of the main building of the new hospital, David began to feel optimistic. This building was low and sunny with large windows and a wide veranda. A large grassy lawn spread out with rows of trees along its border. Several other buildings were grouped nearby, but each had its own lawn and shrubbery.

Inside there were soft carpets and beautifully furnished rooms. There was no sickening odor of disinfectants to offend the nose from all sides like in the state hospital. Draperies and fresh curtains hung at each window.

The aides were gentle and soft-spoken people. Psychologists came from Johns Hopkins in Baltimore on a weekly basis. Staff doctors cared for the physical needs of the patients. Every week Rachel would have a specially trained psychologist.

After the first week, Rachel was taken to the pleasant dining room to eat well-cooked meals. Soft music played during the meal time, and since the patients conversed in low tones, the music was never drowned out by loud noises. Rachel ate better and began to gain in strength and weight.

As soon as warm weather came, she was taken outdoors to the spacious grounds. She was attracted by seeing some of the patients planting flowers in borders along the buildings.

"Please let me plant some flowers. I love flowers," she begged the attendants. So she was given a kit of gardening tools.

"What kind of flowers do you want to plant?" an attendant asked.

"Are those petunia plants there in the box? I would like to plant the blue ones with the red and white ones. Then it would look something like a flag."

One day she was busy digging in the soil and she could smell the odor of the fresh earth. She looked up at the blue sky, so clear it sparkled. For the first time she thought of her faith. In a loud clear voice she said, "Thank you!"

"You're welcome!" There bending over a flower bed next to hers was a young woman about her age.

"Hello! But I wasn't talking to you. I was saying thank you to God for taking me out of Hell."

"Hush! You mustn't say such a bad word here. It just isn't the thing to do." The other girl looked concerned.

"But I have been in Hell. A good angel has brought me to this place. It must be Heaven. Are you an angel?"

"Oh, my no! I have sinned a great sin. Now I am here to repent. Believe me, it is hard to repent."

"What's your name? Mine is Rachel."

"I am Clara. I drove a woman crazy because I hated her. Her name was Rachel, too. You aren't her, are you?"

"I don't think so. You see, I'm not crazy. I just went to Hell."

"Well repent ye! Repent ye!" Clara's voice went higher and higher.

An aide came by with a watering can and thrust it into the excited girl's hands. "Here Clara, you must not forget to water your geraniums. Come with me and I will show you where to get water."

I wonder who that girl is. Somehow she seems familiar. But Rachel did not dwell on it. Cultivating petunias was too much fun to be disturbed by others on such a beautiful day as this.

The following week when David came, he had a pretty green dress for her as well as a comb and brush set. He brushed her hair until it shone and then he began to sing to her.

"You are the angel that brought me here. You remind me of the dear husband I used to have. He sang "Juanita" to me. I love that song. Can you sing that?"

So once again David sang tender love songs to his beloved.

"Are you really David? You used to sing to me like that many years ago."

"Not so long ago. It's been over a year—in fact it will be two years ago this coming fall."

While they were strolling across the lawn, David saw and recognized Clair, the spiteful daughter of Deacon Cook. She gave no signs of recognition, so he decided not to speak to her. How true was the Bible saying that vengeance was God's!

The warm spring days were followed by hot summer ones. One day while the patients were on the wide lawns and working in their flower beds, a quick thunderstorm came up. It came so fast that the aides could not gather up all their charges inside before the heavy rain came. Peal after peal of thunder followed sharp charges of lightning. Rachel huddled under a hedge, too frightened to move. Then she heard a mewling cry, and there was Clara, shielding a geranium in her hands.

Forgetting herself in seeing the helpless girl, Rachel called, "Come, Clara, come on. Take my hand and let's run inside!"

The frightened girl held on to Rachel, and both reached the veranda just as heavy hail started to fall. Thus a close friendship was begun. The two girls managed to eat at the same table for their meals, and since neither had previous recollections of the other, they weeded and planted happily all day long.

By autumn there were still some whirling vertices in Rachel's mind, but not as frequent as before. One day the psychiatrist suggested she tell him again the story of the buzzards field. So once again Rachel went over the well-worn path of the buzzards field, across the stone bridge, up the long, dusty road, to the pink and white cottage.

"Why don't we go inside the cottage today. Who lives there?"

"Miss Lucy. She is very pretty."

"What did she do there?"

The vertex stopped. Suddenly Rachel broke through her wall of secrecy. "My baby was murdered there."

"Your baby? How old was it?"

"It hadn't been born yet. I asked Miss Lucy to take away my baby."

"Do you want to tell me why you did that?"

So quietly Rachel told the whole story. Once again she lived through her grief, but some thought of David's love kept her from becoming wild in her grief at losing Anton.

"Does your husband know about this?" The doctor was watching her very closely.

"No."

"Why don't you tell him?"

"Do you really think I should?"

"I believe he would like to know what has been making you sick. Then you can get well."

"He won't hate me then?"

"I'm sure he won't hate you."

"But the church people won't need to know. Only God and your husband are concerned about this."

"But I have been punished by God."

"No, Rachel, you have been punishing yourself. Talk to your husband when he comes again."

On the next visiting day, Rachel wore her green dress and had her hair arranged in a very becoming fashion by one of the aides. As she was waiting for David, she was a little frightened and pale. But when he came he held her so close she could hear his heart thumping.

She cleared her throat and started, "David, my dear husband, I have tried you so much with my foolishness."

"What's this? You sound like you were going to preach a sermon. Come on, Rachel, I would like a big hug and kiss instead of a sermon."

"Not before I rid myself of something I should have told you long ago. If you hate me, then I will have to stay here the rest of my life."

"Come on, you funny girl. I would never hate you. You are dearer to me than life itself. Tell me if you must, but I warn you, I will never hate you."

So once again Rachel relived the long and sad story of how she had met Anton in the woods, and wooed by his exquisite music, had succumbed so readily to him. She told of her heartbreak when she had learned of his being married and the father of seven children.

"Did he know that you were going to have a baby when he left you?"

"No, David, I never saw him after that. Aunt Sally knew what was wrong with me and she sent me to Miss Lucy's place." She went on to describe the buzzards field, the stone bridge, the pink and white cottage, and the narrow, white bed.

"There on the narrow, white bed Miss Lucy took away my baby and hurt me so much that I was sick for a long time. My parents never knew any of this, and I never want them to know. A doctor guessed what was the trouble. He told me I could never have any children."

"Rachel, that's not true anymore. The doctor that operated on you told me you had all the chances any normal woman has. So we won't worry about that. But what did Deacon Cook have to do with it?"

"Please, David, it is hard to speak of Deacon Cook. Don't ever tell what I am about to tell you. He came to Miss Lucy's place while she was busy with me. He wanted to spend the night with her, but he didn't know I was there until in the morning. I was too weak to walk home, so Miss Lucy sent me home with him. This is the first time I ever told anyone, and since he is dead, I don't want it ever to get out."

"Well the old hypocrite! And to think his family blamed you!"

"That night in church when I tried to make a confession, he thought I would tell about him. His conscience was too much for him, and he blurted out words that sounded to people like he was guilty with me. But he had run after Miss Lucy so much he couldn't face the church anymore, so he killed himself."

"You poor child! Imagine carrying around all that guilt. God has forgiven you, so now you must forgive yourself and get well so that you can come home."

"David, you know I hate to think of going back to that place where so many bad things have happened to us. I wish you could find another farm to live on, but wherever you go, I will go."

"The next time I come I have wonderful news to tell you. I can't tell you today, for you aren't strong enough for it yet. Goodbye now, my pet, and I will see you next week."

CHAPTER 26

After Rachel told David of her deep-seated secrets, she no longer had dreams about the pink and white cottage nor of the narrow, white bed inside it. She spent her days in gladness helping her new friend, Clara, with the flowers.

A newfangled gadget called a radio had come to the hospital and the patients were enthralled with the sound of music traveling through the air from hundreds of miles away. In spite of its crackling static, Rachel spent many hours listening to the orchestras of large cities.

David was now convinced that she was on the way to full recovery, so the first thing was to get the house in readiness. He fixed up Rachel's room first. He had a blue, velvet carpet put on the floor and bought a new bedroom set of furniture. The workmen painted the walls a pale blue and then Hilda hung dazzling, white curtains at the bedroom windows. He went to town and bought a lovely white bedspread. He bought copies of two famous paintings in gold frames, one was *Blue Boy* and the other *Pinkie*. He had these hung about Rachel's bed. A rose-colored vase with pink rosebuds stood on the dresser. Other touches of pink and blue were placed about the room.

David slept in a small guest room until his wife could come home.

New living room furniture in muted tones, a new gray and small, neutral-figured wallpaper gave the room a restful feeling. An old fireplace that had been formerly blocked up was now opened and the carved oak mantel was refurbished. It formed the nucleus of the room.

Hilda and Aunt Virgie were happy with the roomy bedrooms off the dining room. Hilda chose the green chair from the old parlor set to use in her room. That gave David an idea, so picking up the rose brocade chair he carried it to the second floor and placed it by the window in Rachel's room. It was just what the room needed to relieve it from the blues.

It was late spring when Hilda fell on the stepping stones leading to the springhouse and sprained her knee so badly that she had to go to the hospital for a week. During that time David and Aunt Virgie tried to cook for themselves, but it was too much for the old lady. After inquiring around, David had the good fortune to find a young widow, Mrs. Ada Highbee and her two little girls, Ruth and Naomi, who came to work for him.

There was a roomy space over the summer kitchen that David decided to renovate for living quarters for Mrs. Highbee and her daughters. She was given the isinglass stove from the old place, and with other necessary pieces of furniture, she was soon very much at home.

The children's happy patter made the new home come to life. The tension that had been a part of David now began to ebb. He felt that he only needed Rachel for life to be perfect.

David's tenant farmer was very capable and the new harvest promised to be an abundant one. Elmer Bain and his wife had taken the tenant house, which looked like a miniature of the big house, even down to the fanlight over the door. The compound was shaped like a triangle with the big house in the apex. The barn, also made of limestone, and the tenant house formed the other two points. A wide, grassy lot was in the center of the triangle.

Elmer's wife, Lucy, was a pretty girl but very delicate. She became pregnant soon after they came to the place and so was not able to keep the charming graystone cottage as it should be kept.

Hilda was especially sympathetic. "Poor little mite, she looks like a bar of soap after a hard day's washing."

Aunt Virgie became very restless and found strength to go to the tenant house. She was appalled by what she saw. She came back in tears.

"David, we must share with those poor folks. We have so much it is only right that we help them. Why, the poor girl doesn't even have any baby clothes yet."

"Aunt Virgie, it isn't lack of money, for Elmer makes good wages. It's because his Lucy is too weak to have the energy to keep house. She should never have gotten in the family way." David was worried about the young couple.

One day soon after that, he asked Mrs. Highbee if she cared to go over one or two days a week and give Lucy a hand. He and his two womenfolk could do for themselves those days.

Harvest time was drawing near. After the wheat was cut, David helped Elmer haul the golden harvest to the barn where it was stacked. In a few weeks he would have it threshed. The bobolinks were whistling from the fields. The quail answered, "Bob White, wheat's ripe!"

It wasn't until the latter part of July that David warned his womenfolk, "Thursday's threshing day. Do you need anything from town?"

Hilda hobbled over to the cupboards, and after a lengthy search, decided that nothing was really needed. She got David to bring up one of the big smoked hams from the smokehouse.

Early on Tuesday morning there came a long whistle from a steam engine coming down the road. It turned into the farm lane, and once again the long blast sounded, scaring little Ruth and Naomi so that they ran into the house and crawled under the table.

Aunt Virgie came from her room so delighted to help that she trembled. Hilda was well enough to do a good bit but could not be on her feet too long at one time. So Aunt Virgie pared fallen apples from the orchard while Hilda stood long enough to roll out pie dough for ten apple pies.

"Do you think there will be enough pies?"

"David said there would be three extra men not counting Elmer and David himself. Then there will be three of us women."

It was decided to set the table in the large kitchen, for the dining room was too elegant for threshers. Mrs. Highbee was given the task to set up the table, to slice the big ham, and to supervise the frying thereof. She went to the cellar for pickles—dill, sweet and beet pickles. From the jelly cupboard she brought strawberry preserves and raspberry jam.

By this time Hilda started to knead the rising bread dough. No one else could get a light loaf of bread like she could.

By the time the clock struck twelve for noon, all was in readiness. Mrs. Highbee mashed the potatoes and fixed the garden lettuce salad. Hilda seasoned the dried corn while Aunt Virgie tottered out to the dinner bell and rang it with all the vigor she had.

While the men were washing up in the summer kitchen's sink, the meal was ready. The threshers ate with so much gusto that Hilda wondered if there would be enough for the women and children.

The wheat turned out to be better than thirty-five bushels to the acre, and with the market price at its best in four years, David calculated he would have enough money from his wheat alone to care for them all and Rachel, too.

By nightfall the granaries were full and a mountain of straw stood in front of the barn coming up nearly to the big open door that opened from the second floor barn floor.

That night David whistled, "Just to think, Aunt Virgie, I have paid all my debts and have enough to take care of us all—even Rachel. Oh, Lord, how much I miss her. If she could only come home soon. But aside from that, how blessed we are!"

Aunt Virgie looked very pleased and that night she renewed her urgency in prayer for Rachel.

CHAPTER 27

The golden summer days went sliding by, one week leading into another. Rachel loved her gardening, and the flowers bent in answer to the little endearments she gave them. Many times she and Clara stole outside into the soft twilight evening to inhale the exotic odor from the night-blooming nicotina. Arm in arm they strolled along the garden paths looking up at the moon and stars. They both felt within themselves a strong sense of loyal friendship, yet each was eagerly awaiting the end of her stay there at the hospital.

The day following a lovely picnic with David in one of the distant areas of the hospital grounds, Rachel decided it was time to take out the sweet peas she and Clara had planted.

"Over here in this corner behind the wall is a big pile of brush. Let's get some and put it to the sweet peas. It will be a lot better than putting up strings for them to climb."

Clara was agreeable to the idea, so the two set out to break the brush according to their specifications. They tramped on the sticks and sent them back, snapping the dry sticks off for their purpose. They were not allowed to have knives or hatchets. Suddenly the world stood still. There, coiled in front of the horrified girls was a large snake. Rachel tried to warn Clara, but her voice only came in a rasp.

The snake uncoiled its evil length and struck at Clara's hands, but missed. Lunging again, it struck her above her ankle. Then both frightened girls got their voices and peal after peal of screams went across the wide lawn to where the resident doctor was resting momentarily on the porch. Running to the screaming girls, he got a glimpse of the snake. It was a copperhead, beautiful but poisonous.

Drawing a case of small instruments from his pocket, he gave Clara first aid by making cross incisions and drawing out the poison through oral contact.

Rachel continued screaming, and the frightened attendants helped her to her room where they administered a sedative.

Clara's leg was swollen, but by the next day she was out of danger. A few days' rest and she seemed no worse for the experience.

The gardeners killed the snake and a mate they found when they removed the trash pile and made a huge bonfire. That night some of the patients went out to see the flames rushing up out of the middle of the pile. But Rachel did not go. She gave one glance out of the window then turned back, shaking with fear.

"There's the flame of Hell right here in Heaven!"

That night she again saw the stranger with the long, yellow eyes and the snake coiled on his arm. He leered at her. "So you think you have destroyed me, do you? Watch out, I still have another chance at you!"

Rachel's screams woke the whole east wing, and once again she tried to pull out her hair. The concerned staff doctor gave her another sedative, and she went to sleep, sinking under its comforting power.

When the psychiatrist talked with her a few days later, she was quite pale and subdued. Even her sparkling hair seemed to be under a veil.

"Why did the snake frighten you so much, Rachel? Clara was the one that was bitten, and she has recovered."

"I don't like snakes."

"Few people do, especially women. But your fear seems to be overabundant. Were you ever frightened by a snake before?"

"I don't think so."

"What did you think of when you saw the snake?"

"I thought of the DEVIL. He did appear three times to me you know."

The doctor leaned back in his chair. "Three times? Tell me about the first time."

So Rachel dredged up from her memory the time when the Bel Snicklers came to the farm. She recalled the tall stranger with the coiled snake tattooed on his arm.

The psychiatrist interrupted. "That is a common sight among some classes of men, especially seafaring men."

"But after he had tried to manhandle me, he promised to come back for me, and he did. He came back a few days later when David had gone to a stock sale. He tried to get me to come into the haymow with him when I was taking little Jonathon for a sled ride on the barn bridge. The DEVIL caused Jonathon to lose his way and freeze to death."

"How did he do that? Weren't you watching him?"

"I couldn't." Rachel bowed her head and clasped her hands over her eyes. Tears ebbed out from between her fingers.

The doctor handed her his own handkerchief. "Now, Rachel, tell me why you couldn't watch the child."

"The DEVIL grabbed me and tried to force me."

"Did he actually get it done?"

"I don't remember that, but I jabbed him real good with a pitchfork."

"What happened then?"

"I don't really know except what I read in a newspaper. It said I was beaten and raped. I suppose that means the DEVIL forced me when I was unconscious. I was sick a long time and had to go to the hospital."

"Thank you, Rachel. I'll see you again on Thursday. Meanwhile keep the thought of devils from your mind. Think instead about the good things in your life. You might start with that husband of yours."

The doctor called David to the home that afternoon. He was told to go into the doctor's office before he saw Rachel.

"Mr. Lowe, can you tell me about your wife's experiences with a tall stranger who had a tattoo on his arm?"

David related the story of the Bel Snicklers and the tall stranger. He confessed his doubt of Rachel when the stranger seemed to be taken by her and had attempted to manhandle her. Bitter tears fell when he told of how he had misjudged his wife.

"How soon afterwards did this fellow return?"

"About a week later. He'd been hanging around the neighborhood. As soon as I had gone to the stock sale, he appeared at my barn and savagely attacked my wife after dragging her into the barn floor. My retarded son, Jonathon, was trying to reach the house while this was going on. He made a wrong turn and his body was later found in the fields, frozen to death."

"What happened to the fellow?"

"In the struggle, Rachel seemed to have stabbed him with the pitchfork, but it only aggravated him. He beat her, raped her, and partly mutilated her. He then escaped over the fields only to fall over the side of a stone quarry. He broke his neck, and I found the remains weeks later."

"Did anyone know who he was?"

"No one. He had mysteriously joined the Bel Snicklers, and one of the girls saw a tattoo of a coiled snake on his arm. Rachel said he was the DEVIL, and I am inclined to believe her."

"Do you then believe in the supernatural?"

"It seems like I am forced to believe in this awful creature when I think of how much Rachel and I have suffered because of him."

The doctor questioned Rachel several times and always got the same answers. She had lost weight again and had regressed to the point that she stayed in her room and refused to go out at all.

Clara came by time after time to coax her out. Finally Rachel said, "I'm afraid of the DEVIL outside. His snake is there, and he'll be there, too."

Dr. Ekid saw Rachel three times a week, and on one of her visits she told him about her third experience with the DEVIL in the garret.

"There sat the devil, beating on the floor with his hooves. He looked like a goat this time except for his head. He also had hands, and there coiled around his wrist was this snake. He said if I went with him I'd never hear the baby again—my dead baby, you know. So I listened to him and I went."

"How did you go?"

"He told me to tie a rope around my neck and jump off of the chair. I did it and I landed in Hell. I would still be there if David hadn't come and brought me here."

"Rachel, think once. Weren't you sick for a very long time? Many people get hallucinations when they are sick. That is what you had after a horrible experience with this bad man. Yes, he did attack you, but he's dead now."

"Did I kill him?"

"No, you had nothing to do with his death. It was an accident that he fell over the edge of the quarry."

"But a voice on the telephone called me a murderer. It blamed me for deacon Cook's death, too."

"Forget that voice on the telephone. Believe me, that person has been very sorry about that."

"What's to happen to me? Will I stay here forever?"

"No, you will be going home as soon as you forget about snakes and devils and crying babies. You must forgive yourself now."

"But I'm afraid to go home. I'm afraid all those things will come back."

"Wait and see. Now run along and have some fun. You are perfectly safe here."

CHAPTER 28

Ada Highbee, the woman David hired to help Hilda, was a young widow of twenty-five. She had been a widow for three years. Her two little daughters, four and six years old were as badly in need of a father as their mother was in need of a husband.

David enjoyed hearing the little girls playing about the yards and often wished he had some children of his own. He left the house one moonlit evening and walked about. He looked at the light streaming from the tenant house where Elmer and his child-wife were living, and a feeling of envy enveloped him. He saw the lighted windows above the kitchen where Ada and her children were getting ready for bed. He looked back at his own beautiful but empty house, except for Aunt Virgie and Hilda, and thought, *What hollow mockery it is to have wealth when my beloved cannot share it with me!*

He sank onto the bench by the grape arbor and groaned. His head rested in his hands and big tears rolled down his cheeks.

A swish of a woman's skirts roused him and when a soft hand caressed his shoulder, he looked up in startled amazement.

"Why, Ada, what are you doing here? I thought you were with your children."

"It gets might lonely for me, too. I've had no husband now for three years, and no one knows the loneliness better than I do."

"But you have your children. I have nothing. Oh, sure I still have Rachel, but she has regressed, and I'm afraid she will have to stay in the hospital for a long time yet."

This time David felt Ada's cool hand in his, and she reached over and kissed his cheek. Only the thought of Rachel kept him from returning the kiss.

"I think, Ada, it is best if you go inside now. I appreciate your sympathy, but I want to do the right thing, so good night now."

After that he tried to avoid being alone with Ada. She flirted her skirts about as she served at the table to the chagrin of Hilda, who could only hobble about.

Aunt Virgie was able to leave her room for the noon meal, but her old eyes did not overlook the languishing eyes that Ada cast on David. She and Hilda talked it over.

"I ain't rightly strong on my feet yet, but I'm going to suggest to the Mister that he send her packing."

"I don't think we can let her go. She's been helping the tenant farmer's wife, too, you know."

This conversation was interrupted by a loud pounding at the door. It was Elmer Bain. His eyes were wide with fright.

"It's Lucy! She's acting like she's going to have her baby, and it ain't time yet. I'll have to phone her doctor."

Hilda got her cane and hobbled down to the tenant house. She found Lucy a writhing, screaming, sobbing girl.

"Hush! That's taking all the strength you need for birthing your baby. Now let's get you into a clean nightgown and I'll fix your bed up just right. Elmer, you put on a pot of water on the stove to heat and then run over to get Ada to help here."

So between Hilda and Ada, they calmed the frightened girl and made her as comfortable as they could.

The doctor came and delivered a tiny, wizened little boy, two months premature. Hilda gathered the hot water bottles that were on the place and fixed a basket for it. The doctor said the baby would have to be taken to the nearest hospital to be kept in an incubator for a while. He left in the morning, gray and spent, with David holding the baby and the doctor driving for the nearest hospital, fifteen miles away.

The poor little mother was comatose. Her breath was so light it could scarcely be discerned. After several hours of Elmer hanging over her, Hilda sent him out of the bedroom. She massaged the woman's hands and feet.

"Ada, come here. Do you see how blue she's getting?"

"Yes, but what can we do? That doctor should be here."

"He can't be in two places at once."

Just then Lucy gave a gasp and that was the end. At that moment, a barn pigeon fluttered up against the window. It was white.

"There goes her soul, back to her maker!"

Elmer came in as soon as he was called and not getting the full significance of what was happening, picked her up and cuddled her in his big, brawny arms. Her head lolled back.

So once again tragedy had struck the little community, this time double, a dead wife and a helpless, premature infant.

When David returned home and heard of the tragedy, his mind went back to the day they had all moved in and the devoted Hilda had salted the house. Too bad she had not thought to have salted the tenant house, too!

After the funeral, David took Elmer into the hospital to see the little one in the nursery.

"What will you name him?"

"Lucy wanted to name the child Elmer if it was a boy. She had no name picked out for a girl, for she felt sure that it would be a boy. My full name is Elmer Benjamin. I hate to think of such a long name for such a tiny baby."

David patted his shoulder. "Never mind. We'll call him El until he grows big enough to be Elmer Benjamin."

"What's more important than his name is how will I raise him without a mother?"

"You leave that to me. I have two hired women in my house, and my Aunt Virgie claims she is not worn out yet. Surely between them there should be enough help to take care of one little fellow like yours. At least until you can make some permanent arrangements, I mean."

From these words Elmer found a degree of comfort. He took up his daily life and worked with renewed effort, but the gladness of life had gone out of him. There was no child-wife to greet him when he reached his little cottage.

David was amused to see how often Ada had to go to the tenant house after working hours. She would slip down to feed Elmer after her two daughters were fed and put to bed. David gave her credit, she was a good mother and never cheated her children of her attentions.

It was about this time that the doctor told David about Rachel's fear of going home. They decided that a day's visit to the new house would help to dispel her fears.

CHAPTER 29

Ⓘt was a golden autumn day when David got dressed in his best suit and set out for the hospital where Rachel was being treated.

The sumac and maple trees along the wayside were blushing a furious red. Squirrels were gathering acorns in an oak grove, and David drew in the good smell of the trees. How good to be alive on this wonderful day!

Rachel came down from her room wearing a new dress that David had bought her, a robin's egg blue. One of the attendants had brushed her beautiful hair and had arranged it very becomingly. She was still a little thin but some color was beginning to show in her cheeks. David still thought there was no more beautiful girl alive. She was nearing twenty-one, having spent over two years in mental institutions.

"David, how glad I am to see you!"

"Hello, sweetheart. I have something here in a box for my best girl."

"What is it? Please, I can hardly wait! Open it for me!"

As David opened the box she lifted out of its bed of tissue paper a lovely, gray coat. She quickly put it on. It had a rich, velvet collar. She whirled around for his inspection.

"Oh, David, I don't deserve this nice coat. I have no place to wear it."

"Yes, you have, for I am taking you out for a long drive. Where would you like to go?"

"Do you think we could go to the Winers' place? That was such a happy day when we were there on our wedding day. Do they live far from here?"

David's throat got a lump in it. How could he tell Rachel that the Winers were in their graves?

"All right, but put on this scarf. It is a little nippy out."

Rachel obediently put on her scarf and they set out. David drove silently, his mind too occupied with thoughts. Rachel edged over to sit close to him.

"Why are you so quiet, David? Did I say something wrong?"

No, dear heart. I have a surprise for you and don't know how to tell you."

"Another surprise! Don't tell me that the Winers have moved!"

"Just wait and see. It isn't more than ten miles from here."

As they approached the driveway bordered with pine trees, Rachel's face grew more joyous.

"Oh, look! Children! Whose are they?"

Aunt Virgie opened the big front door with the fanlight above it. Rachel's eyes flew open.

"Why Aunt Virgie! Is it really you? Why are you here?"

"I live here. We all live here. Here is Hilda. Remember her?"

"Do I remember her? Of course I do! But why do you all live here? Where are the Winers?"

"This is your home now, Rachel. We all live here. Elder Winer and his wife gave us this house and farm. They went away to live someplace else," David hurriedly filled in the gap.

"Then this big house and the farm are all yours. How wonderful for you, David. You always wanted a farm of your own." Rachel sat down and cried a little in her weakness. David patted her on the hand and wiped her eyes.

"Take me around and let me see everything."

"Not yet, Rachel. You see dinner is ready, and Hilda and her helper, Ada, have prepared us a banquet. Come on and sit by me."

So the roast chicken and gravy and dressing were receiving all the attention they deserved.

After dinner they went on a tour of inspection. First of all the restful living room was admired. The blazing logs in the fireplace set up a cascade of sparks that delighted Rachel so that it was hard to tear her away to see the kitchen with all its gadgets. A long table at one end was used for preparation of food as well as the place where the hired help was fed on special work days.

Hilda's and Aunt Virgie's rooms were admired, and Rachel thought that many things looked familiar, having come from the old house.

By the time they had reached the second floor, the rest were left behind. David had the chance to lead Rachel into the four beautifully outfitted guest rooms with their baths. Then they reached the pink and blue room which she would someday soon occupy.

"Rachel, sit here in your rose chair. Remember it from the old house. You'll never have to go back to that old house again, but the rose chair has happy memories. Remember how I helped you in it as we watched the fire in the isinglass stove? So come here and let me hold you again."

"All right, David, but sing to me as you used to. I love you so much."

After a long time David quietly told her about the Winers' sudden death, glossing over it as much as possible. Through her tears she said, "How wonderful that they could go together."

Darkness was falling when David reluctantly returned Rachel to the hospital. Promising that she would soon be coming home for good, he kissed her gently at the foot of the staircase and gazed longingly as she slowly climbed to the second floor.

The weeks went on, more swiftly now that Rachel had something to hope for. Her health steadily grew better, and along with good physical health, her mental health became better. She seldom cried anymore. She and Clara went on long walks through the golden days. Milkweed silk was floating over the goldenrod, and the zinnias along the garden walks held up their russet and yellow blossoms to the sun. Purple asters brought out an aesthetic sense of delight to Rachel. The air was heady and invigorating.

"I feel so good, Clara, that I believe I may get home for Thanksgiving. What do you think?"

"I agree with you. I will be going home by then as my mother needs me, but I will miss you."

"But we don't live that far from each other. We could often get together. How far do you think it really is?"

"Only a matter of twenty miles or so. Now that everyone goes by car, that isn't very far. But Rachel, I have noticed that it isn't the distance that affects friendship. Once a person parts from a friend, it isn't the same again."

"I am so glad that David has moved from the old place where I was so unhappy. I know I will never get the same feelings I had there."

"Rachel, my doctor says I shouldn't think of the past. He says, 'Think of today and look forward to tomorrow, for we can't undo the past.'"

"That's a good rule. We have to forgive ourselves for what is past since God has done so. Then we must go forward and 'sin no more,' as Jesus said. We must put hate and sorrow away from us."

It was a misty day in mid November when David drove up to the hospital and carried out the bags that Rachel had accumulated. When she came out of the building she was followed by a number of staff and patients. It was a real going-away party. As they drove through the gentle hills, David's voice carried over the sounds of the engine as he sang to his Rachel. They were going home.

CHAPTER 30

Not long after Rachel's return home, David took her for a short visit to her parents. Mother was showing her years in her graying hair and thickened body. Papa was beginning to bend over like Grandpa Miller had in his later days. Her two brothers were getting to be so tall that it seemed only a few years could not have caused so much change in them. Everyone seemed glad to see her, but David noticed a wariness in them.

What were they thinking about his beloved? Are they ashamed of her? The stigma of insanity hung heavy over the consciousness of people.

As soon as the dishes were done, David made an excuse, and they were off for home. He did not want Rachel to remember too much of the past.

The late fall days slipped by until it was nearly Christmas. At David's suggestion, they went into the county seat and shopped for gifts for everyone. Rachel had noticed the high regard that David had for the two daughters of Ada's. So she chose some dolls that would open and close their eyes. David insisted on warm coats and hoods for the little girls and lengths of silk for Hilda and Ada. The new baby was thought of as they shopped, and they decided on adding to the layette his dead mother had provided during the months preceding his birth.

It was hard to shop for Aunt Virgie, but they finally decided on a basket of fancy fruits and a beautiful poinsettia for her room. Rachel insisted that David needed a new overcoat, and as for herself, she could not think of a thing she needed. However David slipped away from her long enough to get her several warm and brightly colored sweaters to wear during the winter months. He also remembered Elmer by getting him a new wamus to wear to the barn and around the farm. These denim jackets were lined with heavy flannel.

When they arrived home with the many bundles, Hilda declared that Santa Claus had taken up his abode on their farm.

On the day before Christmas, late in the afternoon, Rachel and David went out into the woods at the edge of their farm and there found a small, well-rounded cedar tree. They cut this and were admiring it when they heard a baying of hounds.

"The Everlasting Hunter! I didn't think he came this far south!"

"But this is a part of the valley where we used to live. Don't forget, Rachel, that this valley extends through three states."

They remembered how they had first heard the Hunter's hounds the first fall they were married. The Hunter had gone out for some game over two hundred years before and had vowed he would never return until he found game. The valley people declared they could still hear him and his hounds.

That night the little sisters wanted to go to the barn to see the animals on their knees in prayer at the time when the Christ child was born. But Ada refused to take them outdoors at midnight, so they went to bed with fond expectations of the morning when their stockings would be full.

On Christmas morning David and Elmer set out for the hospital where the baby had been cared for ever since his mother had died. Just as the clock was striking twelve noon, Elmer walked in bearing a bundle of flannel and muslin. Little whimpering sounds came from it. Ada hurried forth to receive it. A bassinet was pushed out of the shadows and little Elmer, Jr. was among friends.

Ada held a proprietary air about him, but Rachel got one chance to hold him before they day was over. She had never held a real live baby in her arms before. The experience gave her a sensation of such pure delight, she was unable to explain even to herself. She made up her mind she would try to give David a child before she was very much older.

Rachel was bewildered at the attitude Ada took with the baby. She never allowed anyone to do anything for the motherless tot except to hold him for a minute or two. Ada got up early every morning to come to the room across the hall from Rachel's and David's room where the baby was kept at night. During the day little El was kept in his bassinet near the fireplace.

Ada came in every morning from her apartment over the summer kitchen. She bathed him, fed him, and diapered him.

By the time the child was six months old, Elmer wanted to take the little fellow to his own house, so Ada was found there most waking hours. David thought ruefully that he was paying her to take care of the tenant farmer's child and house. Then he shook off the thought as being unworthy of a man to think of it.

Hilda was getting quite vexed with the thought that she had very little help now. David thought long and hard about it, but no solution came to mind. Rachel was happy to get into the kitchen and do some of the tasks that needed doing. For a time this worked out well.

One day as David was resting on the bench under the grape arbor he noticed little Ruth coming from the tenant's house. A flock of geese was parading through the yard near the barn. The gander was noted for his ferociousness, and most people carried a stout stick when they had to go through this part of the yard. Everyone had had a run-in with this sultan of a harem of gray geese. Every time he would advance, blowing his trumpet, his harem would follow him screaming and helping their master to nip and beat the hapless victim with their wings.

Little Ruth refused to be daunted by this display of arrogance. Pulling her knitted stocking cap down over her eyes, she waded right through the middle of this gaggle of foolish birds. Sir Gander made a feeble feint in her direction, but seeing no display of fear, he retreated, and the brave little Ruth came up to David and sat down beside him.

"Oh, Uncle David, I am so glad you're here. These old gooses wanted to spank me, but they didn't because I couldn't see them."

"Is that the reason you pulled down you cap over your eyes?"

"I'm not afraid of them when I can't see them. I don't like gooses. But Mama says they are good to eat and that their feathers make nice pillows. I slept on feather pillows last night. Mama said that Lucy had pulled the feathers out of the bad gooses and put them into a feather pillow. I sure do sleep good on them."

"Why were you sleeping on Lucy's pillows?"

"Cause Mama takes Nomy and me down to Elmer's house to sleep. That way we are close to little El if he wakes up at night."

"Does your mama sleep there, too?" David hated himself for this question.

"Mama sleeps on the couch with Elmer. He has a big couch in his parlor."

David was sure this was happening, but now his suspicions were confirmed. He must have a talk with Elmer and get this situation straightened out.

That evening while the two men were milking, David said, "Elmer, I think this is the time to have an understanding. Since Ada seems to have taken over you and your child, how about it if we gave you a small wedding? That way your life would be settled."

"I've thought about it, but it's been only about seven months since Lucy's death. What will people say?"

"You can't live with a dead wife, Elmer. Not only that but you need a mother for your child. My wife and the women in the house were willing to help with the baby, but Ada took over. So I got to thinking. I need more time with Rachel. She is getting better but I want her all together well. I can't spend time with her and work on my farm, too. So here's what I suggest. You take over the farm for a third interest. I'll furnish the seed, fertilizer, and a hired man. You do the work and feed the hired man. He can stay in the rooms over the summer kitchen that Ada had.

I'll put in more cows so that you can have a good income from livestock and grain. I'll even furnish you with your winter's meat. Think it over."

David was milking his third cow by the time Elmer caught up with him. He was red-faced with embarrassment, but he managed to stutter out, "I will accept your offer, providing that Ada agrees, of course. But I have a suggestion. How about selling whole milk to the dairy if you're going to put in better milk stock? By some investment, we could put in a cooling system in a modern milk barn. Then, too, the newfangled milking machines would double our profits. We would all benefit."

David thought this was a sound reasoning, and he talked it over with Rachel in the privacy of their bedroom.

Like a typical woman, Rachel thrilled to the thoughts of a wedding, so when morning came, she had some plans to discuss with Ada.

The following Sunday, the family assembled in the living room. There in front of the fireplace, Elmer took his second wife and little Elmer had a new mother. A preacher from a nearby Methodist Church joined the couple in bonds of holy matrimony. Hilda served up one of her luscious dinners, and the couple rode off in Elmer's second-hand car. The little girls and the baby stayed with Rachel and Hilda to look after them for a few days.

CHAPTER 31

One rainy April day David found a little shivering puppy out along the highway. It had evidentially been dumped there by some heartless person who felt the best way to get rid of animals was to take them out to the country and dump them out to fend for themselves. They try to appease their consciences by saying, "Oh, it will find a home someplace. Some farmer will take it in."

The chances of such an animal finding a home are very slim, but this little mutt was lucky. David carried it to the washhouse and gave it a warm, soapy bath before he showed it to Rachel.

Elmer was amused to find his boss bathing a dog and said so.

David turned on him in a forceful manner. "There should be a special Hell for people who do such things as to dump out a helpless animal to try to fend for itself. Now that humane societies are organized, that's the place to take them if they are unwanted. True, the animals will be put to sleep eventually, but in a painless way. They won't starve to death under cruel conditions."

Elmer remarked, "Nature is cruel to some animals."

"But not as cruel as mankind is to them. When our Lord said, 'Inasmuch as you have done it unto one of the least of these, you have done it unto me,' that means animals as well as humans. I have seen so-called *good Christians* neglect their pets in a scandalous fashion. It would be best that they had never been born. But until it is easily available for people to have their pets fixed so that they don't have little ones, we will always have the problem." David finished drying the puppy and carried him to Rachel.

"Why it has copper-colored hair, almost as bright as mine. Can I keep him? I'll name him Copper."

It was a joy to see Copper lapping up milk and then crawl into Rachel's lap to sleep wrapped in an old, fleecy blanket. So Rachel at last had a "baby" to care for. The haunting shadows of her mind were lifting more and more, and the sunshine of sanity flowed throughout her being.

She thought now that she was home again with David that perhaps she could have a son for him. On one of her weekly trips to see her psychiatrist, she told him about her hope.

"If I got into the family way now that I am home, would the baby be all right? It wouldn't be born with a defective mind, would it?"

The psychiatrist shook his head. "No, Rachel, it would not inherit anything like that, for the form of your mental problem has not been a congenital disease. But it would be much better for you if you waited for a few years. You have your husband come in so that I can talk it over with him."

David came out of the doctor's office looking very resolute. He and Rachel talked it over on the way home. "Rachel, you are still a very young woman, and we have a great deal of time before us. So wait before you get such ideas into your head. Be content with Copper and me."

So the days went by, busy ones and serene. The seasons changed and the fields were soon ready for harvest.

David had not been attending church since Rachel returned home from the mental clinic. He had been going as regularly as possible before to the church where Elder Winer and his wife attended. He usually slipped out of a side door into the graveyard to pay a silent tribute to the two people who had entrusted him with their worldly goods. What a difference it had made in his and Rachel's lives!

It was with pleasure that he saw Rachel dress for church early one Sunday morning. "I have not been to church for so long I guess I wouldn't know how to behave. Tell me, David, how do you like me in this new bonnet I made recently?"

David looked at her small, neat, black bonnet that seemed to frame her beautiful hair. She wore a blue dress under her light wrap, for the spring days were getting warmer.

In this congregation, men sat with their wives so that the sharp division of sexes was not as apparent as it was at the last church they had attended. It was recognized that the children needed both parents for their guidance and for the enforcement of good church behavior. The young people sat farther back in the congregation. Many of the young men had the girl of his choice with him. It was seldom that anyone went outside of the church body to choose a wife. If he did, it was usually a girl from a neighboring congregation.

Rachel knelt with David during prayer, holding his hand. She felt a great welling up of emotion from within her and she whispered a prayer, "Thank you, dear Heavenly Father, for my husband. May I become a well woman, and thus be in your service."

At the dismissal of the service, many people came around to meet Rachel. They gently kissed her, while the men "saluted" David by a kiss on the cheek. A young farmer and his wife invited them home to dinner, but David said, "Brother, I thank you for your invitation. Someday I hope to take you up on it, but this time we will have to pass it up. My wife is not very strong and needs her afternoon rest."

A pleasurable warmth spread throughout Rachel's body as they drove home. "How nice those people are. I really believe they are trying to live as the Bible teaches. They seem to have a great deal of charity anyway."

All week long, Rachel felt a stirring of her spirit. She began to think of how she could be of some benefit to others. She felt that the past few years would never have happened if she had been aware of others and not been so self-centered. *I have accepted help from everyone, David, Hilda, Aunt Virgie, and even Minnie,* she thought. Her mind went back to Minnie, that frightened little waif who was with her at the first hospital, the state institution. Where was she now?

The next day she wrote a letter to Minnie and sent it to the hospital. It was not likely that she had gotten out, for there was no place to go.

She studied all week on how she could help others. David saw how quiet she was. Finally one night as he was brushing her hair, he asked her what had been troubling her.

"David, I feel that I have been thinking about myself for such a long time that I have become a very self-centered person. The preacher said last Sunday that we each have a talent. Some people can preach, some are prophets, some can teach, and some are healers. But what am I? I can't even keep my own house. I'm not any good for anything."

"Oh, come on, girl! You are my own dear wife. You take care of the flowers and the shrubbery. Look how beautiful you have made the yards. You help Hilda and you keep Aunt Virgie cheered up. And another thing, you take good care of little Copper. The girls are happy when you play ball with them and help them swing. There, I have named a great number of things that you are good at."

"But, David, I feel that I will never be a real person until I have given you a child. But the doctor says I must be patient."

"My beloved, if I didn't have you, I would be like a barren wasteland. You give me a reason for living. You are such a part of me that when you are not with me, I feel that I have lost my right arm."

So mollified, Rachel went off to sleep. Sometime during the night she awoke with a start. What was that sound? Merciful Heaven, not that again! She recognized the sound as being that of an infant crying. Its wail was heard in the blackness of the night like the sharp slash of a sword. She sat up in bed.

The sound of a crying infant was heard through the blackness of the night. The sound did not come from the garret like it did that time when she came close to losing her life. This time it seemed to come from the front of the house. This was no hallucination, at least she did not think so. To make sure, she touched David and called him softly. He awoke instantly.

"Yes, Rachel, what's the matter?"

"Do you hear something?"

"Yes, I do. It sounds like—well it really does sound like a baby. Come on, put on your warm slippers and housecoat and let's go down and see what is going on there. Better let me go first. Sh—h—h! Don't wake the whole house."

Creeping softly down the wide staircase, they passed the big clock just as it struck three o'clock. David unlocked the massive lock on the front door, and there sitting on the front porch was a willow clothes basket. David recognized it as coming from the washhouse which was never locked. Peeping inside the basket, they saw a small infant crying lustily and waving its arms.

"Merciful Heavens! A real live baby! Someone went to some trouble to leave it on our porch. Look David! See its pretty blanket!"

"Whoever did this is no ordinary criminal, Rachel. They went to some trouble to get our basket to put the baby in so it wouldn't get cold. I wouldn't be surprised to know the person isn't far away."

Rachel clumsily diapered the little stray. It was a girl, and David estimated it to be two or three weeks old.

"I think we had better fix a bottle like Ada fixes for little El. I believe we can do it, only make the formula a tiny bit weaker than for El, for he is older than this baby."

Rachel was delighted in doing what she had been denied before. In a little while the baby was sleeping after drinking her formula. "Just to think, David, we now have another motherless baby like El was and the puppy!"

CHAPTER 32

It was Hilda who was the first to notice that there was a mysterious visitor on the farm. She went into the living room where Rachel sat rocking the little foundling. No one had given the child a name because they decided to wait a while to do so.

"Missus, something pee-culiar is going on. Either we have a big rat or else Copper has turned into a thief."

"Why, Hilda, what's the matter? What's happened?"

"Something happened! I should say so! I had cooked off a ham for our dinner. You know how the Mister loves sliced down boiled ham. Well I had set it on that old table in the washhouse to cool, never thinking anything would happen to it. Well I just went out a bit ago, and here it has come up missing. Oh, yes, the plate is gone, too. A person would think that a varmit wouldn't take the plate, too. It's too early for the six-week's tramp, for I just fed him two weeks ago. And if there is any other tramp around, I haven't seen him. What do you suppose it is?"

"You don't think the children would take it, do you?" Rachel felt uneasy.

"Not those blessed little ones. If they were hungry. they'd ask for something to eat."

David had some ideas on the subject, but said nothing. He picked up his hat and went to the barn. He looked through all the stalls not in use, then quietly climbed the rough steps that led to the haymow. He stood as silent as he could, listening. Over the cooing of the barn pigeons he heard a rustling of the hay. Quietly he stole in that direction and found what looked like a shoe partly hidden under the hay. Grabbing it, he gave a tug, and out came a woman.

"Leave me be! I ain't done nothing! I just needed a place to stay for the night. I mean no harm." It was a woman, perhaps thirty years of age or more. Her pale face was drawn and her eyes looked red from weeping.

"Where are you headed? Do you have a home?"

The woman plucked at an old shawl that she had wrapped around her shoulders. "I'm looking for work. I heard of a place down this part of the country that wanted a housekeeper. I've been walking for two days."

David spied the ham bone lying on the hay. "You can't be very hungry after eating up Hilda's ham. There was enough ham there for our dinner yesterday. Well come on inside. I believe we can give you something else besides ham to eat. You must come from up north by the way you said, 'down here.'"

Tears welled up in the woman's eyes. "Yes, sir, I come quite a distance."

David asked her, "Are you in some kind of trouble?"

"No, sir, just as I said. I'm looking for some work. I ain't got no money and I hadn't eaten in some time. I hadn't ought to have stolen that ham, but I was hungry and couldn't help it."

"What's your name?"

"Bessie, Bessie Jones."

"Are you married, Bessie?"

"Not now I ain't. My old man died five years ago come this July. I lived on a small place near the mountains. It got so lonely there I just had to get out. I can sew and cook and do housework. Know anybody needing a person like me?"

"Come inside the house and we'll see. How long did you say you have been in my barn?"

The woman blushed and said, "A couple of nights. I felt so weak from all that walkin' I just couldn't go no farther."

"Have you seen anyone with a small baby since you came to my place?"

"No, sir, I ain't seen nothin'. I stayed in the haymow because I felt weak from all the walkin'. I just couldn't go no further."

"Well, Bessie, you might as well come meet my wife. She might be able to find some work for you to do. First we'll get you into some clean clothes after you get cleaned up her in the washhouse."

David left her alone and went to find Rachel. "Do you have some clean clothes this woman could wear? She looks as bad as the six-week's tramp."

Rachel left the baby and went to her room and rummaged into a closet. She brought out one of her dresses the Visiting Brethren wanted her to wear. She left off the cape and the result was a plain dress with a gathered on-skirt with an apron to match. Since it was blue, the woman's eyes lighted up. The dress matched her eyes exactly.

Rachel felt a great sympathy for this woman who seemed to be so destitute. "Bessie, would you like to work for us? Of course, Hilda will always be the boss in this house as far as the work goes, but now that we have a little one, she needs help. It takes me a long time to look after Baby here."

"Work for you? Oh Missus, you don't know how much I would like to work here in this grand house. How many children do you have?"

"We have just the one, and I suppose when the sheriff is notified we won't have her. She is a darling little girl, and it breaks my heart to think she will probably be taken away from us. We think she is a little Italian girl that someone left on our porch a week ago. I don't see how anyone could abandon a baby."

"When will the sheriff come?"

"I guess as soon as my husband calls him. We are going to try to get him to let us keep her." Tears welled up into Rachel's eyes.

Bessie went about her household duties with a vengeance. But Hilda noticed that she tired easily. She started formulating suspicions in her mind. She told her suspicions to Aunt Virgie when she carried her breakfast tray into her room. "I don't have much to go on except she looks like she's been through the mill. But it doesn't seem possible that a woman that old could have a baby. She looks like she must be forty years old."

"Well you know, Hilda, there's always a possibility as long as the flower is blooming. She says she's been a widow for five years. I've heard that some widows get pretty lonely."

Bessie never seemed to be paying attention to the baby. She seldom went near the little one. A month had gone by, and the baby was filling out and beginning to be so winsome that David kept putting off calling the sheriff. Finally one day he got dressed and started for the door. "I'm going to see a lawyer about the baby. I think we're in enough trouble now. If we knew who the mother was, we wouldn't need to let the law in on it." He was watching Bessie out of the corner of his eye.

"Oh, David, what if they came and took away our baby? What would we do? I've wanted a baby so much, and it seemed like Heaven sent this little brown girl to be ours."

Bessie sank down on a chair. Her chest was heaving and a scared look was in her eyes. "Oh, Mister, do you have to get the sheriff here? Where will he take the baby?"

"To a foundling home, I guess. That is the law. We might be able to get her back, but we would be running a chance."

"I guess there is no help for it. I guess I'll have to tell you. I am the baby's mother."

"I thought as much!" David handed her his handkerchief. "Now go on and tell us about it. Come here, Rachel and Hilda, you may as well hear this."

"Well as I told you, my husband died five years ago come July. He left me with very little—just the place were we lived. I took in some washing and did a little housework for the farmers. My place is the only one on a lonely mountain road close to a settlement of colored and mixed colored people. I never did neighbor with them, 'cause they stick to themselves. One day a young boy came by. He was light skinned, so I knew he was mixed. He came to the door and asked if he could have something to eat. I fed him and noticed what a good looker he was. He wanted to work for wages, but I had no money. But I told him he could stay a few days for his board and bed. I fixed him with a cot to sleep on, but after the first night he slept with me. I am so ashamed that I did this, but nobody knew how lonely I was. The boy fixed my roof and mended the fence and cut up some wood for me. He finally left after some of his friends drove by one day. He was afraid he would get into trouble with his people.

"I never thought anything would really happen to me, but the first thing I knew, I found out I was in trouble, real trouble. I kept it quiet and didn't let nobody know anything was wrong with me. I kept on with my washings, but after I started to show, I was too ashamed to go out to people's houses to do housework. I got along on what I grew in my garden and the few dollars I made with my washings.

"I realized I was more to blame than the boy. He was only eighteen while I am thirty-two, old enough to know better.

"When it was time to have the baby, old Granny Shoemaker came and helped me through it. You'd better believe it, I had a hard time of it and I am still not quite right. I get tired so soon. Well anyhow, I saw that I couldn't keep the sweet little thing there in that place near the mountains. I decided to come down this way to find work. I decided on your place, but thought if you saw the baby first you'd let me stay."

"Well that is quite a story. Do you mean to say that Baby is partly colored? She doesn't look like it to me. She even has blue eyes."

"Hilda, don't you know that all babies have blue eyes when they are born?" David was relieved to hear the story. It meant there would be no need to see the sheriff after all.

"Bessie, are you quite satisfied to stay here?" Rachel was very anxious to keep the baby. She was so darling, and regardless of her ancestry, would certainly grow up to be a beautiful person.

"Oh, please, I would feel like I was in Heaven if you let us both stay. I'll let you care for her and she will belong to us all. Oh, please, Mister, let us stay!"

David thought for a while. "We can always give it a trial. Since Rachel gets so much enjoyment from the baby, we will let her take it over during the day when you are helping Hilda. We will raise her and look after her like we would do our own. But she will always be yours. Why don't you sell that little place of yours and put the money into a trust fund for yourself and the baby? And another thing, it is high time to name her and send in a record of her birth."

Bessie formed a strong affection for Aunt Virgie, and one day she said, "I've decided on a name for the baby. I asked Aunt Virgie this morning, and she has given her consent. I am going to name her Virginia Nancy after Aunt Virgie."

The old lady was so pleased that she started to get out of her room more. One day she announced that she was going to make a quilt for her namesake. "I'm going to make Martha Washington's flower garden. I might not get it quilted, but someone here will look after that for me."

It was real encouraging to see little Virginia creeping about the floor and tumbling about with the puppy, now half-grown. Aunt Virgie sat by the fireside sewing away on her bits of colored cloth. Even though it was late spring, a low fire was kept burning on the hearth.

The serenity of those days did so much for Rachel's condition that the psychiatrist said he felt he could see her on a three months' basis rather than the monthly visit he had been seeing her.

Rachel behaved so normally that David nearly forgot that she had been otherwise. But he realized too that there was a thin edge between violent reaction and peaceful existence.

CHAPTER 33

From her rocking chair on the screened side porch, Rachel could see down over the neighbor's farm as she was rocking little Virginia. She could hear the guinea fowl clacking away and hear the geese screaming in the barnyard. A red dominecker rooster flew to the top of the rail fence and let out a blast on his bugle loud enough to wake the baby. She whimpered a little then turned her head and was soon fast asleep again. Although Rachel felt a great sense of security here with a baby in her arms, she did not feel fulfilled. The baby was not flesh of hers and David's.

Each week the baby was filling out and her dark skin was becoming lighter. As she looked down on her glossy ringlets and tan skin, Rachel marveled at the child's beauty. She looked like a sleeping cherub on a Christmas card.

Bessie liked to sing as she worked. Her spirits seemed overflowing since she had reached this haven where she could have her child and be protected. It was far enough from her old home that her former neighbors would never find her, and as for the neighbors here at the Lowes, it did not matter to her what they found out about her. Not many of them came to visit with the Lowes anyway, for they all lived a quiet life. She had been honest with the Lowes and the Missus was taking good care of her baby. So what more could one want? The future would take care of itself. She sang a popular tune she had heard over the radio, "Who takes care of the caretaker's daughter while the caretaker's busy taking care?" It was a silly rollicking song, but then at this post-war period of time, many things moved at a feverish manner.

Rachel started humming the gay little tune to the sleeping baby. She really should take her and put her to bed, but the pleasure of the child's body was so great she could hardly lay her down.

Unwillingly she thought back to that dreadful night when she nearly took her own life in the garret on the old farm. Her arms felt so empty then and again she seemed to hear the terrible sobbing of her murdered child.

"I must not think of it! I must think of something else. I know—I'll help Hilda get dinner on the table. It is nearly time, and she has harvest hands today," she muttered to herself. "What can I do for you, Hilda? Shall I slice the bread?"

"Sure thing, Missus. The bread board is over there on the sink. Slice it a little thinner than Bessie does it. I always say she will make a good stepmother. They always say that when a woman slices the bread too thick."

David had hired a second man to help with the wheat. That made four men for dinner. It looked like a heavy yield of wheat and the price was good. The younger man had a bold air about him, and David caught him eyeing Rachel as she was passing the bread after he had returned thanks for the meal. Rachel felt uncomfortable, for once again that morning her thoughts had turned to the past. She and the other women would eat at the second table, for no self-respecting farm wife would eat at the same table with the hands.

The new man held out his cup for a second cup of coffee when Rachel saw his bare forearm. There, tattooed on it was a coiled snake. The boiling hot coffee filled the cup and continued flowing down over his arm and over the coiled snake.

Rachel gave a horrified gasp as she recognized this symbol of the DEVIL. She was not conscious of the scalding coffee going down the fellow's arm.

With a loud yell he jumped up and screamed at her, "You bitch, you lousy, confounded bitch! You did that on purpose! I'll get you for that!"

David grabbed the coffee pot and set it down. Then turning on the enraged man he said, "Leave the table! Hilda, get some of that salve we use for burns and put it on him. Then, Mister, I'll see you outside with your wages."

Taking Rachel in his arms, he carried her upstairs to her room, the weeping Bessie on behind. "There, Bessie, I'll leave her in your care for a while. Maybe she'll come out of it, but we'll let her sleep awhile. Meanwhile I'll have to rid this farm of its snakes!"

Going to his desk, David unlocked a drawer and took out some money. Out on the side porch the man sat and smoked. "I want you off this farm inside of ten minutes. I don't want anyone around that uses such ugly language to and about my wife."

"But she deliberately scalded me!"

"No, she did not do it on purpose. She's been sick a long time and the very picture of a snake upsets her. Now, go!"

The man took his money and muttering curses, tramped off to the south. David had an uneasy feeling that he had not seen the last of him.

Rachel slept very heavily, and when she awoke, was very confused as to where she was. She started to cry and to call for little Jonathon. Her mind was on the old farm with its tragedies. In spite of the efforts to rouse her, Rachel started to sob convulsively.

In spite of the need to gather his wheat harvest, David decided to let Elmer and his hired hand, Jake, finish the wheat by themselves. It was more important to get Rachel to the doctor at the hospital.

Hilda dressed hurriedly in her second best dress, the one she called her "scuff dress," and she went with David at his insistence. They presented themselves to the authorities at the hospital. Rachel had stopped her crying and was in a daze, so gave no recognition to any landmark along the way.

Fortunately Rachel's psychiatrist was in that day and after a short wait, was able to take care of her. David waited in the outer room with Hilda.

This time Rachel did not respond, so David was forced to leave her behind when he left for home. How fair his farm looked as he turned into the driveway! How desolate it seemed to him since he had left his heart in the mental hospital.

Bracing his shoulders, he stopped the car, waiting for Hilda to alight. "I know how you must feel, Mister. Don't forget, you have the responsibility of four children and six adults besides yourself. The good Lord willing, she'll be all right in no time," and wiping her tears, Hilda went inside to take up her duties.

"How is she?" was the first thing Aunt Virgie wanted to know when her nephew came into her room.

"She's not responding at all."

"Then I must postpone leaving you when the quilt is finished. I still want to welcome Rachel home again—just like I did before. I'm not going to die until she gets well, and get well she will, for I will spend my time praying for her, night and day."

The days ran together. David went about his daily chores in an absent-minded way. He was not fully aware of those about him until one day he heard a voice coming from a clump of hollyhocks. He tiptoed curiously to the edge of the long-stemmed flowers that came higher than his shoulders.

"And Mr. God, please help Rachel to get well so she can come home soon. Then she can see Mama's new baby she told us she would get by Christmas." There kneeling on a board lying between the yard fence and the hollyhocks was little Ruth, his favorite of Ada's two little girls. He stood there silently, then stole away. Now he had two people praying for his beloved, the very old and the very young. Surely God would hear the one so soon to go to His Kingdom and the one so lately coming from His Kingdom.

He went to the mailbox to get the mail and there on a postcard was a brief message from the little scared Minnie who had meant so much to Rachel when she had been in the state asylum.

Dear Rachel, (she wrote in a childish scrawl) *I am all well now and hope you are too. I have to stay on here for I have no other place to go. Love, Minnie.*

As David read this pathetic little card, wells of sympathy came from his generous heart. As usual, when troubled, he went into Aunt Virgie's room and consulted her.

Aunt Virgie wiped her eyes. "Poor thing, how I wish we could have her here! But we already seem to be running a home for the homeless. Where could we put her?"

"Well Elmer and Ada will soon be needing an extra room when their baby comes. I've been thinking about adding a few extra rooms onto their house. That way it would give them extra room as well as giving Jake, our hired hand, a bedroom in Elmer's house. Then we could move Bessie and her baby out to the rooms over the summer kitchen, leaving us another bedroom here in the house. That way we could accommodate Minnie without any trouble."

"But in the meantime, Nephew, where could we put her?"

"Oh, so you have already settled that she is to come? Well I trust it to you, Aunt Virgie. Yes, we will try to get her, and when she comes, we'll put her into that small room I slept in before Rachel came home the first time."

"Do you reckon that the authorities would let her come out of the state to live with us?"

"I'll go tomorrow to see the state's attorney at the courthouse."

"David, when you go up to that asylum, take Hilda along to help you with Minnie. It would look better if a mature woman like Hilda was along. Sometimes the law can be pretty tricky."

After consulting the state's attorney at the courthouse where he used to live, David and Hilda struck out one day to go to the state capital to the asylum where Rachel had first been taken. It was a glorious day in August and the signs of harvest and reseeding could be seen in all the fields as they went along the road.

Hilda had brought along a small suitcase with shoes, underwear, and a nearly new dress that had belonged to Rachel. They would have to do until more suitable clothing in Minnie's size was found.

When David and Hilda came to the hospital, they were ushered into the office of the superintendent and told to wait. When the superintendent came in, he seemed pleased to read the legal order that the state's attorney had prepared for David. They were taken to the day room to wait for Minnie. The door was carefully locked after them. David drew a deep sigh when he heard cries and moans coming from the wards nearest him. No wonder Rachel had declared that she had been in Hell.

Minnie came in, sliding around the door so self-effacingly as to nearly blot herself out of the beholder's eyes. She was even slimmer than Rachel and her hair was so colorless as well as her face that they seemed to be all one. Not even her lips showed any color. Her hands shook as well as her knees.

"Minnie, we are Rachel's family. Do you remember her?"

The girl nodded her head slowly. "Where is Rachel?" she whispered.

"We couldn't bring her, but we want to take you to her. Would you like to come home with us and live in our big house?" David found himself pleading.

"Oh, yes! Can I come today?"

"Right away. We brought some clothing for you. They may be a little big in size, but we can buy others in a few days. Here they are. Now run and get dressed." Hilda handed over the small case, and Minnie scuddered out to her room like a happy, little kitten.

David went back to the superintendent and told him of their plans. He said, "I wish more of our patients had such a happy ending. Too many of them have been dumped here in this hospital just to be rid of them. In many cases their mental ailments could be cleared up with a little tender loving care."

The ride home seemed to be shorter than it had been earlier. Minnie kept her eyes open, and now and then asked what something was along the way.

They stopped at a little store adjoining a filling station where David filled his gasoline tank and then brought out some snacks, including large ice cream cones for them all. Minnie's eyes lit up as she saw the treat and she slowly started to eat it. To say that Minnie was ecstatic when they reached home was an understatement. She jumped out of the car and ran to look at the beds of flowers that Rachel had prepared with David's help. There were zinnias, marigolds, and gladioli, all in riotous bloom. A row of monthly roses in bloom caught her eye next, and David found her on her knees smelling them, tears running down her face.

"Oh, Mr. David, I feel I've finally reached Heaven! Is this beautiful home really going to be mine?"

"As long as you want. Come on now and meet Aunt Virgie. Then there's Bessie and her baby. In fact we have another baby at the tenant house as well as two pretty little girls."

So this homeless girl entered into a new life—and David had no inkling of how valuable that life would be to everyone.

CHAPTER 34

R achel's response to the doctor's treatments seemed to be slow. She seldom cried, but she was always cold and shivered even on the warmest days. The medical doctor found her blood pressure was very low, and she seemed to be anemic.

Inside her head a gray cloud seemed to fold and unfold its sinuous length across her brain. Then it gathered itself into a ball, pressing across her forehead until she felt she were sprouting knots over her eyes. Her ears would stop up, and she was barely conscious when these attacks came to her. She opened her little Testament that had been given to her when she first entered this hospital. She missed Clara so much.

She turned to the back of the book near the end and read in St. James, *Is any sick among you? Let him call for the elders of the church: and let them pray over him, anointing him with oil in the name of the Lord: and the prayer of the faithful shall save the sick, and the Lord shall raise him up, and if he has committed sins, they shall be forgiven.*

Rachel read and reread this last chapter in St. James. When David came, she read it to him. "David, I'm calling for the anointing. Will you please see to it? I truly believe I will get well then."

So faithful David looked up the elder of his congregation and explained the circumstances. "Elder Martin, I need not tell you that whatever my wife discloses is to be kept confidential.

"Brother Lowe, both my deacons and myself will have sealed lips. It's always been so in the church, but sometimes people will talk too much. Knowing the prejudices of people concerning mental disturbances, we will keep confidential that Sister Lowe has these problems. We will meet you tomorrow at this hour at the hospital."

David had hunted up Rachel's prayer covering, and telling his household what was to take place the next day, he said in a choked voice, "I'd take it kindly if you were to pray for Rachel at the time of the anointing."

By three o'clock the next afternoon, the three of them, David, Elder Martin, and Deacon Smith gathered in Rachel's room. She was sitting in an armchair, dressed in a soft, blue dressing gown, her beautiful hair still hanging loose. David put her covering on her head, and the service began.

The elder read the passage of scripture that Rachel had been reading, and after an earnest and rather lengthy prayer for Rachel's health, he handed the vial of sweet oil to the deacon while he spoke to Rachel.

"Sister Rachel, if there be any sin on your conscience not confessed to God or the church, I so admonish you now to ask our Father's forgiveness."

Rachel's head dropped. David took her hand, and after a mighty effort she said, "Brothers of the church, and dearest husband, I have searched my soul. I have asked the Lord's forgiveness for my youthful sin of fornication. I have asked for His forgiveness for ridding my body of an unborn child. No one can understand the agony I have suffered over this, unless it is David. I know I have been forgiven but the DEVIL has sent his hellish imps three times to harm me, to torment me, and to frighten me. Pray that the Heavenly Father will cost these devils out of my mind and out of my body. I cannot endure them any longer."

The elder bent his head and murmured a short prayer. Then taking the vial, poured a few drops on Rachel's forehead. The soothing sweet odor was so wonderful to her that she closed her eyes in rapture.

"Oh, thank you Lord!" Little by little she felt the tension leaving her body. The elder touched her forehead with his cool fingers and a shiver of pure delight went through her. David felt her body tremble.

"Oh, the bumps that have been rolling inside my head are gone. I truly believe I am healed. Thank God!"

"Amen!" the elder and the deacon responded; and so they left leaving David and his wife together. He picked her up from her chair and carried her to the bed where he tucked a rosy, satin quilt around her. After kissing her tenderly, he left.

Twilight was beginning when she awoke. From the chapel she could hear an evening song sung by the patients who gathered there each evening. The last rays of the dying sun touched her rose crimson quilt, turning it into a glory of its own. Her window faced the west, giving her a view of the distant mountain range. The sky was covered with a mackerel formation of clouds. Each little cloud was touched with crimson and faced with violet and royal purple. In the center of this splendid sunset was the sun itself, the end half circle of its faded elegance. It resembled a ruby throne with mottling splendid colors beaming out from its edge. It seemed like a throne for a Heavenly being.

"My Savior and my Lord!" murmured Rachel. "I know now that I am healed! Show me now how to help others."

All of the lovely sounds of life came through the open window. A bird sang its vesper song; children called to one another on the street next to the hospital; a bell rang hastily in a farm woman's hands calling her loved ones to the evening meal. Rachel shut her eyes and thought of her mother's brown flour potato soup. Why was she thinking of food in the midst of these splendid delights of living?

An attendant came in with a supper tray. Ah! That was it! She was hungry. "Why, Mrs. Lowe, how happy you look! You must be feeling good!"

"I am, Mary, I feel fine. I've had such a wonderful experience this afternoon. It only comes to a person once in a while."

"But isn't it wonderful that we can have such happy experiences now and then? It makes life more endurable. Mountain-top experiences would soon grow common if we had them every day."

When David came the next day, he found Rachel on the porch, laughing and talking with her associates. She seemed so animated that he realized that she was a new person.

"Rachel, I believe you will be able to come home for good very soon. We have a surprise for you when you get home."

"Oh, David, tell me what it is! Please tell me."

"It wouldn't be a surprise then. You'll find out soon enough. Don't worry."

It was another two weeks before David took her home. The doctors were very pleased with her progress. Her physical health was very good and her mental outlook was a miracle.

"What is my surprise?" she demanded naughtily.

"I won't tell you until we get home."

Entering the driveway, Rachel was surprised to see a gang of carpenters hammering and sawing at the tenant house.

"What are you building there?"

"That's part of the surprise. We are adding four new rooms onto Elmer's house. Now that he's getting quite a family, he will need the extra space."

"Oh, that's no surprise. I know that Ada was expecting. But why four rooms?"

David helped her from the car. "We are letting Bessie and her baby take the rooms over the summer kitchen that Jake had. He will go and live in one of the upstairs rooms at Elmer's. That way we will have two extra bedrooms upstairs."

"Two? Who is sleeping in the other big bedroom? Certainly you aren't going to move out of my bed!"

"Hush! Of course not. Here's Aunt Virgie. She refuses to die until she can finish the quilt for her namesake and until she can greet you at the door."

The trembling old lady leaned heavily on her cane as she came out onto the porch. Her chin was trembling and the tears ran down her withered cheeks.

"Oh, my dear child! Welcome home! Welcome home! How thankful I am to have once again seen this day—that you have come home, and this time for good!"

Holding the ancient woman in her arms, Rachel said, "Aunt Virgie, we can't let you go yet. We need you around to advise us and to pray for us. Without your prayers I wouldn't be here."

"Nonsense, Rachel! The Lord healed you in His infinite goodness. I just helped a little."

"Now here is your surprise." David brought a smiling Minnie to Rachel. She had on her new pink and white checked gingham that Bessie and Hilda had made between canning peaches.

Rachel looked at her blankly for a few minutes, then with a cry of pure joy shouted, "Minnie! My friend Minnie! My dear one friend I had in Hell! How did you get here?"

"Your David and Hilda came to the asylum and signed papers to take me out. You see my mind had been good for over two years, but I had no place to stay. I would have had to stay there forever if David hadn't come and taken me out."

"David is too wonderful for words. He took me out of Hell, too, and after a time brought me to this heavenly place. I'm very glad you are here."

After greeting Hilda, Bessie, and Baby Virginia, they all went indoors. Soon Ada came with little El and her little girls. Little Ruth said, "Aunt Rachel, could you feel me praying for you? I prayed in my hollyhock church. I know Jesus heard me."

Hilda came in just then carrying a large tray of homemade ice cream with a huge chocolate layer cake. Bessie brought in a pitcher of lemonade. What a party they had!

"I do declare! I do love a happy ending!" laughed Rachel.

"But my dear girl, this is only the beginning. You'll see."

CHAPTER 35

It was another month before the new addition to Elmer's house was finished. On the day it was ready the family spread the furniture around the new part, the hired man took his few possessions to his new bedroom. Then Bessie and her baby moved into the small apartment over the summer kitchen. That left a large, airy bedroom for Minnie. She and Rachel had fun redecorating the room with new wallpaper and drapes. It was done in a rosy pink color and faced the west so that it seemed to have a permanent sunset. The two smaller guest rooms were left as they were. Rachel looked dreamily at the one across the hall from hers and hoped that the day would come when she could make this into a nursery.

Cornhusking came again, and Rachel, begging to go into the fields with David, was allowed to go one bright October day. They had hired another man by the day to help husk corn, so seeking privacy, David took her into the far end of the cornfield where they could be alone. The crisp air, the blue sky with cumulus clouds lazily drifting across, the cawing of the crows, and the rustling of the dry corn in the shocks gave Rachel the greatest happiness she had experienced for weeks. She breathed in great breaths of air scented with the odor of the tarry binder twine and dry corn. Once again she asked David to sing to her.

She was quite proud to have husked three shocks of corn, but the next day David said, "I feel this is too rough of work for you to do. Remember it's been only a few weeks since you were so sick. Wait a few days and then we will see how you make out."

Rachel pouted like a spoiled child, but was appeased by David's promise that she and Minnie could bring a lunch out for the four men at noon. That would save the time taken to go the distance to the house to eat.

"How can we carry victuals enough for four men?"

"Do you remember the little wagon that Jonathon used to ride in? You and Minnie can haul our dinners out to the field in that. Be sure to bring along a keg of fresh water, for it may get hot this afternoon. One of you can pull and the other one can steady it." David put on his wamus and left before Rachel could put up a reaction to this.

Hilda fixed a bountiful meal for the four men. She and Bessie had baked that morning, so she sent several dozen light rolls and two big apple pies. She sent along a generous dab of freshly churned butter and a small jar of apple butter. Slices of sugar-cured ham fried a golden brown and a jar of red beet eggs filled out the big basket, too big for either Rachel or Minnie to lift. A stone jar of hot coffee and another one filled with cold buttermilk filled the last bit of space in the basket. Calling to little Copper, the two girls went down the farm lane, laughing with the sheer joy of being alive.

Rachel pointed out the wildflowers called butter and eggs because of their yellow and orange coloring. She picked one and holding it between thumb and forefinger, showed Minnie how the tiny flower would open and close its mouth. "It is a cousin of the snapdragon," she explained to the delighted Minnie. A purple thistle grew nearby, and a mass of honeysuckle covered a low stone wall.

Minnie sighed in happiness. "I don't know which I like better, these ordinary wildflowers or the ones you grow by the house."

"No flower is ordinary," Rachel said. "Each one was created to give pleasure to the world. Even the lowly dandelion is beautiful."

"Is it true that some people eat dandelions, Rachel? I heard in the asylum that people even make wine from the yellow blossoms. Do people ever do that?"

Rachel picked a tender dandelion plant, discarding the exterior leaves and handed it to Minnie. "There, taste that. This isn't the season to eat dandelions because they are slightly bitter now, but imagine it with a bacon dressing garnished with egg and vinegar. We like to eat it with fried potatoes on the side. Many a dinner have I made with this."

"But dandelion wine—is it good?"

"Our church doesn't hold with drinking wine or any other alcoholic drinks. But now and then some wine is made. When I was first married, Aunt Virgie had made some elderberry wine for the summer complaint. It was good, too! I remember she had a little dandelion wine in the cellar. It had a sweet, lemony taste because she always put some lemons in it. David wouldn't let me have but a little taste since more would cause a person to get tipsy."

The men stopped their work and came over to the buckeye tree where the girls had pulled up the wagon. They all sat down and waited politely until David had asked the blessing. The two girls accepted a light roll each, but told them they had each had a "piece" before they had started.

"Let's go the long way home through the woods. We might find some chestnuts if the squirrels haven't gotten them all."

"Do you think we could? I would like to see a squirrel. I don't even remember if I ever saw one." They got deeper into the woods.

"Sh—h—h! Do you hear the rustling? It sounds like something big coming through the woods. Here, Copper, keep real still. Come on, Minnie, stoop down here beside me."

"Is it a bear? Oh-h, Rachel, I'm scared!"

"Sh—h—h!"

Scarcely breathing the girls stared fascinatedly at a man shuffling along among the dry leaves. Copper started to growl, but Rachel held him close while she stared in terror. He crouched at the edge of the woods, then ducking around through the trees, he ran across the cornfield next to the road, keeping the corn shocks between him and the next field where the men were working. When he reached the road, he vanished from Rachel's sight.

Minnie was sobbing in her terror but stopped when she saw Rachel's face drained of color.

"Do you know who that was, Rachel?"

"Yes, he was one of the devils that are out to get me. But this time he can't hurt me. You were with me and besides that, the Lord won't let anything happen to us. Come on, let's go home."

David sensed the tension in Rachel and Minnie when he got in from the field. "Well, girls, what happened? I know something has, for both of you are acting like you have seen a spook."

Minnie just toyed with her food and said nothing. Then Rachel said, "All right, I'll tell you. Minnie and I came back through the woods and we saw the DEVIL there."

"How do you mean that? What DEVIL?"

"The DEVIL that called me the ugly name when I spilled the coffee on him."

"You mean that fellow is sneaking around here? Did he see you?"

"No, he didn't. We hid down behind a cedar tree. He went on out of the woods and through the cornfield next to the road. I couldn't see which way he went after he got on the road. Did you, Minnie?"

"Yes, he turned left so that he didn't go by the house."

David felt very uneasy, but he told Rachel and Minnie he did not want them to go out to the woods again unless he was with them. "And another thing girls, I want you to stay close to the buildings. Hilda and Bessie, keep a sharp look out at all times when you are outdoors."

He expected he would have trouble with Rachel having bad dreams that night, so he spent a long time brushing her long hair. He carefully tucked her in after they knelt with their prayers. He kept his arm about her all night. To his great relief she did not have the horrible nightmares she had so often experienced before she had her anointing. He felt now that she was truly healed since she had faced an emergency and had come through with victory.

The next day was cloudy and promised rain, but David and his men were out in the cornfield early. He told Rachel she was not to bring out any lunch because he would be coming in to get it and he would carry it out to the men. He would be starting to haul in the golden ears of corn and store them in the corn crib.

The corn crib was built so that there were inch-wide openings between horizontal boards for ventilation. Mice were delighted with this arrangement, and they came in swarms from the fields to winter off at the farmer's expense. Farm cats were likewise charmed, for they had the duty of catching and eating the mice. When the farmer was finished milking, he always was careful to fill the cats' pan with the sweet, foaming milk. Such a high protein diet with the milk gave the feline population a glossy, well-fed appearance.

By four o'clock the weather had worsened so that the men came into the house early. Hilda had been expecting them and had a chicken potpie in the oven ready for an early supper. The milking and feeding were postponed for an hour so that the men could feed off this delicacy while it was hot.

David did not go into the barn right away but talked to Hilda privately. As a result, she went to every window in the house and saw to it that it was securely fastened. Then she pulled each shade to the bottom of the window. Rachel did not see these maneuvers, being busy with little Virginia. But Minnie saw what was happening and a chill came over her. She murmured to Bessie as she was helping with the dishes, "They must be expecting trouble."

"Yes, but don't say anything to Rachel. She seems to have forgotten the trespasser you two saw yesterday. Best thing for her, too."

David came in early from the barn, wet and tired. "Come on, Rachel, let's go to bed. I want a hot bath and to turn in."

"I'm agreed. There's nothing quite as soothing as hearing the rain on the roof, especially if it's a tin roof like the one over the porch roof right outside our bedroom window."

During the night David woke up sensing something not quite right. He cautiously stole out of the bed, then slipping into his pants and picking up a flashlight, he crept down the stairway.

But still with all of his stealth, Rachel heard him and ran after him in her bare feet. There was a light in the kitchen, the one that hung over the sink, but there was no one in sight.

Just then there was a terrific clutter that came from the pantry and a muffled cry came from there, too. David raced across the big kitchen and slammed shut the pantry door. Then he called out, "All right, come out with your hands up!"

Slowly the door opened and a sorry figure emerged, hands in the air and the rest of the body covered with flour.

"Who are you? What are you doing in my kitchen?"

"Why, Mister, you've scared me out of my growth! It's me, Hilda!"

"Hilda, for pity's sake, what are you doing in the pantry in the middle of the night? If you wanted to powder yourself, I'll buy you some talcum powder."

"Now, David, don't make fun of her. She's all upset. What were you trying to do?"

"Just settin' my bread for tomorrow. Everybody was in such a rush to go to bed that I plum forgot to set the yeast. I should 'a knowed better than to go into the pantry without a light on. That Bessie never puts things where they belong, but that's her only fault. Anyhow I spilt a whole crock of flour, and now it's wasted."

It was this comic relief that showed David how the tension caused by the skulking stranger had affected them all.

CHAPTER 36

"Come on, Copper. I'll put you outside before I go to bed." Minnie did not often take care of the dog since Rachel usually performed these services. The dog ran for the barn and started to bark in an excited way.

The fear of an intruder seemed to have leveled off since a month had gone by and no further sign had been seen of him, so Minnie assumed that Copper had spotted a rabbit on the last of the turnips in the garden.

"Come on, Copper! Come on to bed!" Minnie had a fear of the dark and hated to think she might have to go out into it. But no Copper came, and she could hear his barking from the barnyard. There was no help for it, she'd have to go get him, for everyone had gone to bed. What an exasperating dog! Grabbing her sweater from the hall closet, she put it on and got a flashlight and set out to bring back one spoiled dog to his dog bed in the kitchen.

As she got closer to the barn and unhooked the great wooden barnyard gate, she could smell smoke. She forgot her fears of the darkness and ran through the muck that is found in any barnyard, and there saw that the near-side of the straw stack was on fire. The stack stood about fifteen feet from the stables and was used for bedding for the cattle and horses.

There was a flame rising high and smoke coming from the other side. The flames would soon blanket the doors. Already the horses were setting up a whinny. They would be burned alive unless she did something.

This naturally scared girl quickly opened the horse stable doors and going inside, yelled, "Get out, you beasts! Get out!" But she realized their fear was greater than hers and so it was up to her to drag them out by their halters. She grabbed old Bess's halter first, then tugging with all her slender strength, succeeded in getting her outside and into the barnyard.

She ran and opened the barnyard gate, then giving the horse a slap on her side, sent her galloping into the farm lane. She screamed with all her might for David, but only succeeded in arousing Copper to greater activity.

She ran back into the stable and grabbed the halters of two more horses and led them without too much trouble to the farm lane leading to the pasture. This time she was near the farm dinner bell, which she rang so vigorously that the rope broke. She was yelling loudly enough this time that David heard her while he and Rachel were at their nightly prayers in their room.

This time there were more horses to rescue from the billows of smoke that poured into the stable so thick it was hard to see through it.

Minnie had heard of heroic rescues and always in these stories the hero had to mask the horses' eyes to lead them to safety, so she took off her sweater and wrapped it as best she could around the stallion's eyes before she attempted to lead him out. That left two colts, so frisky she dared not approach them. But Copper distinguished himself by nipping at their feet and driving them right out into the smoke but past the fire. Thank goodness, when they were on the outside, they had sense enough to keep on going.

Now for the cow stable. She turned on the electric lights and searched the stable as best she could through the smoke. In the far corner was the latest calf with its mother. The rest of the cows were in the pasture. Now to get old Brownie out! She had nothing to make a blindfold of. Wait! Yes, she had—her panties. So stepping out of them she immediately tied the two legs around the cow's eyes. Then smacking her smartly, drove her outside with the wobbling calf bawling on behind.

David came running through the barnyard gate just in time to see this rescue, but putting aside its incongruity, grabbed a hose connected to the barn cistern and tried to put out the blaze. Just then Elmer as well as Ada, followed closely by Jake, came running. When Bessie came they saw how ineffective one hose was, so she ran back into the house and brought the water bucket from the well. She doused the contents over the fire, but by now it had the makings of an inferno.

"Ada, go to the telephone and call the fire company or the whole barn will go! Then stay inside and look after your baby!" David could still think logically.

Minnie ran inside and got Hilda and Rachel to help her collect all the buckets they could find. Going to the well, they filled the buckets and formed a bucket chain from the well. Rachel pumped the big iron handle to the well, then ran to Hilda who in turn ran to Minnie who dumped the water onto the burning straw stack. Elmer was checking the stable for livestock, but seeing none, joined in the bucket brigade.

Before long the welcomed siren sound came from the village fire company's engine. Ada had gotten through.

"Minnie, run inside and see that Aunt Virgie is all right. Calm her fears and tell her that we think the barn will be saved now that we have more help."

Obeying David's suggestion, she ran for the house, then became conscious that she was not wearing many clothes. "I hope no one sees my panties on the cow. I'll never live it down," she said to herself.

She got up over the porch in time to see a dark figure enter the door that had been left open by Hilda and Rachel in their excitement. An intruder! Was it the fellow they had seen in the woods that October afternoon? Quietly she entered the house and looked about for a weapon. Ah! There was one—a heavy-headed cane that Aunt Virgie never cared about, saying it was too heavy for her. Minnie grabbed the cane and followed the movements of the fellow. He was going upstairs! Why? Oh, to be sure—he was after David's cash he kept in the bureau drawer. There must be several hundred dollars there for the running expenses of the farm.

She tiptoed to the first landing and there took a position beside a big, old-fashioned chest at the turn in the staircase.

The fellow did not take long. She could hear the opening of bureau drawers, then a pause—one so threatening it caused her to feel nauseous with fear, but soon she felt his presence drawing near.

He started down the steps, but as soon as he reached the bend in the stairway, Minnie rose from her hiding place and with all her might hit the fellow on the head with the metal knob end of Aunt Virgie's cane.

The sound of his fall echoed and re-echoed throughout the house so that Aunt Virgie came trembling from her bed. She saw an awesome sight, a man lying half off the bottom of the staircase with money scattered its full length. At the top of the stairs was poor frightened little Minnie, keening like a lost soul.

"Did I kill him? Oh, Aunt Virgie, did I kill him or just knock him out?"

Aunt Virgie called on reserves she did not know she had and tottered over to the stricken man. She knelt and felt for a pulse beat when he stirred and moaned.

"No, he's not dead, but Minnie, you've got to help me. Cut down the clothesline. We've got to bind him. What's going on outside? Is the barn burning down?"

"No, Aunt Virgie, the fire company is here now and has the fire under control. This fellow here must have set the fire, for I can smell kerosene on his clothes."

"Hurry, child, or we'll have a dangerous man on our hands. Quick, get the butcher knife and cut some rope."

So these frail women bound the man's hands behind him and then bound his feet together. There he lay like a trussed-up turkey. The two women, holding each other, laughed hysterically and then cried.

Thus it was when Hilda came in sopping wet that she saw the situation and also saw what the other two had overlooked—a coiled snake tattooed on his wrist. It was the former hired man who had cursed out Rachel.

Leaving the money lay where it was, she went to the telephone and called the sheriff, then she went upstairs to see how much damage he had done there.

When she turned on the light in Rachel and David's room she recoiled in horror. Lying on the bed was a snake, a large garter snake. Thank Heavens she had seen it before Rachel did! Gingerly, she picked it up, for she knew it was not venomous. Its head was crushed, but the tail was still moving, showing that it had been recently killed and put there only to frighten Rachel.

She took up the wastebasket and deposited the snake in it, then hastily changed the bed linen. Cleverly she disturbed the covers the way they were when Rachel and David had left them so precipitantly when the fire was discovered. She ran downstairs and out into the garden where she buried the snake.

By the time Rachel came into the house, Aunt Virgie was being helped to her room by the valiant Minnie. Hilda took her by the hand and said, "Come into the kitchen, Missus, and help me make some coffee for the firemen. Will you see if there's any cake left in the box? I'll get out some sugar cakes I made yesterday. How many men are there?"

"Good gracious, Hilda! We're all soaking wet and we should get into some dry clothes. Look at yourself, and here you stand prattling about sugar cakes! There's plenty of time for that. David and the men are hauling away the remainder of the straw stack before it blazes up and sets the barn on fire. I wonder how it caught fire! Where is Minnie? That brave girl saved our barn and the stock. I never thought she had it in her!"

"Missus, don't go through the hall just yet."

"Why not, Hilda?"

"There's something there that will just upset you. Better to be in wet clothes than to be upset."

"Oh, come on, Hilda, I won't get upset. Remember the good Lord healed me and I won't let myself get upset. Besides that, I'm cold, and I know you are, too. Let the coffee boil a few minutes and get into something dry."

"All righty, Missus, but you can't say I didn't warn you! Don't scream!"

Rachel, by now thoroughly curious, went into the hall and saw the trussed-up man lying there. He was still unconscious.

"Why, it's the hired hand who said he'd get me!"

Hilda was conscious of the term *hired hand* and not *DEVIL* as Rachel had described him before. So the Missus was really healed! The Lord be praised!

By the time David, his employees, and the firemen came into the house, they made such a sopping mess of the floor that Hilda flinched. But they were all grateful for the coffee and the cakes she set out.

"We have the straw stack scattered over the corn stubbles so it won't do any harm. Elmer and Jake got the horses rounded up and back into the stables, and here is Minnie's sweater. But old Bossy surely wore something strange over her horns. Hey, Minnie! Where are you? You should have seen old Bossy's sunbonnet, only it wasn't a sunbonnet! By the way, where is Minnie? She saved our barn and our stock! How can we thank that brave girl? I never saw one little woman get around so fast!"

"Not only that," added Hilda, "she saved your money, too. Look in the hallway and up the staircase."

The men crowded into the hall and were appalled by what they saw there.

"Who did that? Who tied him up? Why that's Joe Lance, the fellow I discharged sometime ago. So that's how the fire started! I thought one of us was careless with the lantern. Say, Hilda, did you capture him?"

"Not me, Mister! It was Minnie. She seemed to be everywhere at once. She and Aunt Virgie tied him up with the clothesline after Minnie knocked him out with Aunt Virgie's heavy cane."

"Well I never!" David sat down, numb with the shock. The men all stood with mouths agape.

"Say, we'd better call the sheriff!" was all David could add.

"No need to, for here I am," and the sheriff came walking into the house. "Who captured him?"

"One of the family here, the smallest and weakest of the bunch. She lives with us and has repaid us a hundred times over for anything we have ever done for her. Where is she, Hilda?"

"In Aunt Virgie's room. She's too shy to come out. You'll have to talk to her alone, Sheriff, for she's a very scared person."

"She must be quite a person to have knocked out this character and then tied him up."

Shivery and scared, little Minnie came out of Aunt Virgie's room when David called her to talk to the sheriff.

Aunt Virgie called out to David. "You're not to scare her, David. I won't allow it! She's the bravest girl I ever saw! I'm going to do something nice for that girl. I'm going to set to work in the morning to make her a rainbow quilt. I've never made one of them before." Aunt Virgie's voice was so strong that the ones in the kitchen could hear it. "Besides that, anyone who can help tie up a burglar the way I did has no business lying in bed all the time!"

So Aunt Virgie, at the age of eighty-five, decided she was going to live on a while. Life was getting too interesting to die!

The sheriff took away the unconscious intruder and took him to the hospital. After a two-day wait, David went to visit him. A policeman was guarding the door. We found Lance still suffering from the blow that Minnie gave him. He lifted his head from the pillow then sank back and closed his eyes.

"Go away! I don't want to see you or any of your filthy family ever again."

David went away, but when he got back home he drew Minnie to one side and told her that the fellow was conscious and would be all right within a few days.

"David, please take me with you to see him. I want to apologize for hitting him so hard."

"There's no apology needed. But he will have to have a lawyer when his trial comes up. I will furnish him with one. I'm sorry that you will have to go to court to testify against him."

The trial took place three months after the attempted arson. It was against David's pacifist ideas that he and Minnie had to testify. When it was David's turn to testify, instead of taking the oath that the clerk of courts attempted to administer, he said, "I do not take an oath. Instead I will affirm that I will tell the truth."

When Minnie gave her testimony, she looked so distressed that the jury and judge were both very impressed. The sentence pronounced was a light one—six months in the house of correction.

Every month David drove to the penal institution to visit Joe Lance. At first the hardened young man cursed him and turned away. But David followed his conscience and continued to visit him. He took Joe a copy of the New Testament as well as other religious publications. Joe only threw them to the floor and stamped on them. Then he spat in David's face.

David took his clean pocket handkerchief and wiped his face. Then he left. But the next week he was back. This time he brought some of Hilda's good coconut cake. Joe took the cake and crammed it into his mouth like a beast.

When he had finished it, he said, "Haven't you had enough of me? What kind of man are you?"

"I hope I am a man that pleases God. I want to make it up that you are in here. I want to see you repent. I want to be your friend."

After several more visits David was gratified to see that Joe accepted him. He said, "If your intentions are to convert me, you have nearly done so. I have read your Bible and understand now why you bother with me. But tell me, why did your wife pour hot coffee over me?"

So David explained how a man wearing a tattoo of a snake had violated Rachel that eventually led her into insanity. "She is now making a complete recovery, but it has been touch and go with her. She regresses every time she sees a snake or even the picture of a snake. She is dearer to me than life itself, so now you can understand why I ordered you off the farm."

When Joe was released he was a much better man. David helped him to find work in another community. Before they parted, Joe asked, "Do you think I can take off this tattoo? I want to be rid of it."

No one knew about David's compassion toward Joe except Minnie. Because of his example she decided she wanted to join the church that David and Rachel belonged to. One beautiful Sunday in May, she was baptized in the creek that flowed in back of the farm.

The elder, wearing wading boots, entered the water first to a place where a little pool eddied. He then went to the edge of the stream and helped Minnie to the pool. He lowered her into the water and he baptized her according to the dictates of the church affiliation. He helped her to her feet, then placing his hands on her head, he prayed.

Such a feeling of gladness came over her. It seemed to her that all of Heaven's glory surrounded her.

CHAPTER 37

Hilda was frying mush for breakfast when Jake opened the kitchen door and walked in.

"Morning, Jake. It's a little early for breakfast here, but you are welcome to stay."

"No, thank you. I didn't come for breakfast. I've already had mine. Is David up yet?"

"I think I hear him upstairs now. He should be down any minute. Here, Bessie, will you set the table?"

With heightened color, Bessie did as she was bidden. Soon David entered the large, sunny kitchen.

"Why, Jake, you're out early this morning. Already finished at the barn?"

"Not quite, but I want to talk to you before I go back to finish. Elmer and I were just talking. I'd like for you to make me a partner in the farm here."

"A partner! What capital do you have?"

"How much did Elmer put in?"

"Well he's not exactly a partner. He farms on the share. You get paid wages. What's this all about anyway?"

"Bessie and me have decided to get married, only we won't have a place to live. I want to keep on working for you, so there's the hitch. We thought if we could make some kind of bargain with you, we could build a small house on the other side of the driveway and still keep on working here. We both have some money we have saved to build the house. I want you to study on it."

David talked it over with Rachel, and a few evenings later called in Bessie, Jake, Elmer, and Ada.

"It seems that another romance has sprung up here on the farm. Now here's what we'll do. Rachel and I have talked it over. We have enough fieldstone here on the place that we've been picking off to build a bungalow for Jake and his family. We think stone will harmonize with the rest of the stone buildings."

Jake and Bessie both blushed. Then they looked at each other with eloquent silence.

"Since Elmer didn't have to pay for his house, I'll finance Jake's, providing you two fellows help to haul stone and give a hand with the building. Of course, we'll have to have stonemasons and carpenters, as well as electricians and plumbers. But there will be the cellar to dig, cement to pour, grading to do, and that's where we all can come in to help. We won't need any lawyers to draw up papers unless you insist. We'll be partners in the profits and expenses of the farm. You'll not get paid by the month, Jake, as before. The land and the buildings belong to me, but the taxes will be everybody's share. Now does that suit you?"

Both of the men came up and with a handshake, sealed the bargain. They knew David to be a man of his word. They needed nothing more.

They started to haul in rocks from various fence corners. Bessie decided she wanted a fireplace and went along on the wagon to find the best stones for it.

When the stakes were driven laying out the house, Bessie and Virginia went out every day to watch the cellar being dug. Part of it would be for storage and part for a washroom and playroom for the little girl.

Bessie would continue working for Rachel but on a daily basis, and then but two or three days a week.

Rachel said, "I'm strong enough now, and with Minnie's help we ought to lighten Hilda's load considerably."

Bessie and Jake decided to have the wedding in the new house when it was finished.

"I'd like to stand in front of the fireplace to be married. I've always dreamed of having my own fireplace with fall flowers all around. To be in my own house will seem like being in Heaven. I never dreamed my life would turn out this good. Just imagine what I've been, and now," her voice trailed off into a joyous sob.

The news of the stock market crash had of course reached these happy groups of people, but this had happened so far away that it could not concern them. Then one day a letter came from David's bank. He read it without comprehending, then reread it. It told him that half of the stock left him by Elder Winer was valueless.

He took a trip to town to inquire about his bank stock, finding the banker in an agitated frame of mind. "If this keeps up, we'll have a depression so bad that all industries will have to shut down."

As far as David could find out, his inheritance had shrunk to about half its value. "But," he thought, "we'll still have plenty, for we still have the farm."

That summer their same style of living still existed. Many people who were out of work stopped by to inquire as to doing a day's work in exchange for food. In his usual generous manner, David never turned anyone away from the door hungry. Rarely did a week go by that someone did not seek refuge in the haymow of the barn for a night's sleep. David insisted on but one thing—to empty their pockets of matches.

One cold night the family was about ready to sit down to eat supper in the dining room where Hilda insisted on serving them when there were no farmhands. Copper started to bark hysterically at the door. On opening the door, David was surprised to see a tall, gaunt man in ragged overalls and a floppy straw hat surrounded by a most bedraggled family. A tiny woman was holding a baby that looked to be about a year old. Assorted sizes of children were peering out of the gloom at David. He figured there must be five partly grown children, not counting the baby.

"Mister, could you please take us in for the night? We're on our way south to Tennessee where we have kinfolk. Our car gave out just down the road a piece, and we can't git no further tonight. I'll chop wood, milk cows, or do anything you have to do just so's my kids and woman here git in out of the cold and git a warm bite to eat."

Hilda and Bessie straightaway started to set the kitchen table before David could even answer the man.

"Certainly, neighbor, come in, all of you. Here is a place where you can all wash up. We even have a toilet in this closet for anyone who needs it."

"Hey, Pop, looky there. They have a privy right in the house like the swells in town has," spoke up a scraggly haired boy about ten.

While the family was performing its ablutions, Hilda hastily cut three more slices of ham while Bessie and Minnie pared more potatoes and started frying them. Rachel ran to the cellar for several jars of peaches they had canned during the summer, and by the time the family was clean, a bountiful supper was set on the long kitchen table.

A silence fell over the group as David bowed his head and reverently prayed, "Lord, for thy bounty set before us we do truly thank You. Bless us and bless these strangers who have come under our roof. Guide and direct us all. Amen."

The hungry little ones set to. Hilda beamed to see the food disappear. Just as they were being seated she hurriedly stirred up a huge corn pone and put it in the oven. By the time the platter of golden fried ham was passed, the pone was ready. How fragrant it smelled as she cut it into generous squares and passed it around.

The tired little woman had tears in her eyes as she broke open the steaming corn bread. "I declare, I never thought I'd get to eat some good corn bread tonight. That's better than any cake you could bake. Down home in Tennessee we allus had sargam sirup to put on corn bread. I'll bet you all never heard of such stuff here but us'n allus just pure loved it."

The woman stopped talking and her eyes got so big and round that everyone stopped eating and stared. Hilda was passing around a pitcher of sorghum syrup!

"Oh, Lordy! I's almost home. We'uns bin up nawth here so long I nearly lost the remembrance of sargum sirup and corn bread."

The man said in between bites, "May I have some more of that red-eye gravy? You folks sure do know how to set a good table. I never did git your names. We'uns are Mr. and Mrs. Billy Stitz, formerly of Flowerdale, Tennessee. We bin up nawth workin in the factories of the city. The baby is a year old today, though he's a bit small for his age. We've not had a roof over his little head these past two days nor had any vittles."

David said, "We have two extra rooms upstairs we'll put you in. The Good Book says to entertain the stranger at the door for by doing so we may be entertaining strangers unawares."

"Well Mister—what did you say your name is?"

"Lowe, David Lowe. This is my wife, Rachel. That good cook over there is Hilda, and this is Bessie and her little girl, Virginia. That big fellow over there is Jake, one of my partners, and that pretty girl is Minnie. Most of us have different last names but we are just one big, happy family. My Aunt Virgie is in her room and asleep by now. My other partner and his wife and four children are across the yard there. There's fourteen of us all together."

After that long speech, Bessie said, "Since your little one is a year old today, let's do what we did at my little one's first birthday. It's seeing what the future holds for your boy."

Quickly she gathered some articles and put them on a round, braided rug, then took the Stitz baby, and placed him in front of these articles. The little one, frightened by the numerous faces looking down at him, started to whimper. He soon straightened up and crawled over to a bottle. Good Lord, no, not that. It would foretell a life of drunkenness. He passed over the bottle and fastened onto a carpenter's rule. A long sigh was heard from his mother.

"Of course I would rather he'd picked up a book, for none of us'ns is book larned. But a carpentry is a good, honest trade."

"I'm glad of that. Friend, I started to say a bit ago that you ain't entertaining angels. We're just tired-out hillbillies. So if you all point the way, us'ns is ready for bed."

David and Rachel set up two folding cots for the weary children in one bedroom, and in the other one the weary parents bedded down.

After a hearty breakfast of flannel cakes and pudding, David went with Billy Stitz to get the car. "You're a long ways from home, Billy. Better take time now and let's look her over."

After a few hours of tinkering, the old car perked up and the family packed in and was ready to go. Hilda thrust a big bag of lunch into their willing hands, and David, taking Billy aside, put two twenty dollar bills into his hand. The tears began to flow.

"Lord bless you, neighbor! The Good Book says 'Cast thy bread upon the waters and it will return to you again.'"

"That's all right, Billy. The Lord has been good to me and has blessed me many times over. Oh, it hasn't always been rosy with me, but you'll get yours someday."

By the middle of the summer, Jake's house was just about finished. The money he and Bessie had saved was spent on household furnishings. They visited country auctions and came home with some good pieces. Some needed refinishing, so night after night they spent sanding and varnishing.

During the winter months the women spent the long evenings braiding a large, room-sized rug for the living room. What a turning out of the attic! Some woolen blankets had been stored there from the Winer's occupancy. Practical Hilda went to the summer kitchen with its big iron pots, and there she boiled and dyed the blankets brilliant hues of red, green, and yellow.

"What color hands do you have today?" teased David as she passed the food at the dinner table. "That Jake won't be able to wear his shoes indoors on such a fine rug."

Hilda and Minnie cut the long strips of cloth after it was dyed, and Aunt Virgie turned in the raw edges with thread and needle. Even Ada came in several afternoons to help in spite of her new son, David Lee. He was just over a year younger than Elmer's son, little El. Both boys were now at the toddling stage and found so much mischief that it was decided that she would be of more help if she kept the little boys at home.

There were five strands of cloth plaited into a wide braid. Elder Winer's old black overcoat, his wife's blue dress, and a strand each of red, green, and yellow was woven through the rich-looking braids.

"This rug should last you a lifetime if we sew it tight enough. I've heard tell of some folks that use fishing line to lace between the braids. That should keep it from coming apart."

Finally the twenty-fifth of November came. It was a few days after Thanksgiving, and such a smell of baking and cooking came from Hilda's kitchen.

Aunt Virgie decided if she bundled up well she would allow the family to carry her across the driveway to the new house, sparkling in the autumn sunlight.

The living room was filled with some of the church friends, for both Bessie and Jake were now members of David's church.

"Since no one lives his religion any more than David and Rachel, we want to belong to the church that preaches that way," was the terse way Jake expressed it.

The fire burned bright in the stone fireplace. Masses of fall roses or chrysanthemums banked both sides, and there the couple stood to take their vows until death parted them. Little Virginia held roses in her hands that were picked from the south side of the bushes by the summer kitchen. She tightly held on to her mother's beautiful blue wedding dress with the other hand.

The happy couple took no honeymoon but simply moved their personal effects from their old rooms into the new house. For the first time in her short life, little Virginia had her own room. At first she was excited, but soon started to cry when she found herself in her little bed, spread with Aunt Virgie's lovely quilt. Her mother's door was closed, but soon she fell asleep with her shaggy bunny clutched in her arms.

For the second time the apartment over the summer kitchen was empty.

"We've had two brides leave that apartment. Now it is your turn, Minnie, if you want it."

"Not me, David. I like my room where it is."

So the two rooms were fitted up with extra cots for the homeless people that drifted in and out of the place. They had travelers every few days, for the Depression was growing worse.

David found that farm prices were sinking to such a low that neither he nor his partners were barely making a living. When the following spring came, they faced a drought. They plowed and planted the fields, but without rain, the tender plants died. The vegetable garden gave out with a few onions and radishes, but the potatoes, beans, and cabbage all withered and died. They dared not use any more water than necessary. Hilda took the water remaining in the water glasses and watered the few houseplants they allowed themselves. Baths were restricted, and then the bath water was diverted from the sewer and allowed to go to the nearby garden. But in spite of their best efforts, the vegetables died.

"Now what to do?" wondered David.

"We still have a good many jars of food left over from former years. That should help a bit, providing you don't give it all away," said Hilda.

There was a light rain in July, too late to do any good except for the turnip patch. They yielded luxuriously, their green tops contrasting so beautifully with the dried stalks of the other plants.

"Guess we can eat turnip greens as well as the rest of the turnip," smiled Minnie.

When weary travelers came to their door, they were welcomed to stay and to share in the turnips. Hilda had a little lard left, so she stirred some of it into the turnips to give them a meaty flavor. There was still cornmeal, so many a pan of corn pone or cornmeal mush was served to the family and the Depression-hit person who would be sharing their meal that day.

The Depression became worse, and seldom did the Lowes sit down without company. Hilda automatically set several extra places at the long, kitchen table.

Many people stayed overnight. Some stayed several days after resting from the grueling days in the northern cities. Everyone was heading south, for all signs pointed toward a hard winter.

David decided they would butcher early in November in spite of the fact that the shoats were not fat. All available corn nubbins were sought out and fed to the hungry hogs. Even the acorns were scarce this fall. There was very little lard to be gotten from the butchering.

"Hilda, you will have to hold off baking pies this winter. Instead, why not use the canned cherries and make us steamed puddings in a bag. That's always good." David smacked his lips.

The cows were turned out into the empty fields to forage for themselves. Milk production had fallen to a minimum. Half of the herd was only giving strippings, which were not considered suitable for human consumption. The breeding sow and boar got this. There was barely enough milk for the three families.

At last a three-day rain fell, causing the thirsty pasture land to grow green. The herd was saved for a time.

David was faced with the fact he would have to draw out his money on interest. Elmer and Jake knew the money would be a loan to them, but they were not prepared for David's return. His face was white. "When I got to the bank there was a long line of people all drawing out their money. At that rate the bank will soon have to close its doors. Then what will we do?"

Sure enough, the next day the bank ran out of cash and closed its doors. There was a deep gloom over the land, and the heavy dust storms from the middle western states caused a pall to hang over the sky.

David called the three families together for a conference, and they started to pray. While they were kneeling by their chairs, a little noise was heard at the door.

"'Cuse me, please. I's just passin' through and was just wonderin' if I could fish in the crick in back of the barn. My name's Sam, but some folks call me Fishin' Sam."

David rose from his knees and saw a young, black boy holding a ragged coat together in front and a battered hat on his head.

"Certainly, Fishin' Sam, come right in and have a bite to eat first. We're praying to the good Lord to show us the way how we can feed fourteen people that live on this farm plus the animals. For the first time the land won't support us."

"I don't know nothin' about supportin', but when I'se gets hungry, I always catches me a fish, but I guess I'll help you pray awhile, then go catch us some fish."

The family rose to its respective chairs and started to eat the turnip greens and corn bread with its lean bacon on the side. Hilda had made a peach cobbler from the canned peaches left over from two years ago. There was no sugar, so honey was used for a sweetener. The three families often ate together now to save food, so today's peach cobbler was made from the last of Ada's flour.

"What are you white folks so skeered about? You-all had a dinner fit for a king. You-all ain't so bad off yet. Come on, let's go fishin in that there crick."

The men took their cue from the smiling lad and hunted up lines and hooks. To their amazement, they caught enough fish for several meals.

It was at this time that Roosevelt took office and the bank reopened. David drew out enough money to finance a new seed time. When April came with its rain there was rejoicing, although the western plains had little joy. Many of their farms had blown away.

CHAPTER 38

It was at this time when the world seemed at its lowest that Rachel became
pregnant. As was the custom, only David was told of her wonderful secret. At
last God was hearing her.

One day Aunt Virgie said, "My, oh my, Rachel, you look so good. There's
a look about you that tells me you have a secret. Am I right?"

"Yes, Aunt Virgie, but only David knows it. I'm about three months gone
and no morning sickness yet."

Aunt Virgie clucked, "Ach huh, I don't like that. The old grannies always
said it was a healthy sign to have morning sickness. But then not everyone is alike."

A cold shiver ran down Rachel's back. *Am I being too glad?* she thought.

The long, hard winter ended and so did Rachel's hopes for a baby. Her
sorrow was so deep that David feared for her sanity again. It was during this period
that she dreamed again of the little pink and white cottage. In the dream Miss
Lucy was surrounded by flying buzzards. She woke up shaking.

"Another baby is lost!"

Her fit of despondency lasted for several weeks. Then one day little Virginia
came in. She was nearly four now and had the run of the farm. "Aunt Rachel, why
are you so sad? You're crying. Don't cry. I'll take care of you."

The child's visit brought a surcease to her grief. There was work to do. It
was spring after the harrowing winter. There were flowers to tend, a vegetable
garden to get into condition, and a house to clean. Minnie helped her outside with
the flowers and vegetable garden while Bessie came over to help Hilda with the
housecleaning. Meals were skimpier than usual.

The rains came and the winter wheat sprang up greener than grass. There was hope in the land. The Depression continued but the farmers rejoiced. The could raise crops again.

After the house was cleaned and the vegetable gardens well on the way, Aunt Virgie decided it was time to get the rainbow quilt set together and quilted.

"I haven't seen my old friends very many times since we moved down here. I want to have a quilting bee, Rachel. Would it be all right to have about five or six people come in? Of course we would have them for the day, so we'll have them for dinner at noon. What do we have good to eat?"

Hilda pondered, then said, "We have a fat goose out there in the chicken yard that isn't laying. How would roast goose taste?"

Aunt Virgie just beamed. "That will be fine. Now could we set the table in the dining room, and I'll come out there to eat? We'll have to set the quilting frames up in my bedroom. It's big enough to accommodate them. That way we won't make any mess in the living room."

Rachel was pleased that Aunt Virgie felt so ambitious. "Of course, Aunt Virgie. We are happy that you feel well enough to have in your friends. I'll phone them right away."

On the appointed day there were three plain Brethren buggies driving carefully down the pike that was the main route from the state line. They drove carefully on the side shoulder of the road where the crushed stone was left.

Each of the seven women tried to outdo the other in making tiny stitches. It was agreed to use the crisscross quilting pattern over the small blocks of rainbow-colored patches. On the wide border, Fannye Wolgum suggested that they put a scroll. She was a short, crippled woman who had suffered a hip and back dislocation ever since anyone could remember. She had a sunny disposition and seldom gave way to self-pity.

The noon dinner was a culinary triumph. The seven elderly ladies sat around the table with Rachel at the foot of the table and David at the head. He courteously asked Aunt Virgie to pronounce the blessing, which she did in her cracked and trembling voice.

The dining room never looked more charming. The silver and cut glass gleamed in the firelight. Even though it was May, Aunt Virgie asked for a fire.

"I want you to see the girl we are quilting the quilt for. Here she comes now." Aunt Virgie proceeded to tell her friends about Minnie's saving the barn from fire and then capturing the trespasser. "I never thought I had so much courage. Why just the two of us bound the man and the sheriff took him over."

"Do you know where he is now, Aunt Virgie?" David decided it was time to tell her the rest of the story. "While he was in prison, he had a change of heart. He decided to give up his wild ways. I even heard he has been converted and is holding down a job as a fireman in the city. He wrote to me at Christmastime."

"Well it is nice to hear good endings to stories. Now I want each of you to write your name on the lining. Then the youngest of you can embroider over the name and we'll put in the date."

So Fannye, a mere sixty-eight, quickly outlined these names in embroidery floss on the yellow lining. Aunt Virgie decided she would hem the quilt all by herself and then she would give it to Minnie, the apple of her eye.

A week later David decided to replace the rope on the dinner bell. He let it dangle to within four feet of the ground. "Now that bell is to be rung when it's time for meals. I don't want to hear of any of you children ringing it unless there is an emergency. Do you all understand that?"

Elmer's two boys and their elder sisters all nodded their heads. But Virginia was not as sure as her friends. "What's a 'mergency, Uncle David?"

"Virginia, it means if something bad is happening. We hope such a time won't come."

Aunt Virgie stayed in bed after her quilting party, feeling too weak to sit in her rocking chair. She asked for the quilt so she could finish the hem. Rachel came in to see how she was. She looked at Rachel with shining eyes.

"My dear child, you have been such a comfort to me and to us all. I want to tell you something. I dreamed last night that I saw you with your baby girl you are going to have. She will come in God's good time and she will have your beautiful hair and David's compassionate brown eyes. I always thought that David must have the same kind of eyes as Jesus. He follows our Lord in so many ways."

"Oh, Aunt Virgie! Hair like mine! Well I hope she won't have to put up with all the jibes I've had as a girl. People don't act so nasty about red hair anymore."

Aunt Virgie's head sank to one side as Rachel was talking. Heavens! Was she dead? But no, her frail chest rose and sank, so Rachel knew she was only sleeping.

That afternoon a little sparrow flew up against the window pane with so much force that it knocked itself out. "An omen! A death omen!" and Rachel hurried to the bedroom in time to see Aunt Virgie gasp her last.

Immediately the bell started to ring. The men came running from the field where they had been cultivating corn. They stopped in time to see little Virginia still pulling the bell rope.

"I thought I told you that you must not do that except in an emergency." David angrily surveyed the small culprit.

"But this is a 'mergency. Aunt Virgie called me while I was asleep and told me to ring the bell."

Hilda came to the edge of the porch, holding a dishcloth to her eyes. "She's gone! Aunt Virgie has just died. But no one told the child to ring the bell—no one that's alive, that is!"

It was a seven days' wonder how little Virginia knew that Aunt Virgie was dead. Had her soul communicated briefly with the child in her sleep? David put it down to one of the mysteries of life.

Aunt Virgie's church friends came out in full force. The body lay in state in the living room, the simple casket unadorned saved by a cluster of ripe wheat tied with a black ribbon. A black crepe hung on the front door.

There were several dozen black, box-like buggies and their horses tied to the front fence. David went to a great deal of trouble to borrow several buggies to take as many of the family as could be spared to the cemetery. He even had the undertaker bring his horse-drawn hearse.

The services started at ten-thirty, and after an hour of preaching, came to a halt with dinner being served in both the kitchen and the dining room. The food was the traditional food served at the funerals of these people: cold roast beef, pickles, both cucumber and red beet, bread and butter, coffee, and raisin pie. It was a standard joke among some people to call raisin pie "funeral pie."

After dinner the people got into their buggies and followed David and the horse-drawn hearse. They slowly went back across the state line. The long line of buggies extended for a half mile.

The end of the funeral came when the body was interred in the old cemetery where Aunt Virgie's people lay. There they faced the east, all waiting for the Judgment morning.

CHAPTER 39

The household settled down. There was promise of an abundant harvest. One day there came over the radio the terrible news that there was a war in Europe. Then the talk of a draft was heard. David looked around at his big family and breathed a sigh of relief. Neither of his farmers would be eligible for a draft since they were busy producing food for the war effort. The young men in the church were torn by decisions. Many were signed up for alternate service since they were members of a pacifist church. This was guaranteed by Congress. There were many who could not bring themselves to work in hospitals or other institutions, so these young men were sent off to training camps. Each man made his own decision.

The months slipped by. The three partners recovered their losses. Some of David's stocks that he thought were lost revived and once again he found he was a rich man. The guest rooms in the summer kitchen loft fell into disuse since no one tramped the roads looking for work anymore. The defense plants in the cities were crying for workers.

One golden October day Rachel teased to be allowed to go to the cornfield and help with the husking. Elmer and Jake were cutting corn in another part of the farm, so David gave his consent. The field where they would be working had matured earlier than the rest of the corn crop.

As usual they carried a heavy bucket of lunch and a wooden keg of water. Rachel found her old band of eel skin and wrapped it around her wrist to strengthen it when she snapped off the husk.

The sky was nearly cloudless, the crows were cawing over a distant pile of corn, and the gentle breeze brought the intoxicating odor of ripe corn and the tarry odor of binder twine. David sang all of Rachel's favorite tunes. She thrilled to the goodness of life and the glory of the day.

The ate their lunch and then lay back on the dry corn shock to rest.

"David, dear one! Come on and make love to me out here under this beautiful sky. Maybe this time we'll be successful for a baby."

"Out here!" David looked all around and saw how isolated they were. "All right." So the happy couple clasped each other in their arms and found out once again the beauty of discovering the love man had for woman.

Breathless but completed, they rested a few more minutes, then opened their eyes. A rabbit was crouched a few yards away, ears twitching and eyes curious. A crow flew off a nearby corn shock with a loud Caw! Caw! The embarrassed couple laughed until the tears came to their eyes.

"I'll bet you showed them a thing or two!"

It was a few weeks later that Rachel whispered into David's ear, "I think our little one has started!"

"Be careful this time, Sweetheart. I don't want you to lose this one."

During the next few months Rachel spent many days in bed. Morning sickness made her very uncomfortable, so she left all the Christmas preparations to Hilda and Minnie. She sought out a doctor early in her pregnancy, and he calculated that the little one would be born during the latter part of June or early July.

Hilda was full of advice. "Don't stretch up or you'll have the baby's cord wrapped around its neck and strangle it. Be sure to keep from touching the body anywhere when you are frightened or the baby will be marked. I had a sister-in-law who stood watching a monkey in a store window. Sure enough when her baby was born, there on its left arm was a big furry patch exactly like monkey fur."

"Aw, Hilda! That's just a coincidence."

"Well you remember old Grandmother Slater? Remember how the left side of her face was? It was all red, and it is called port-wine marks, but no one can deny the fact that old Grandmother Slater's mark was caused by her mother getting so scared when the barn caught on fire. She put her hand up to her face and screamed. So don't take any chances."

"I promise! I want this child to be perfect. I pray every day."

It was in her fourth month that she felt safe enough to accept her mother's invitation to come and spend a day with her family.

Her brothers were both grown. Amos had married young and was living in an addition to the house. His wife had already produced a healthy infant. Jacob was a conscientious objector and was doing his alternate service in the state hospital, the same one where Rachel had once been confined. He served there helping the patients as best he could. He seldom got home but he wrote his parents every week. He also wrote to Rachel whenever he got the time.

Mother Miller did not seem as energetic as she had once been and she never went out nursing anymore. Rachel's father was bent over from his years of toil but he was still able to assist Amos on the farm.

Where had the years gone? The place seemed to be familiar if she did not look at the new addition. She wondered if her mossy fairy ring was still in the woods. She thrust aside the thought in a guilty fashion.

The short day as drawing to a close when David announced that it was time to be going home. But it started to snow before they could get started.

"Better not start out in a snowstorm. You are welcome to stay overnight." Mother Miller was apprehensive.

"It probably won't amount to much. If we stay off the main roads, we won't be in danger from the big old trucks going over the main road. It is only an hour's drive, and we have a heater in the car. Don't worry about us. We'll call you when we get home."

The snow became heavier and by the time they reached Black Creek Hill it was so dense it was hard to see through the windshield. They drove down a slope and were nearly ready to cross the bridge when the car went into a long skid, lurching down over a bank and slid into a big, ghostly white sycamore tree. There was a sickening sound of breaking glass, and the last thing Rachel remembered was the sound of someone moaning.

When she opened her eyes, she wondered where she was. Her first thought was for her baby, so she felt her abdomen. Yes, the little one was still there, but she could feel nothing. She heard another moan, and there was David slumped against the steering wheel. There was barely light enough to show that there was an ugly gash in his head.

"I've got to get help! I must be strong. It is up to me now," she muttered as she set about trying to stop the bleeding. She used her handkerchief as well as David's to wrap around the wound. Where would she get help? She peered through the falling snow and saw high up on the hillside a feeble light. Then she remembered that there was a house sitting along the road at the top of the hill. She would have to climb that long hill in all the snow that had fallen.

Pulling the fur robe over David, she set out. She had no boots for this kind of weather and she wondered what effect the cold and wet would have on her baby.

"Mother always said that babies in the womb are a lot tougher than we think," she kept talking to herself in order to keep from hysteria.

The first few steps wet her shoes and legs, but she forgot her own condition in the greater need for finding help for David. She floundered across the bridge, then turning right she followed the road up the steep slope. Large pine trees grew on both sides of the road, and she was reminded of the time she was racing away from the buzzards field and across the bridge to Miss Lucy's.

The whirling wind and snow hit her and the pine trees swayed and moaned.

"Oh Heavenly Father, help me now. Don't let David die. Save the child in my womb."

Sobbing, she marched on. Her feet felt numb in her wet shoes. Her legs were like two icicles. Then she saw a form coming out of the swirling snow and she rushed up to it. It seemed to be an old man, but it was difficult to make out any facial features.

"Please, sir, please help me! I'm so afraid! My husband is back there and he is badly hurt."

There was a sighing in the trees. The old man peered into her face. "Don't be afraid, Rachel. God will help you. He will keep your child safe, too. Keep on. It isn't far now. Give me your hand, I'll show you the way."

Suddenly Rachel felt a warm glow being diffused throughout her body. Then the babe in her womb gave a lurch, and she felt movement for the first time. She walked on, lightfooted as a doe. Why this was really a beautiful night! She could see into the woods now and see how each twig held its mound of snow.

A gate loomed out of the gloom and a light showed through the snow. She was nearly there. She turned to the old man by her side to thank him, but he was nowhere in sight! How did he get away so suddenly? She had no recollection of his releasing her hand. How did he know her name? How did he know she was pregnant? The hand that he had clasped was still warm but the other one was cold.

When the people in the house answered her knock, they were amazed to see her coming in out of the storm. While the wife chafed her hands and feet and fixed her a hot drink, the husband got into boots and heavy coat.

"Abigail, while I go down the hill to find this man, you might be heating some bricks in the oven and get some hot water bottles ready. I'm going to blanket the horses and take the bobsled to town. No ambulance can make it through this storm."

"Well, Papa, just as you say," the wife answered while she scurried around trying to do three things at once. Rachel raised herself out of her lethargy and poured a cup of coffee for the man before he went out.

"Our name's Pitcairn. You didn't tell us yours yet."

"Lowe—David and Rachel Lowe. If it hadn't been for the old man, your neighbor, I would never have made it up the hill. He left me at your gate."

"Neighbor! We have no near neighbors. What did he look like?"

"I didn't get a good look at him, but he seemed to be old and bent over. He acted as though he knew me—at least he called me by my name. I don't know how, for we don't know anyone in this community."

"What did he say?" Mrs. Pitcairn's voice trembled.

"He just said that God would take care of me. He took my hand and for the first time my baby moved. I felt warm and happy all over. I knew then that everything would be all right."

Abigail and her husband exchanged glances. "Old man Lee! This hill is named for him. There used to be a house across the road where he lived. One night it burned down in a snowstorm such as this. The old man was asleep and perished in the blaze. This happened about fifteen or twenty years ago. People have always said that he comes back in stormy weather. Some have even claimed to have seen him. But this is the first proof that he does come back."

"A hant! Do you mean that I saw a hant? Do you mean that a hant guided me to your door?" Rachel was startled yet not really afraid. "Whatever it was, I believe it was sent by God to guide me through the storm."

Mr. Pitcairn wrapped several mufflers about his neck and taking the bricks wrapped in newspapers and a hot water bottle, called to Rachel, "Come on now, Mrs. Lowe, we will save time if you come with me now. You scrooch down there in the straw and keep chafing your husband's hands and feet. It will take us several hours to get to the hospital. Abigail, you watch out for the livestock and take good care of yourself. I'll be back in the morning. Don't worry, for if old Mr. Lee was on the job, then we know everything will turn out all right."

David was still breathing when they reached the bottom of the hill. Mr. Pitcairn lifted him from the car and laid him on the straw on the bottom of the sled. Rachel surrounded him with hot bricks, keeping one for herself and one for Mr. Pitcairn. Tenderly she covered David with the fur robe. They set off to climb the hill again and headed in the direction of the nearest hospital.

The horses were headed into the wind, but they were blanketed so that they did not seem to mind the weather. At first Rachel gasped for breath, but she lay down in the straw under the fur robe next to the unconscious David. She rubbed his hands and feet as best she could under the robe. Mr. Pitcairn stamped his feet from time to time and took a drink from a bottle.

"Better take a drink of this. It will keep you warm. I never drink the stuff except in emergencies such as this."

Rachel shook her head. The snow became heavier, and she kept on praying. At last the lights of the town could be seen through the snow. Within a half hour David was being wheeled into the hospital with Rachel keeping close to his side. Mr. Pitcairn went to find shelter for himself and his team.

Three days later when David opened his eyes, he had no recollection of anything that had happened. Rachel touched him and the tears rolled down over his pale face.

"I thought I'd died and had gone to Heaven without you. You must tell me how I got here."

"Not until after you have had your dinner. Then after a long nap I'll tell you all about it."

"Dinner! I haven't had breakfast yet!"

The nurse in charge brought him a light meal and so his strength was built up.

Jake came for him a week later, and David found that life at the farm was going along smoothly.

CHAPTER 40

This year spring came early. The young wheat had wintered well and gave a promise of a bountiful harvest. It seemed to be one of the fairest springs that David had ever seen. The locust blossoms hung heavy from the trees bordering the fields. The clover in the east hay field was a carpet of red blossoms, and the bees were busy flying back and forth in their commuting to the hives under the big willow trees down by the highway. Dandelions were so golden that it seemed the sun had transferred one of its rays to the Lowe farm.

When the lilacs had put forth their exotic blooms of purple clusters, Rachel spent a great deal of time in that part of the lawn. She was getting along well, but her back troubled her a number of times. Her figure was rounding so much that Hilda declared that she was going to have a girl child. "If you came to a point in front, that means you will have a boy, but this just has to be a girl."

Decoration Day came on a Sunday this year, so Jake took his little family accompanied by Elmer and his family and they decided to drive to Mountain Lake for an all-day picnic.

Minnie and David went to church. It was not customary for women in the "family way" to go abroad the last months of their pregnancies. Rachel felt so enormous and uncomfortable, yet she felt envious when she saw Minnie looking so demure in her pretty blue dress and black bonnet. She looked longingly after the shining black car as they drove down the lane to the highway.

As soon as they returned, Minnie ran to change her dress and was slicing ham for frying when her knife slipped and she found her wrist covered with blood. She gave a sharp gasp.

Hilda looked up in time to see her fall to the floor in a faint. "Mister! Come quick!"

David ran to the kitchen, and with a white face quickly grabbed a dishcloth and bound her arm tightly. "She'll have to have that arm taken care of right away or she'll bleed to death. Hilda, call the hospital and tell Dr. Scott that we're on our way. Rachel, I don't want you to stir from the house. Lie down and be a good girl. I do not want anything to happen to you with me gone."

The house seemed to be hot, but it was cooler than the outdoors. Rachel lay on the couch, and Hilda tried to fan her. But she was so restless that it seemed like wasted effort.

The sky was darkening and mutterings of thunder could be heard to the west. A hot wind swept across the side porch.

"Do you know, Missus, we haven't eaten yet. Come to the table and I will fix you a nice coddled egg with a piece of toast."

"No, Hilda, I feel like it would choke me. I feel so short of breath. Ah, there's a car coming into our driveway. Is it David so soon?"

"No, can't make out who it is. He seems familiar, too."

"Anybody home? Mrs. Lowe?"

"Who is it, Hilda?"

"You seem to be familiar, but I can't place you. I'm Hilda, the housekeeper."

"Yes, I know. I'm Joe. I worked here two years ago. I'm sorry to say that I'm the one who tried to burn down your barn and steal Mr. Lowe's money. Is Mrs. Lowe at home? I want to tell her how sorry I am for everything that happened."

Rachel got up from the couch and went to the door. "Why are you here again? Why don't you go?" Her voice became higher with fright.

"Mrs. Lowe, you have nothing to fear from me. After the dirty tricks I tried to pull on you folks, I don't wonder at your feeling the way you do. I was passing by and I wanted to tell your husband again how much he has meant to me. He came to see me many times while I was in jail. He loaned me money to get a fresh start after I had served my time. Seeing how he practiced his religion, I too became a Christian. One of the first things I did was to take that tattoo off my arm. The snake is gone but it left a scar." He showed Rachel the scar. The fright on her face turned to one of compassion.

"The DEVIL has tried to get me, too, but through David's patience and goodness he has gone." Rachel reached out to shake hands when a loud clap of thunder followed a sharp bolt of lightning. Was it Satan's anger at losing these human souls?

Just then a little spasm touched Rachel and to her embarrassment, she started to pass the amniotic fluid of childbirth.

"Oh, my!" she gasped. "Hilda, help me to Aunt Virgie's room. I feel so strange. I can't make it upstairs."

Joe looked calm. "Never mind, Mrs. Lowe. I'll call a doctor. It looks like your time has come. The water has broken.

"Young man," scolded Hilda. "What do you know about such things? It ain't decent."

"Hold on there, Hilda. I am an ambulance driver in the city. I had to take special training in childbirth and I have delivered at least a dozen babies these past few months. Your phone seems to be dead. Probably there is a tree across the lines. Whoops, there goes the electricity!"

Hilda was busy getting Rachel to bed, but she took time to gaze apprehensively out the window. The rain had slacked off enough that she could see a big willow tree had fallen across the road. She went out to the next room and told Joe it looked like there was no way to call a doctor nor could Rachel be taken to the hospital. The baby was not due for six more weeks.

"Hilda, don't you know that babies have a way of arriving in the midst of storm or shipwreck?"

"Well if you are sure you know what to do, get out there in the washhouse and wash your hands in plenty of soap and water. I will get the hot water handy. It looks like we will have to deliver this one ourselves."

Rachel started violent pains, and Hilda comforted her as best she could. She ran to the kitchen for a sharp knife and laid it under the bed to cut the pains.

For a matter of three hours the horrible pains lasted. Joe shook his head and went to the kitchen while Hilda draped her with sheets. Placing a kerosene lamp on the bureau, Joe made an examination. Then he whispered to Hilda, "Come into the kitchen." Rachel's screams were so cutting that no one could even hear the violent storm on the outside.

"The baby isn't coming right. It's a breech."

"Oh, merciful Heavens, no! Do you think we can save her? Can't you turn it around?"

"No way, Hilda! But if I only had my instruments, there would be a good chance. But they are with my ambulance in the city. The only thing we can do is to pray!"

The minutes became hours and Rachel was so exhausted she could only make a rasping noise in her throat. She was about ready to give up when the little feet arrived. Joe and Hilda scolded and coaxed. Finally Joe pulled a tiny baby forth and cut the cord. He put the tiny baby girl over his shoulder and patted it until it cried.

"There, Mrs. Lowe, do you hear that? It's the most wonderful sound in the world. She looks like a healthy baby, and look, she has your beautiful hair, or will have it when the fuzz on her head grows."

Rachel was too weak to answer. Hilda took the baby while Joe finished up with his patient. By the time the baby was cleansed and wrapped in a blanket, Hilda started to clean up the mother and her bed. Rachel fell into a deep sleep and never noticed when the storm ceased.

It took several hours for David and Minnie to reach home. The last mile they had to walk and climb over uprooted trees across the highway. Minnie was wearing a bandage over her arm. Both she and David were soaking wet from the rain. They were surprised to find Joe and Hilda cozily drinking coffee in the kitchen while funny little sounds were coming from Aunt Virgie's old room. There David found his new daughter and his sleeping wife.

He heard the incredible story of how Joe accidentally happened in and how the two of them saved Rachel and helped to bring the new child into the world.

"What a day it has been! Don't tell me that casting bread upon the water doesn't bring its own reward!"

"But who wants to have water-soaked bread?" quipped Joe.

"Now what shall we call the new baby—Josephine Hilda?"

Joe looked alarmed. "Heaven forbid! I like the Hilda part, but spare the poor child the Josephine part."

Rachel woke in time to hear the discussion of a name. "I've decided on Abigail in honor of the woman whose husband saved David's life. May I put Hilda's name in it, too?"

"Sure thing, Missus. Now if I was your Aunt Virgie, I would make her a quilt, but I ain't aiming to do that just yet. We will enjoy her for many years until I start to piece quilts."

Thus Abigail Hilda Lowe made her appearance on Memorial Day, and indeed it was a day to remember.

Epilogue

It was Memorial Day again, and Abigail insisted that her parents take her to visit Grandma Miller. The slender little girl had the warm brown eyes of her father, but to Rachel's dismay, had inherited her red hair. Her curly red hair added to her pixie-like charm. The curls were seldom still while the child was awake.

"Why did she have to inherit my red hair?" Rachel moaned.

"Times have changed, my dear. People now find red hair to be beautiful. I know I always did think so."

"Yes," Minnie added, "according to the latest magazines, many women are dyeing their hair red."

When they came to the Miller farm, Grandma came to the door holding out her arms. "Little Mary Jane is here to see you." This was Amos's oldest child. "Come inside and see the big birthday cake I have for some little girl who is having her tenth birthday. Does anyone know who she is?"

"Oh, Grandma, how I love you!"

The delighted child ate so much of her grandmother's dinner that she gave a great sigh of contentment.

The old homestead seemed empty without her father. Rachel missed his quiet ways. He had died the year after Amos had built on an addition to the old stone house where he and his family now lived and farmed the homestead.

After the dishes were washed and put away, the little girls begged to be taken for a walk. David had gone out to see the farm, so Rachel was elected.

"Come on, Mummy! We want you to take us to see the cave where Uncle Amos and Uncle Jacob used to play when they were little boys."

"That's too far for us to walk. I'll tell you what, I'll take you back into the woods to see the fairy ring."

"What's a fairy ring, Mama?"

"In the shadiest part of the woods is a perfect circle made of the greenest moss you ever saw. It always looked like the best velvet carpet ever made."

"Oh, that sounds nice! Do fairies really come there?"

"That's according to your imagination. I used to like to think the fairies came there to dance by the light of the moon."

"Take us there, Aunt Rachel!"

Rachel remembered with pain the times she had met Anton there. Would she be haunted forever by this? Yet she would like to see the mossy ring again.

The three crossed the little brook that flowed from the spring. Its water was as icy as ever when they dipped their bare feet into it.

"Best not to wade too long in it. We might all take colds. Come, put on your shoes and stockings. On your way back we will gather some of the watercress that is growing over there in that eddy. I know that Grandma would like some of it."

When they had followed the little path that led into the woods, Rachel saw that this was not the pleasant place she had once loved to roam. The woods were full of high bushes hung with spider webs. Poison oak was rampant, and someone had been using the once beautiful glades for a dump. Tall poke bushes bearing their bloated purple berries blocked the path. A small snake glided away from them, and for a moment the old horror seemed to be closing in on Rachel. This gloomy evil place was no longer the beloved secret place of her girlhood. It seemed like a symbol of her past life.

"Come girls, we will have to go back. The woods are no longer beautiful, and they aren't safe. I could cry!"

Sadly they went back. When they came to the stile, they walked down a little path where once there had been a pond. The girls gave a cry of joy.

"Oh, look! Johnny-jump-ups! We'll gather some for Grandma!"

What Rachel had remembered as a swamp was now a grassy meadow with clumps of wild flowers dotting it. She found a bank of sweet clover and sank down into its perfumed depths to await the children. A yellow butterfly lighted onto a purple thistle. The breeze softly waved the grass. She felt the warm sunshine on her body. Off in the distance were the blue mountains. Big, white cumulus clouds floated over them.

She looked again. A dear familiar figure was coming across the field. It was David! She had passed from evil into the light. There was her heart's desire!

Yes, happiness was a sunlit meadow, for this was where her loved ones were.